E2
?)

The Gloriou

By

Thorne Smith

The Echo Library 2006

Published by

The Echo Library

Echo Library
131 High St.
Teddington
Middlesex TW11 8HH

www.echo-library.com

Please report serious faults in the text to complaints@echo-library.com

ISBN 1-40680-372-3

CONTENTS

CHAPTER I

CONGRATULATIONS

THE old gentleman with the resplendently starched cuffs moved into the room. In the kindly half light of the long, low apartment he stood poised like an ancient ramrod, worn and polished from long years of campaigning. About his person clung a pleasantly subtle suggestion of good soap and even better cigars. An expensive and thoroughly masculine smell.

With meticulous care he began to remove his gloves, releasing each imprisoned finger as if the action were an independent and definitely unrelated operation, requiring individual attention.

It was rather impressive, the way he took off his gloves—that is, if one's nerves and patience were in good working condition. But the woman sitting in one corner of the huge divan had never been heavily endowed with patience, and at present her nerves were not so good. They were very bad nerves indeed.

"If you don't take those gloves off," she said, "I'll drag them off with my own two hands. Your fingers aren't made of china. Why do you wear them, anyway? They make me feel like sweating."

"Give full rein to your animal impulses," suggested the old gentleman in a calm, deep voice. "You might lose a few superfluous pounds hither and yon."

Imperturbably he returned his attention to his gloves. He took them off as if he were really fond of them. And he was fond of his gloves. Always he had been like that, a creature whose nature was so ebullient with affection that it was generous enough to include even inanimate objects—all the good things of life. Now, at the age of sixty, he still loved the world, although he had learned to regard its creatures with affectionate contempt not untinged with that inner loneliness that comes from utter disillusionment.

He had loved a lot, and to no good end, so far as he could see, had this old gentleman.

With a slight pat of approval he placed the gloves on a rangy grand piano sprawling in the shadows like one of the less unneighborly monsters of the prehistoric past. Then from under his right arm he took a package and placed it neatly beside the gloves. This he also patted, but with a somewhat ironical gesture. Having attended to these little details with fitting solemnity and obviously to his entire satisfaction, he bent two remarkably bright and penetrating eyes upon the woman who sat watching him with an expression of brooding animosity on her faded but still good-looking face. Noiselessly he moved over the heavy carpet, bent with easy gallantry, and lifting one of the woman's fleshy hands, kissed it quite impersonally, as if it were little better than a fish. Furiously she snatched her hand away. He made little effort to retain it—no more than one would to retain a fish unless one were grim about it.

"How do you do, my antiquated trull," he said with unruffled good-nature.

The antiquated trull—a gamely preserved woman in the unreconciled fifties—answered with restrained passion.

"Don't call me a trull, you crumbling ruin," she told him. "What do you think a body can do at my age?"

The old gentleman gave an unnecessarily refined cough of admonition.

"My inquiry," he explained with exasperating patience "had no anatomical significance. Let's skip your body for the moment and totter up to a slightly higher level, if you don't mind."

"I wish I could skip my body," complained the woman "These days I can scarcely drag the thing about."

"That's pitiful," replied the old gentleman unemotionally. "It's your appetite, my dear. You eat like a wolf. It's surprising. But to get away from that for a moment, I might suggest that you're supposed to have also a mind not to mention a bit of a soul knocking about within that gnarled exterior of yours."

"All I have are corns," said the woman, gloomily surveying her feet. "Toes full of corns. They keep me busy cutting them."

"You disgust me," replied the old gentleman. "Honestly you do—actually disgust me."

"Rex Pebble," the woman told him, "don't stand there like an old hypocrite. For twenty-five years I've been trying to disgust you without the least success. I'm too tired now to try any more."

"I don't know about that," Mr. Pebble reminiscently observed. "At times you've been fairly disgusting, my dear. I might even say, revolting."

"But not to you," retorted the woman. "You were born demoralized."

Mr. Pebble selected a long cigarette from a box on a low table, then lighted the slender tube as if from afar he were watching himself perform the act with profound admiration.

"Birth," he observed through a scarf of smoke, "is a demoralizing transition. Much more so than death, which has at least the dignity of something definitely accomplished. Birth—I don't know—it always strikes me as being so tentative and squirmy."

"You do love to hear yourself talk," said the woman. "Especially when you know it annoys me."

"Sorry," said Mr. Pebble complacently. "If you don't care to talk, Spray, my old decrepit, what do you want to do?"

"What did I ever want to do?" she demanded. Mr. Pebble started slightly.

"Let's not go into that," he said with some haste. "You appall me. This is becoming most difficult. At our time of life we should sublimate sex into an anticipation of an air-cooled existence on wings."

"Nonsense!" snapped the woman called Spray. "I'd turn in my wings without a qualm for one good shot of sex."

"How debasing," said Mr. Pebble. "Unadmirable in the extreme. You, Spray, are about the most unreconciled old voluptuary it has ever been my misfortune to encounter."

"You're just a string of long words," Spray retorted. "And that's all there is to you. There's nothing else left. Not," she added regretfully, "that it would do me any good if there was."

"Really," objected Mr. Pebble, "I shouldn't be allowedto listen to this sort of thing. It's far too low for me. My natural elasticity of spirit becomes rigid in your presence."

"Twenty-five years ago——" began Spray.

"That reminds me," said Mr. Pebble. "I called this evening especially to offer you my congratulations."

"For what?" asked Spray in surprise. "For God's sake, don't tell me I'm another year older."

"No," said Mr. Pebble. "It's not as bad as that. Tonight is the twenty-fifth anniversary of your first seduction. I'm rather sentimental about such things. For a quarter of a century now you have had the honor of being my mistress."

"What's honor without pleasure?" Spray demanded bluntly.

"That's a very difficult question to answer honestly," Mr. Pebble admitted.

"I'm your mistress in name only," went on Spray, her eyes clouding. "I've outlived my usefulness." She paused and smiled maliciously at the man. "How do you know," she asked, "I was first seduced by you?"

"I don't," replied Mr. Pebble. "Knowing you as I do, I think it highly improbable. But, if you don't mind, allow me to retain at least one harmless illusion. I'm an old man, you know."

The woman looked up at him thoughtfully. He was tall, slim, and straight, and faultlessly groomed. About him there seemed to linger still something of the insinuating, care-free, insatiable young devil she had known and loved in her way. But his face was lined now; his fine hair was white, and his eyes, though keen and alert, gazed down at her from a lonely height as if from another world. This much she could understand, for she too was lonely now that her fires were spent. Swiftly and regret. fully she traveled back through time, and yet a little proudly. This man had loved her and kept her, and although she had failed him more than he would ever know —at least, she hoped so—she was glad to remember he had never done a deliberately unkind or dishonest act so far as she was concerned. The years washed about her, and memories drifted among them. Perhaps not admirable memories, but happy ones. And there were some she refused to admit even to herself, for women are made that way. She had been a fair, ripe figure of a girl, and she had not wasted much time. This man still meant more to her than any man who had ever come into her life, although she still regretted a certain young doctor who had been so stupidly decent her charms had left him cold. What a fool that young doctor had been. She had liked him the better for it. Her face softened as she held up a hand to the man standing above her.

"You are an old man," she said, her voice taking on a richer quality. "A distinguished old devil of a man. Sit down. You make my corns ache."

"To relieve those corns of yours," said Mr. Pebble, sinking into the divan beside her, "I would grovel on the floor. Gladly would I grovel."

"And gladly would I let you if it would do any good," she told him. "But nothing helps corns, really. When you grow old your feet grow tired all over. They ache and make you mean."

"I know," he said sympathetically. "I am not without my twinges and disconcerting cracks. There is no sense in crying out against nature, yet I fiercely resent my aged body and its lost powers. The mental tranquillity that comes with age may have its compensations, but one has to be damnably philosophical to attain them. It grows tiresome at times, being philosophical."

"Give me a cigarette," said Spray.

He lighted her cigarette, and for a moment the woman leaned back, puffing thoughtfully.

"Tell me about it," she said at last."About what?" asked Rex Pebble.

"About my first official seduction," Spray replied.

"Don't you remember?" asked Mr. Pebble.

"I might," she told him, "if you'd just give me a start."

"It was quite all right," began Mr. Pebble. "As a matter of fact, it was hardly a proper seduction at all."

"Are any seductions proper?" she wanted to know.

"No," admitted Mr. Pebble, "but some are highly salutary—greatly to be desired, you know. What I mean to say is that both of us knew exactly what we were doing."

"I'm glad I didn't think I was flying a kite," Spray observed innocently. "First impressions are so important in such affairs."

"As I remember it," went on Mr. Pebble, "you seemed to be quite favorably impressed. I hope you don't think I'm bragging."

"A sensible pride in achievement is perfectly permissible," said the woman. "Especially at your age. It's all you have left to brag about."

"You depress me," said Mr. Pebble.

"Go on with that seduction," Spray reminded him.

"Then don't interrupt," Mr. Pebble objected. "And stop making me feel my years. It was a glorious night, as I recall it. Such a night as this. There was something a little mad about it—something that made important things, such as honor and loyalty, seem quite remote and futile. I had been married to Sue about three months at the time."

"That's a long time for a man to remain faithful," observed the woman.

"Sue never gave me a chance to get started," replied Mr. Pebble without rancor. "The little devil was up to her tricks six weeks after we were married. As a matter of fact, I don't know to this day whether I'm the father of my daughter or not. Neither does Sue. It doesn't really matter. She's a decent sort, anyway, and, thank God, she doesn't take after either of us."

"Then her father must have been a nice man," said Spray. "He couldn't have been you."

"I've about come to that conclusion myself," Mr. Pebble admitted judicially. "He must have been much too good for Sue. Probably didn't even know she was married. I like to think so, at any rate."

"You haven't much of an opinion of either of us, I suppose?" Spray suggested.

"Not much," agreed Mr. Pebble, "but that doesn't keep me from liking you both—I might even go so far as to say, loving you both."

"Even knowing we've both been unfaithful?" Spray asked softly.

For a moment Rex Pebble stared unseeingly into space, then passed a hand across his eyes as if to brush away an unpleasant vision.

"Even knowing that," he replied. "It isn't sinning that counts so much as the concealment of the sin. You, Spray, and Sue, have been fairly honest with me in so far as your natures would permit. As for me, I have scarcely had the time or inclination to be unfaithful, what with two healthy women at my disposal. You know, the flesh is the frailest of our possessions, and yet we expect it to be the strongest. I'm inclined to believe that too much idealism leads to the cruelest sort of bigotry. Where was I?"

"I was in a fair way of being seduced," said Spray, "and you seemed to think it was a nice night for it."

"It was," said Mr. Pebble. "Couldn't have been better. You were singing at some Egyptian-looking cafe then, and showing as much as the law allowed. Very good stuff it was, too—song and all. I admired your voice as well as your body."

"How about my brains?" asked Spray.

"There was very little about your brains," said Mr.Pebble. "You didn't need any. But to continue. I was exceedingly low in my mind that evening and was finding it difficult to get drunk. So I gave up the attempt and solaced myself in you instead, which was much wiser."

"I remember now," said Spray. "You drove me to your home and introduced me to Sue, then you borrowed some of her things for me, and we went for a cruise on Long Island Sound. She was very sweet about it."

"There was a reason for that," observed Mr. Pebble with a faint grin. "She had a boy friend almost suffocating in the cellar. I nearly packed his trousers by mistake."

"Edifying, we were," said Spray, "the three of us, weren't we?"

"Perhaps not," admitted Mr. Pebble, "but at least we had both the good taste and the good sense not to waste the evening in noisy melodrama. Sue told me later she had spent a very pleasant week-end. She was pointed about it. You may never have realized it, Spray, but it was you who kept my marriage with Sue from going on the rocks. You actually held us together. It was only after I had provided you with a home that she felt inclined to provide me with one."

"Glad to have been of help," said Spray. "And so I was seduced."

"And so you were seduced," agreed Mr. Pebble. "You were even good enough to return my wife's nightgown."

"It was a lovely, daring bit of stuff," Spray observed.

"Yes," said Mr. Pebble almost sadly. "She would never wear it for me."

"So you got another girl to wear it for you," said Spray.

"It seemed the most reasonable thing to do," said Mr. Pebble. He paused and took a small square box from his pocket. "And," he added, presenting the box to the woman, "if you don't mind, I am going to ask you to wear this, also."

Spray opened the box and gazed down into the flickering fires of a black opal. The glowing beauty of the jewel was transmuted to her eyes.

"When the sun went down behind the green islands in the Sound the sky looked a lot like that," she said. "Cool fire and disturbing beauty—beauty that almost hurts. Thanks, Rex, I'll wear it." She took his hand in both of hers and held it against her cheek. "But I'd much rather be able to wear that nightgown for you again," she added.

"Still harping on the same old subject," said Mr. Pebble, fastidiously brushing some powder from the back of his hand.

"It's been more than a subject to me," she retorted. "It's been a career."

"How awful," observed Mr. Pebble, rising and walking over to the piano. "Why don't you call it a hobby?" "Hobby, hell!" declared Spray. "It's been a craze." Mr. Pebble looked pained.

"Let's try to forget everything you've said," he suggested, "and start afresh. It would be more fragrant. Here's a present Sue sent you."

He took the package from the piano and carried it to the divan. Spray opened the package and read aloud the card enclosed.

"To Spray Summers," she read, *"my husband's mistress, from Sue Pebble, your patron's wife. Congratulations!"*

Mr. Pebble took the card and looked at it, a faint smile edging his lips.

"Right to the point," he remarked. "No unnecessary words. Rather sporting, I'd say."

A cry of animal ferocity broke in upon his observations. Spray was confronting him with a large pair of carpet slippers in her hands. Mr. Pebble needed only one glance to feel convinced that they were the worst-looking pair of slippers he had ever seen. His wife must have searched with fanatical zeal to find a gift so devastatingly humiliating. He admired her for her perseverance but lamented her shocking taste. He lamented it all the more when he received the slippers with sudden violence in the pit of his stomach. For a moment Mr. Pebble was forced to abandon his impressive poise. The sheer fury behind Spray's arm did much to make up for the softness of the slippers. With a dull, businesslike thud they struck the stomach of Mr. Pebble, and with a look of utter astonishment he promptly doubled up, his hand pressed to the assaulted spot. However, this undignified posture was of short duration. Summoning to his aid the traditional pride and courage of a long line of Pebbles, he immediately snapped erect and stood regarding the raging woman with a calm and imperious eye.

"I would rather receive an honest kick in the seat of my trousers," he said with stoical self-control, "than have one treacherously hurled at me from afar."

"Well, you just show me the seat of your pants," said Spray, "and you'll get a kick there, too."

"Madam," replied Mr. Pebble, "why should I show you the seat of my trousers? That would be literally asking for it. In your present mood it would be more than a foolhardy gesture of defiance, not to say a grotesque one. It would be actually dangerous, even if your feet are the Bull Run of chiropody."

This remark did nothing to restore tranquillity to the heaving bosom of Spray Summers. If anything, it heaved all the more. She snatched up the slippers and prepared for a second assault.

"If you throw those slippers at me again," Mr. Pebble told her in level tones, "I'll be forced to step on your corns—all of them."

Spray's right arm halted in its swing. The threat had proved effective. The very thought of such retaliation sent twinges of pain through her feet.

"You deliberately helped your wife to insult she said. "I'll never forgive you for this. Look at them. Look at those slippers."

With a tragic gesture she thrust out the slippers for his inspection. Unflinchingly he looked at the horrid things, but was unsuccessful in repressing a smile. Although they shocked his esthetic sense, they immensely appealed to his sense of humor.

"Don't be ridiculous," he said. "I knew nothing about those slippers. What's wrong with them, anyway? For a woman with feet like yours I should think they would be ideal."

Spray choked over this one.

"I'm humiliated," she said bitterly. "Humiliated. Do you know what I'm going to do?"

"I never know," declared Mr. Pebble.

"I'm going to buy a Mother Hubbard—a horrid flannel one—and sent it to that wife of yours on her next birthday. And you are going to take it to her for me. Don't forget that."

"I'm afraid I won't," replied Mr. Pebble a little wearily.

"Wonder who she thinks she is!" went on his mistress. "I'm every day as young as she is, if not younger. I am younger. I know it. Five or ten years younger."

Realizing the impossibility of trying to reason with a woman who made such extravagant statements, Mr. Pebble, in spite of years of experience, did the worst thing he could have done. He agreed with her.

"I'm sure you must be right," he said placatingly. "I should say nearer ten."

"To hell with you," blazed Spray. "You chattering old monkey. To hell with you, I say. What are you trying to do, treat me like a child?"

"If you keep on lopping the years off your age," Mr. Pebble assured her, "you'll soon be a babe in arms." "I wish I were," she retorted.

"In whose arms?" asked Mr. Pebble.

"Not in those brittle pipe stems of yours," she answered. "I want to be in my mother's arms."

"Funny thing," casually observed Mr. Pebble, "but I can never picture you as ever having had a mother."

"I never had one," said Spray.

"Then why do you want to be in her arms?"

"Well, you got to be in somebody's arms when you're a mere babe, don't you?" she demanded. "Any fool would know that, even an old one."

"Not necessarily," replied Mr. Pebble. "You could be in a basket or a cradle or a shoe box or even an ash can, for that matter."

"Could I?" sneered Spray. "Well, I wasn't that sort of baby. I was always in my mother's arms."

"But I thought you said just now you did not have any mother," objected Mr. Pebble.

"Will you stop trying to pin me down?" Spray cried fiercely. "I simply meant that we did not carry on long conversations."

"About what?" asked Mr. Pebble.

She started to answer, then stopped with an expression of frustration.

"How should I know?" she said at last. "If we never had any long conversations, how do you expect me to tell you what we didn't talk about?"

"I don't," Mr. Pebble replied rather hopelessly. "I don't even know what we are talking about."

"Neither do I," said Spray. "You've got me completely baffled. Why don't you go home?"

"Aren't you going to give me anything to eat?" Mr. Pebble demanded.

"I don't know where Nockashima is. Haven't seen him for days."

"Is that wretched heathen drunk again?"

"He's always either drunk or telephoning," Spray complained. "Often he's both drunk and telephoning. Then he's just too bad. Also, he suffers from hallucinations. Why don't you take him home to live with you? Whenever I discharge him he simply eats a box of rice and goes to bed. Then he covers his head with the blankets and gibbers back at me in a weird, muffled voice. It's worse than talking to a ghost."

"I should say so," said Mr. Pebble.

At this moment a strange couple entered the room. It consisted of a bloodhound who could not smell and a Japanese houseboy who could scarcely walk.

The bloodhound's name was Mr. Henry, and no one knew why.

"Good-evening, madam," said the more loquacious of these two animals in a slightly blurred voice. "I was shot in leg by baroness while crossing Fourteenth Street."

"That explains everything," exclaimed Spray Summers with a hopeless waving of arms. "What did I tell you? Hallucinations! I might be able to stand a crazy Jap or a drunken Jap, but certainly not the two rolled into one. You talk to him, Rex Pebble—that is, if you want any dinner."

Mr. Henry lowered himself thoughtfully to the carpet. Once seated he pretended he was smelling something by making his nose quiver. The dog was living a lie. Yet it was a harmless form of deception, for a bloodhound who had lost his sense of smell must do something to overcome his inferiority complex.

Deprived of the support of his companion, Nockashima clung to the back of a chair and stood looking with guilty eyes at the tall, menacing figure of Mr. Pebble.

CHAPTER II

NOKASHIMA AND THE BLOODHOUND

REX PEBBLE had lived far too long and had been told far too many lies to take anyone at his or her own word. The most obvious statement was suspect to him. On the other hand, he had lived quite long enough to know that almost anything was possible, especially when it happened on Fourteenth Street.

Therefore, he did not immediately call Nockashima a liar and a drunkard, although he knew the servant was congenitally both. It was just barely possible that some passing baroness had encountered the dissolute Jap on Fourteenth Street and taken a pot shot at him. Knowing the little man as he did, it struck Mr. Pebble as the most reasonable thing for a baroness to do to Nockashima. Probably the woman had once employed him and become, as a consequence, slightly deranged. Mr. Pebble could well understand that.

Accordingly he greeted Mr. Henry, the non-smelling bloodhound, with a casual nod, then bore down on the wavering Nockashima, whose expression of quiet was immediately replaced by one of protective stupidity.

"Nocka," said Mr. Pebble with friendly incredulity, "do you mean to stand there swaying before me and to tell me to my face that you've actually been shot?"

"Yes, boss," replied Nocka with stolid conviction. "I been shot all right. Through and through. Also," he added, so that there might be no misunderstanding, "up and down."

"Literally riddled," murmured Mr. Pebble. "Sure you're not just half shot, Nockashima?"

"That too," agreed the Jap, visibly brightening. "Half shot—all shot. Leg of the worst. There are holes in it."

"But why a baroness, Nocka?" asked Mr. Pebble.

"Titled ladies like me," Nocka explained.

"So they shoot you out of sheer affection," said Mr. Pebble.

"That's right, boss," replied Nocka. "They shoot me up.

"I'd rather they shot you down," observed Mr. Pebble, "and out. However, one can't have everything. Any blood?"

"No, boss," said Nocka. "Just holes. Blood all gone." "Do you mean to tell me you're bloodless, Nocka?"

"Yes," vouchsafed the servant. "I am without blood."

"How do you keep on living?" asked Mr. Pebble, interested in the Jap's mental processes.

"I don't," said Nocka simply. "I am dying. Soon I will be good and dead."

"You may be dead," remarked Mr. Pebble, "but I very much doubt if you'll be much good."

"Oh, I'll be all right, boss," said Nocka encouragingly.

"I'm glad you take that view of it," observed Mr. Pebble. "Of course, after you're dead we can't keep you on here. What do you want us to do with you?"

"Put me in jug," said Nocka, "and send me home as token."

"What sort of jug, Nocka?" Mr. Pebble wanted to know.

"An ash jug," declared the Jap. "I want to be burned all up."

"Nothing would give me more joy," put in Spray Summers. "If I had my way I'd set fire to you right now."

"Only after I am all dead," said Nockashima firmly. "I burn then."

"You'll burn in hell," Spray assured him, "you black-hearted heathen."

"Don't scold at me, madam," Nocka said quite seriously, "or I'll become nervous breakdown."

"Ha!" cried Spray bitterly. "I like that. You'll become a nervous breakdown. Why, you've made me a gibbering idiot. Go on and die, sottish little ape."

"Soon," said the sottish little ape. "But no words, madam."

"No," retorted Spray. "Just cheers."

Mr. Pebble decided that this sort of thing would arrive at no good end.

"Nocka," he said, shifting his attack, "how old are you?"

"I am of no years," replied the Jap surprisingly. "I am all things to all men."

"You're a pain in the neck to me," cut in Spray Summers. "And elsewhere," she added with characteristic abandon.

"Show me those holes in your leg," Mr. Pebble demanded rather hastily.

"What holes, boss?" asked the servant.

"What holes?" Mr. Pebble repeated. "Didn't you tell me a baroness shot your leg full of holes?"

"You thought I did," said Nockashima, now in his most baffling stride.

A groan of mental anguish escaped Spray Summers' lips.

"He can throw you every time," she told Mr. Pebble.

"The horrid little beetle plays ju-jutsu with the English language."

"Are there no holes at all in your leg?" Mr. Pebble asked a trifle wearily.

"In which leg?" was the cautious answer.

"In any leg," replied Mr. Pebble, who was rapidly losing control.

"In some legs, yes," declared Nocka.

"But not in yours?" insisted Mr. Pebble.

"All gone," replied the Jap. "I am weak from the loss of holes."

By this time Spray was laughing comfortably on the divan.

"My god," she said, "how you two can talk. I don't know which is the most unintelligent. The heathen is weak from the loss of holes, is he? Well, I've got a gun upstairs. Shall I get it and make him strong with holes?"

"I'd like to make him nonexistent with holes," grated Mr. Pebble. "I'd like to make him just one hole in space."

"Like baroness," suggested Nockashima. "Cocktail, boss?"

The servant's question was timed to the exact second. Mr. Pebble checked his mounting wrath and struggled back once more to his poise.

"By all means," he said. "That is the best way out of everything. Are you able also to cook dinner?"

"Shake first, then cook," replied the Jap. "We must all be hungary."

"Go on and shake your head off," Spray flung after him as Nockashima left the room, Mr. Henry acting in the double capacity of guide and support.

When Nocka returned with the frosted shaker all sense of guilt appeared to have departed from his soul. His eyes had lost their expression of protective stupidity. They were now alert and gleaming. He even walked with Mr. Henry as an equal.

"He must have made a good one," Spray observed. "How are the cocktails, Nocka?"

"I am all recovered, madam," replied the Japanese. "I have no years at all."

"I feel somewhat younger myself," remarked Mr. Pebble after he had emptied his glass. "That was an honest cocktail mixed by dishonest hands, which goes to show that through evil great good can accrue. How are your wounds, Nocka?"

"I have no holes either," the small man replied proudly.

"I wouldn't brag about that," commented Spray Summers.

"I suggest we avoid the subject," interposed Mr. Pebble. "These cocktails are actually buoyant, Spray. Have another."

Spray did. Then she offered the slippers to the non-smelling bloodhound. Realizing what was expected of him, Mr. Henry came over to the divan and went through the elaborate pretense of sniffing them.

"Too bad he can't smell," Spray observed sadly. "If he could, the scent of these slippers would so infuriate him he'd tear the things to pieces."

"I wonder why that dog can't smell?" Mr. Pebble wondered without much interest.

"He does smell at times," replied Spray, "but never with his nose. I think his mother dallied with a Pekingese."

"'You can cram more unsavory suggestions in the smallest space," protested Mr. Pebble, "of any woman I know."

"Mist' Henry," put in Nockashima, "him must have smell something very shocking when small babe of pup. It stultify his nose."

"Nothing should be too shocking for a bloodhound to smell," remarked Spray Summers. "That's their sole purpose in life—to take it on the nose, so to speak."

"Not when babe of pup," said Nocka. "When smell is too awful young nose declines to play part. It withers like delicate flower beneath blast of sun."

"That's the way I like to have things put," declared Mr. Pebble, pouring himself another drink. "Fine poetic frenzy evoked by a dog's nose."

"Well, I've lived with that dog and that Jap for five long years," said Spray, "and I defy William Shakespeare to do as much and retain one whiff of poetry in his soul."

She too poured herself another cocktail, and looked defiantly about her. Mr. Henry, as if sensing his defective part was under discussion, put an end to a trying situation by taking the slippers in his mouth and stalking from the room. With a quick bow Nockashima followed the dog.

"Exit three unsightly objects," said Spray with satisfaction, "but of the three those slippers are the worst."

"Sue can think up some dirty tricks," observed Mr. Pebble. "She has a perverted sense of humor."

"I don't mind an occasional dirty trick," replied Spray. "I've pulled a few myself in my time, but those slippers were wicked. It's the first time in twenty-five years she has ever got the better of me."

"Wish I could say the same," responded Mr. Pebble. "She's got the better of me more than once—both of you have."

"Oh, I don't know," said Spray. "You haven't been so desperately treated, considering the chances you took. You've had more than most men—two lovely homes with a lovely woman in each. In addition, you've had the privilege of bringing up another man's daughter and of making a home for your nephew. What more could you ask?"

"I've had more than enough," was Mr. Pebble's enigmatic rejoinder. "Lots more."

"How is Kippie, by the way?" Spray wanted to know. "Haven't seen him for some time."

"He's growing more divertingly worthless every day," said Mr. Pebble. "He's twenty-six now, and in the three years since he left college he hasn't earned an honest dime. As a matter of fact, he's virtually ruined that advertising agency of mine."

"If he ruins only advertising agencies," remarked Spray, "no great harm will be done. Does he stop there?"

"I fear not," said Mr. Pebble. "The other morning I took one of the cars out for an early spin and found myself sitting on a pair of so-called step-ins." He paused and sighed a little wistfully. "Women's undergarments have taken vast strides since our day. There's nothing to them at all now except speed. They're very nice."

"I wear all the latest things," said Spray Summers. "For all the good it does me."

"Or me," added Mr. Pebble.

He rose and, taking up the shaker, went in search of Nockashima. In the kitchen he discovered the Japanese engaged in an odd ceremony. With the slippers in one hand and a large steak in the other he was endeavoring to instruct Mr. Henry in the fine art of smelling. From the tense attitude of the bloodhound's rump Mr. Pebble could see that the dog was taking the situation seriously.

"Sniff hard, Mist' Henry," Nockashima was saying. "Which smell more better, steak or slips? Take good sniff now." Here the little man first passed the steak across the dog's nose and then did the same with the slippers. "Which you like," he demanded, "nice steak or delightful slips?" Apparently Mr. Henry had little preference, or perhaps both steak and slippers were equally revolting to him. With a puzzled expression in his limpid eyes he looked adoringly up at the Jap. "Ha!" cried Nockashima, refusing to be discouraged. "Hard to make up mind, eh? Both so good. Take deep whiff now, then wag for favorite."

Once more the steak and slippers were offered to the dog's nose. The sight was too much for Mr. Pebble.

"Oh, I say," he exclaimed. "I wouldn't do that. Don't let him smell the steak."

Nockashima glanced up with innocent concentration. "Mist' Henry," he said somewhat sadly, "him can't smell steak, I don't fancy."

"Well, I don't fancy him getting his great nose all over it," Mr. Pebble protested.

"Mist' Henry's nose is all right outside," explained the Jap. "Inside not so good."

"Nockashima," said Mr. Pebble severely, "I'm not out here to argue with you about the relative merits of the inside and outside of Mr. Henry's nose. No side of that hound's nose belongs on a steak. I don't even care to discuss it. It's not fitting for animals to smell people's food."

"He can't smell anybody's food," replied Nocka with increasing sadness. "Not even his own food."

"Whether or not that dog can smell his own food is a matter of indifference to me," said Mr. Pebble. "That's his hard luck, but I'll be damned if I'm going to allow him even to try to smell mine."

"I let him smell my food," said Nockashima gently.

"I don't care if he eats your food," replied Mr. Pebble. "You keep that dog's nose in one place and that steak in another."

"Where's good place for dog's nose?" the little man wanted to know.

"What?" asked Mr. Pebble, a little mystified.

"Where I keep Mist' Henry's nose?" replied the Japanese.

"I don't see why either of us should be concerned where Mr. Henry keeps his nose," declared Mr. Pebble, "so long as he keeps it entirely to himself. Furthermore, I'm getting fed up with Mr. Henry's nose."

"You feed on dog's nose, boss?" asked Nockashima, with an expression of horror on his wrinkled face.

"Oh, God!" exclaimed Mr. Pebble. "Don't be a fool, Nockashima. I never ate a dog's nose in my life."

"That's nice," said Nocka approvingly. "That's very good. Tough on dog to feed on nose. I take care of Mist' Henry's nose if you not eat."

"I don't have to promise you not to eat that blood-hound's nose," retorted Mr. Pebble. "More for my sake than his, I wouldn't touch his nose. I have a nose of my own."

"And you eat that?" asked Nockashima, now thoroughly interested.

"Certainly not," snapped Mr. Pebble. "Are you deliberately trying to infuriate me?"

"That's nice," said the Jap. "That's very good."

"Are you telling me it's nice that I don't eat my own nose?" demanded Mr. Pebble, his consumption of cocktails having made him a little childish.

"Don't you think so?" asked the guileless servant.

"I don't even have to think about it," replied Mr. Pebble. "How can a man eat his own nose?"

"With his teeth," said Nockashima quite reasonably, and Mr. Pebble was undone.

He began to tremble so violently that the few remaining ice cubes in the shaker tinkled pleasantly against its sides. The sound automatically attracted Nockashima's attention.

"More cocktails, boss?" he inquired.

Once more the servant's question had been happily timed.

"For God's sake, yes," gasped Mr. Pebble. "Don't say anything more to me. Just make the cocktails, then bring them in. That's all. Just make them and bring them in. No more talk about my nose, or that dog's nose, or of any nose in all the world. Understand that. Just make them and bring them in. That's all."

Still mumbling to himself about what Nockashima should and should not do, Mr. Pebble tottered from the room and sank wearily down on the divan beside his mistress.

"What kept you?" she inquired.

"I think," said Mr. Pebble, "that Nockashima was put on this earth just to torture my soul. He has noses on the brain."

"How do you mean?" asked Spray. "How on earth can a person have a nose on the brain, even such an original type as Nockashima?"

"Are you starting in, too ?" demanded Mr. Pebble. "Or is it a plot to drive me mad?"

Before Spray could answer, the small man entered triumphantly. He was carrying a fresh shaker of cocktails.

"Mist' Henry knows difference now," he announced, happily. "He can smell like regular dog."

"How do you know that?" asked Mr. Pebble, intrigued in spite of his determination never again to discuss any subject with this mad Oriental.

"I taught him," said Nocka proudly.

"Still I don't understand," pursued Mr. Pebble. "He ate steak all up," said Nockashima.

Both Spray and Mr. Pebble gazed in blank astonishment at the Japanese servant. This was indeed a stunning piece of information.

"What?" said Mr. Pebble after a dazed silence. "He ate steak all up?"

"Every bit," replied Nocka in a pleased voice. "All. But not these."

He set the shaker on the table and produced the slippers from his pocket. These he extended to Spray. With a choking sound, she covered her face with her hands.

"Take them away," she moaned.

Mr. Pebble was too stunned to speak. His poise was shot full of holes. With fascinated eyes he watched the Japanese pour two cocktails. What manner of man could this be? Mr. Pebble wondered vaguely. Why did God permit the little man to live? Perhaps there was no God. Perhaps life was just one long dirty trick.

"Mist' Henry knows difference now all right," continued Nockashima cheerfully. "He crunch into steak with great enjoyment, but not slips. They're not so good."

CHAPTER III

BAGGAGE CHECKS OUT

NEITHER Mr. Pebble nor his mistress felt in the least inclined to discuss any subject with Nockashima. Time passed in brooding silence which Rex Pebble devoted to the restoration of his cherished poise through the consumption of numerous cocktails. Feeling considerably fortified, he rose at last, and placed a friendly arm round the happy little servant's shoulder.

"How can you bring yourself to touch the vile body of that misbegotten little monstrosity?" Spray Summers demanded.

"Oh well," said Mr. Pebble, none too definitely, then added, for lack of anything more adequate to say, another "Oh well."

"Our dinner has gone to the dog," Spray continued bitterly, "and you more than shake the hand of the telephoning drunkard who fed it to him. You actually caress the withered marmoset."

"I know," said Mr. Pebble with alcoholic tolerance, "but you still have your slippers, and you must admit the marmoset can shake a two-fisted cocktail."

"Get out of my sight, you soiled camels!" the irascible woman exclaimed, "and take these damn slippers with you. Mr. Henry might like them for a little gouté, the dirty dog."

This time it was the rear of Mr. Pebble that received the slippers instead of the stomach. He accepted them there with unflinching heroism, thanking his lucky stars he had been fortunate enough to escape a frontal attack.

"You should join a major league," he tossed back over his shoulder. "Remarkable control."

Gently but firmly he propelled Nockashima from the room.

"Madam no like Mist' Henry to eat steak all up?" the small Jap inquired when safely out of earshot.

"Not all up, Nocka," Mr. Pebble explained. "She's funny that way. Madam likes it better to eat her own steak. I'll telephone for another one."

"Let me telephone, boss," said Nockashima quickly. "I get a steak of most rarefied succulence plenty quick."

Remembering the servant's passion for the telephone, Mr. Pebble interposed no objection, feeling that as long as the Japanese was having such a thoroughly good time he might as well make a night of it. Accordingly, he abandoned Nockashima to the telephone, then quit the kitchen and the house by a side door. It would be just as well, he reflected, to let Spray simmer for a while.

Blending the fragrance of moist herbage with the scent of cocktails, Rex Pebble bore his sixty years along an uneven brick wall that led to a walled garden at the back of the house. And the moment he entered this quiet place the summer twilight claimed him. It was a spacious garden with fine turf pierced by the trunks of trees, and it sloped gently to the brow of a hill which lay without the walls, thus giving the spot a fair, broad view of the valley below and the villages nestling in it. A long green pool, now glowing in the sunset, dreamed tranquilly within the garden and all day long reflected the changing moods of the sky. In the middle of the pool the statue of a naiad stood lightly poised on the surface of the water. A border of flagstones circled the pool, converging at the steps of a little white pavilion which stood partly hidden among the trees. This small but luxuriously appointed structure had been built essentially for privacy, which was just as well, for it had been the scene of full many a revel in those days when sixty years were an inconceivable distance off to Rex Pebble. He gazed at the pavilion now, then certain memories forced him politely to avert his eyes. They rested on the statue of the naiad, and Mr. Pebble seated himself on a bench beside the pool the better to contemplate this wild nude figure.

For many years Rex Pebble had been contemplating this naiad, and for many years the naiad had been contemplating him with the same provocative smile on her half-parted lips. He had given her the name of Baggage because he was fully convinced she was both saucy and promiscuous. And he liked her the better for it, although in his heart he chided her gently for her folly.

Baggage was a lush figure of a wench, the creation of vanished hands that either had known women too well or else had been deprived of them entirely. Certainly the stone had been caressed with desire and fashioned with a hungry ruthlessness that had left it a brazen challenge to the eyes of man. Yet there was something refreshingly honest and direct in Baggage's lack of modesty. Her seeming depravity sprang not so much from weakness or viciousness as from an ordered philosophy of existence—a desire to share with others the good things of life of which she herself was one of the best. If endowed with life Baggage would never be one of those women who tearfully proclaim, "I didn't mean to do it." Not Baggage. She would say instead, "Sure I did it, and if you don't watch out I'll go and do it again." Also, one would always know where to find Baggage. One would only have to look for the nearest man, and if there were two men, no doubt the other one would be waiting for her as patiently as possible.

These unedifying reflections upon the probable character of Baggage passed through Mr. Pebble's mind as his eyes dwelt on the lithe, lovely lines of the full-blown figure.

He had found Baggage in a storage warehouse. She had been sold in default of payment for her keep. Yet even the dusty mantle gathered from her long incarceration had failed to rob her body of its wild pagan grace. Mr. Pebble had an eye that automatically discounted the outer draperies of women in favor of what lay beneath. He had bought her on the spot.

"Wouldn't you like a sheet about her?" the man had asked when Baggage had been deposited in the back of the open motor.

"I might," Mr. Pebble had told the man. In fact, I'm sure I would, but I doubt if the lady would like it."

Leaving the man a little shocked, Mr. Pebble had driven off with Baggage. Later he had presented her to his mistress. Since then she had become a part of the establishment, like Nockashima and the bloodhound, Mr. Henry.

With a slight start Mr. Pebble raised his snow-white head, then shrugged his shoulders as if remonstrating with himself. Had those cocktails made him drowsy, and had his thoughts gone straying into the realms of pure fancy? Surely he had imagined he had seen the tawny, voluptuous form of Baggage step down from her little pedastal and come gliding towards him across the path of the slanting sun now flickering on the still waters of the pool. Surely he had imagined this, and yet— Mr. Pebble half rose from the bench and looked at the spot where the statue had been but where it was no more.

"My god!" he muttered. "Did the poor girl fall in? This is indeed a night of catastrophe."

"Sit down, old man," said a low voice beside him. "I didn't fall in the pool. I have come to pay you a long deferred visit."

Mr. Pebble resumed his seat. Quite calmly he accepted the situation.

"Hello, Baggage," he said. "I'm afraid you've come too late. I'm an old man now, as you have just reminded me."

He glanced at the beautiful figure beside him, then savored as if on the tip of his tongue the full bitterness of his years. There was something so imperatively urgent in the sleek young body of the girl sitting so close to him on the bench, Mr. Pebble felt that a just God should do a little something about it. Either the cocktails or the animal magnetism of his companion was making him a bit dizzy. His old, tired heart was thumping dangerously against his vest. What was it the doctor had told him about that heart—no excitement? That was it, no excitement. How absurd. If the doctor himself were here he would be fit to be tied. In fact, he would have to be tied if only for the sake of propriety. The low voice was speaking again. "You were too busy when you were young to pay any attention to me," said Baggage. "What were you always doing in that little pavilion down there?"

"You know all the answers," Mr. Pebble told her. "Hadn't you better let me get you some clothes?"

"And you know me better than that," said the girl, with a mocking laugh. "I never wore a stitch of clothes in my life. Why should I begin now?"

"Well, times are not what they were, my child," Mr. Pebble answered feebly. "Women wear clothes nowadays —not much of them, I'll admit, but still they wear a few."

"I wish you were young again," said the girl, fixing Mr. Pebble with a pair of wickedly disturbing eyes.

"Oh, how I do," muttered Mr. Pebble. "Don't look at me like that. It won't do you a bit of good, and it's upsetting me terribly. After all, I did you a good turn once. What's the idea now? Why are you trying to torment me?"

"I'm jealous," replied Baggage, "jealous of the youth you've lost. I want you back again."

"Listen, Baggage," Rex Pebble said earnestly. "Nobody wants to get back more passionately than I do, but you can see for yourself, my child, it just can't be done. There's no going back for me. I'm an old man now, with a heart too weak to hold its memories."

"Your memories would overtax the strongest heart," she told him; then asked curiously, "Has all desire vanished from your body?"

"Yes, my dear," responded Mr. Pebble a little sadly, "but not from my brain. That's what makes it so difficult to look upon you as you deserve—to estimate you dispassionately for what you are."

"And what am I?" asked the girl.

"A saucy, impertinent young wanton with a single-track mind," he told her; then added reflectively, "Not that the track doesn't run through diverting pastures."

"You've said it, old man," replied Baggage commonly. "I need a spot of diversion."

"I'm afraid you won't find any here," said Rex Pebble, "unless you'd like to have me try to improve your morals."

"How can one improve what never existed?" Baggage wanted to know. "I never had any morals. That's why I've always remained an essentially honest girl."

"Perhaps you're right at that," observed Mr. Pebble. "Human beings are cluttered up with morals altogether too early in life. A wise providence should wait until our bodies are too old and weak to resent them—to get our backs up, so to speak."

"How do you mean, get our backs up?" Baggage asked in a puzzled voice. She paused, then smiled delightedly. "Ah," she said, "I think I see. What an odd way to put it.".

"You don't see at all," declared Mr. Pebble, "but you're quite right about having no morals. You remind me of my mistress."

"What!" exclaimed the girl. "That old———"

"If you please," Mr. Pebble hastily interrupted.

"Oh, all right," said Baggage impatiently. "I'd remind you of all women if you only really knew them. At heart we're not nearly so refined as you men try to make us, and we know a lot of words, too."

"Don't I know!" replied Mr. Pebble. "Not only do you know a lot of words, but you also love to use them. My life has not been overburdened by too many refined women."

"Then you should know a lot of bad words I've missed," the girl said hopefully. "Tell me some."

Mr. Pebble looked really affronted.

"You'd better talk with my mistress," he replied a little coldly, "or better still, with my wife."

"I won't have any dealings with either of those hags," Baggage retorted. "They had all the youth of you. What have I got? Nothing but an old horrid."

"Why don't you join the army?" Mr. Pebble ungallantly suggested. "You should be able to get plenty of action there."

"I've had my heart set on you for years," said Baggage. "I hate to let you escape me."

She cuddled up closer to him on the bench and put a cool arm round his neck.

"Heaven protect me," muttered Mr. Pebble. "If that woman of mine called Spray finds us together like this there'll be no escaping her."

"I hope she does," said Baggage. "I'd love to annoy her."

"I feared as much," said Mr. Pebble. "She is annoyed enough already."

"Are you?" asked the girl, burrowing her small nose into his neck just behind his ear. "You smell awfully clean. Why don't you take your clothes off?"

With a startled ejaculation Mr. Pebble broke the girl's strangle hold and slid along the bench to momentary safety.

"You can think of the damnedest things," he complained. "Let me point out this to you: I am a clean old man, and you are a vile young woman. We have nothing at all in common."

"I want to bite your ear," said the girl. "That is always a good way to start."

"Keep your teeth to yourself," Mr. Pebble retorted. "What are you thinking of starting, anyway?"

"Something in the nature of a seduction," said Baggage. "That is, if you'll stop flitting about like some nervous old bird."

"I am a nervous old bird," replied Rex Pebble. "A very nervous old bird, indeed. Why can't you talk and be reasonable instead of mauling me about? You have even less consideration for a body than a professional wrestler."

"Then consider my body for a moment," said Baggage.

"What am I going to do with it?"

"Why don't you take it back to your pedestal, where it belongs?" asked Mr. Pebble.

"My body belongs with yours," replied the girl.

"Then it virtually belongs in the grave," said Mr. Pebble. "I'm going to fall down dead if this keeps up." "Let's fall down together," Baggage suggested.

"By God!" cried Rex Pebble. "If I were twenty years younger, or even ten——"

"Yes?" broke in the girl. "Go on. What would you do?"

"None of your damn business," said Mr. Pebble. "I'd teach you a lesson."

"How do you know you could?" Baggage challenged.

"By all that's holy," exclaimed Rex Pebble, now thoroughly aroused, "I will teach you a lesson if it's my last act in life."

He rose quickly from the bench, and ripping off his coat and vest in one ruthless movement, tossed them to the flags.

"Hurry!" cried the undismayed Baggage encouragingly. "Stick out your legs and I'll drag your pants off."

The hard-boiled ardor of the girl was too much for Rex Pebble. With a sudden revulsion of feeling he sank back on the bench.

"What a suggestion!" he muttered. "What a picture! Me with my legs stuck out and you dragging off my trousers. What do you think this is, a game?"

"Sure," replied Baggage. "You can keep your shoes on. I don't mind."

"I'd look crisp with my shoes on," observed Mr. Pebble. "Not to mention my socks and supporters."

"Who's going to worry about your feet?" demanded Baggage. "Snap off those pants."

"Snap them off?" repeated Mr. Pebble. "Oh, my word. Everything is all off. I am definitely beyond seduction."

"You're no such thing," cried the girl, flinging herself upon him and dragging out his shirt tails.

Once more the famous Pebble courage asserted itself. No woman was going to drag out his shirt tails. That was going too far. He rose from the bench and seized the girl by the shoulders. Mistaking his intentions she abandoned his shirt tails to the light summer breeze, and threw her arms round his neck. For a moment they struggled perilously on the edge of the pool, then Baggage with a low laugh wriggled from his grasp and sprang lightly away.

"Pist! She uttered in a piercing whisper. "Look behind you!"

The water of the pool parted smoothly as the even smoother body split its surface. Like a flash of silver Baggage streaked through the green depths, then dwindled and disappeared. Where had she gone? Rex Pebble wondered. Had the whole episode been a figment of his disordered imagination? Or had Nockashima mixed some curious Oriental dream-stuff in the cocktails? From cocktails to shirt tails was not a wide leap in thought. Mr. Pebble took the leap. His shirt tails were out. They were playing havoc with the Pebble poise. That was not a question of imagination. It was grim reality. And equally real was the fact that Baggage, in the flesh, had dragged those same shirt tails from their tender concealment. An impulsive wench.

Mr. Pebble realized with a pang of regret that he could not stand there forever gazing into the pool for a last glimpse of that swift silver body. Baggage had withdrawn from life as remarkably as she had appeared. He hated to turn about and face his mistress. Nevertheless, it would have to be done, or she would do it herself by force. He sighed, and without any unnecessary ostentation, collected his shirt tails and tucked them out of sight. It was not a neat job, but at least he felt less like a flag. Then slowly he turned his back on the pool and faced about to meet Spray Summers who, in spite of her feet, was bearing down upon him like a ship under full sail. Mr. Pebble noted with relief that the good lady appeared to be far more astonished than angry.

"A pretty way to be carrying on at your time of life," she announced, a trifle winded from the unaccustomed speed of her progress. "Tell me without even attempting to lie, you senile atrocity, just who was that naked trollop you were trying to assault before you chucked her into the pool."

"You've got your facts in reverse," said Mr. Pebble. "In the first place, the trollop was trying to assault me, and in the second place, she chucked herself in the pool the moment she saw you."

"Then why doesn't she come up," demanded Spray, "se I could give her a piece of my mind? Perhaps she's drowning. I hope so."

"It was Baggage," said Mr. Pebble. "But she's gone now. Look, Spray. The pedestal is vacant!"

CHAPTER IV

JUST A DIP AT TWILIGHT

SPRAY SUMMERS looked with large eyes at the pedestal upon which the wench Baggage had once stood so gracefully poised, then she sniffed with all the righteous indignation of the most moral woman in the world.

"Good riddance of bad rubbish," she said. "What was she doing?"

"As far as I could find out," replied Mr. Pebble, "she was trying to drag my trousers off."

"What for?" demanded Spray.

"How should I know?" asked Mr. Pebble innocently.

"Who should know better than you?" snapped the woman. "If a man started in to drag off my pants I'd ask as a matter of interest exactly what he was after."

"I was a little afraid of the answer," said Rex Pebble.

"You needn't have been," observed Spray, witheringly. "She must simply have wanted a pair of pants. That's the most you could offer the hussy."

"Isn't that quite enough?" asked Mr. Pebble.

"Empty pants never meant much in my young life," said Spray, dropping wearily to the bench. "From the way that woman was tugging at you it looked to me as if she was after a great deal more than your pants."

"It would look that way to you," remarked Rex Pebble. "Aren't you the least bit interested in the disappearance of the statue?"

"Oh, I don't know," replied Spray, passing a hand across her eyes. "Odd happenings seem to be the natural order of events this evening—such as Mr. Henry eating the steak and Sue sending me slippers and you fighting with a naked woman for possession of your pants. I feel a little odd myself. It might be the cocktails, but I haven't felt like this for years."

Rex Pebble took her hand in his.

"I know how it is," he said. "Almost anything might happen. But," he added with a shrug, "nothing ever does. We just sit here growing older like a pair of spectators waiting after the curtain has dropped. There's nothing more to see and no place new to go, yet here we sit, you with your tired feet and me with my bad heart."

"You were wrestling with a naked woman only a minute ago," said Spray. "Isn't that enough for one evening?"

"No," replied Mr. Pebble decidedly, "it is not."

"How about that precious soul of yours?" asked Spray Summers. "What's become of that?"

"I'm afraid it never clicked," said Rex Pebble. "Just a string of long words. Certainly, I don't care for you with my soul, because now that you're old I think you're pretty awful."

"And I think you should be chloroformed," retorted Spray. "You sit there brooding over the past like an old buzzard on a dead cow."

"Prettily turned," said Mr. Pebble. "And quite right, too, but one can't wrestle with a nude girl, even at my age, without feeling somewhat aroused."

"It would only make me feel tired," observed Spray.

"Obviously," said Mr. Pebble, "but you're not a man, and I am."

"You're merely the crumbling ruins of a man," said Spray, pressing the hand that was holding hers, "but I like you just the same. You're still so much of a fool."

"But you don't care for me with your soul?" continued Mr. Pebble. "Don't tell me that."

"No," she said. "That sort of talk has always been 'way above my head. I don't understand it. If I were a young girl and I came upon you here, I know jolly well I wouldn't fall in love with a white-haired man of sixty, no matter if I was fairly bursting with soul. I just couldn't do it. And now I'm an old woman I don't love you for what you are so much as for what you were—what we were together."

"That's it," said Rex Pebble. "That's it exactly. I keep calling on you and listening to your banalities not for what you are now, but because of old associations, for the things we've done and seen together, the good times we've had and the bad ones we've shared. Like the memory of a dead child, the past holds us together."

"Beautifully but depressingly put," murmured Spray. "The past is the only child I've ever had."

"He was a lusty little devil," said Mr. Pebble. "I wish we had him back."

"Yes," agreed Spray sadly. "He was a very amusing child and always up to mischief." Cupping her mouth in her hands, she turned her head toward the house and shouted, "Nockashima, you heathen! We want cocktails!"

"If he isn't singing aloud to Mr. Henry," said Rex Pebble, "as is his custom, it's barely possible he may have heard you."

As if by magic Nockashima appeared, hurrying busily across the grass. On a tray he was carrying the silver shaker and two long-stemmed glasses.

"That's a real pretty sight," remarked Spray, growing a little esthetic at the prospect of a drink. "The white jacket, you know, and the silver shaker and the green grass and all. Only the man is vile."

Collecting a red metal table on the way, the little servant deftly placed it before them; then, with a clever flourish, he deposited the tray on the table.

"I had drink all mixed," he announced with satisfaction. "Nice evening, madam, for drink. Wine go good with dinner."

"Damn me if I know how you're still able to walk," said Spray, "let alone to think, but for this service, Nocka, I freely forgive you the steak."

Nockashima giggled his pleasure, gave several quick, ducking little bows, and was about to withdraw when his eyes chanced to stray across the pool. For a moment he stood staring with foolish astonishment at the vacant pedestal, then looked inquiringly from his mistress to Mr. Pebble.

"Naked lady all gone?" he asked in a hushed voice. "She no more be with us here?"

"I'm afraid not, Nocka," said Mr. Pebble. "The naked lady seems to have taken flight."

"Too bad," said the Japanese sorrowfully. "She pretty good, I thought. She very nice." Once more he was about to turn away, and once more he stopped as if remembering some trivial incident, "I saw naked lady on next lawn," he announced quite casually. "She look like our one only this naked lady all flesh and no stone."

"What was she doing on the next lawn?" asked Spray Summers, always alert for a little scandal.

"Oh, she just attack chauffeur," explained the Jap indifferently. "Chauffeur called Alfred. Naked lady very determined. She get Alfred down right on grass——"

"Pretty," interrupted Spray sardonically. "And only next door. Go on, Nocka."

"Then Alfred spring up," said Nockashima, "with big howl but no pants. Just drawers for Alfred."

"The poor chap seems to have escaped not entirely without honor," observed Mr. Pebble, "although it was just drawers for him. Were they long, Nockashima, those drawers?"

"Yes, boss, with bags," said the Jap. "Quite funny."

"She may have been naked," put in Spray, hoping to cast a feeble beam of morality into the darkly unmoral jungle of her little servant's mind, "but she was far from being a lady. She actually attempted to take off Mr. Pebble's pants."

"Yes, madam," agreed Nocka sociably. "I saw that, too. Very active occasion. She pretty good."

"Nocka," put in Spray severely, "you can take yourself off without any more personal observations, or I'll chuck you out on your ear."

"Yes, madam," murmured the small man, with one of his quick bows.

This time, when Nocka withdrew he made no attempt to turn back. He had read correctly the danger signals sparking in the eyes of madam.

"That naked lady doesn't seem to be having much luck," observed Mr. Pebble, looking with a faint grin after the retreating figure of the little Jap.

"She's making progress," replied Spray. "She succeeded in getting your shirt tails out and the chauffeur's pants off. Anything may happen when her technique improves. Still, I contend her methods are too disconcerting. They tend to make the subject forget the object of the assault."

"Exactly," agreed Rex Pebble. "A man is accustomed to take the initiative in such affairs."

"But they don't take it often enough," replied Spray Summers. "There should be an open season for unmarried women over a certain age."

"From the little I've been able to observe of the modern young woman," said Mr. Pebble, "assault seems no longer necessary. I have an idea there should be a closed season for men."

"You don't have to worry about that," replied Spray. "Your season is closed for good."

"Yes," said Mr. Pebble regretfully. "My hunting days are done."

"And I am no longer hunted," added Spray. "All I am is an old abandoned quarry whose feet have been run ragged."

"I tell you' what let's do," said Mr. Pebble, seized by a sudden impulse. "Let's strip off our clothes and take a dip in the pool."

"Are you craftily trying to get me to help you look for that naked lady?" demanded Spray Summers. "We haven't been in the pool for years. The shock might kill us."

"What if it does kill us?" replied Mr. Pebble, now reckless from many cocktails. "It would be as good a way to go out as any. My heart is ready to call it a day at the slightest provocation. Let's take a chance. The cool water might soothe your tired feet."

This last possibility did much to break down the woman's resistance, which at best had never been strong.

"Give me another cocktail," she said, "and I might consider it, although I think the idea is perfectly mad." She accepted the proffered glass and polished off its contents with professional celerity. As the potently stimulating concoction was assimilated into her system the idea lost some of its madness and her mood became more yielding. "Your suggestion has its points," she resumed, breaking the short silence. "It might be fun at that. We'll take our last swim, and if we do die it will save us a lot of time and trouble."

"You always were a game kid," said Mr. Pebble approvingly. "Especially where foolishness was concerned. Come on, let's strip."

"I'd like to be foolish again," replied Spray. "And this certainly seems foolish to me."

A few minutes later two mother-naked figures were standing on the edge of the pool. Had Nockashima been watching—as he probably was—he would have found the occasion highly diverting. The years had added flesh to Spray Summers' body and removed it from Mr. Pebble's. Of the two it was the man whose figure appeared the more youthful. Spray was fat and flaccid, given to sagging here and there and bulging in various places. When she had finished with her body she had shamefully let it down, and now it was taking its revenge. Rex Pebble still remained as straight and slim as a boy, but a great deal more knobby.

"I hate you," declared Spray Summers, regarding him enviously. "You remain the same from year to year while all I do is get fatter and more jellified. It isn't fair. I hate my body."

"See that scar," said Mr. Pebble, pointing to a long white line on his right leg. "I got that twenty years ago when you pushed me into the fireplace. The andirons did it. It doesn't seem all that time ago, does it?"

"No," replied Spray. "Look at this one." She lifted her left foot and displayed a wicked scar. "That came from stepping on a broken glass during one of my less responsible moments. It seems only yesterday. I can even recall the doctor's face and how I accused him of not knowing his business. That was a wild party."

"Just a couple of old battlers," said Rex Pebble with a grin. "Weather-beaten and dishonorably scarred."

"I've got some on my head," replied Spray Summers.

"I was always knocking it against things that refused to budge."

"You were terribly unfortunate that way," agreed Mr. Pebble reminiscently. "Always being patched, or stitched, or turning blue in places."

"I bruised so easily," replied Spray, "and you could never learn to keep your great hands to yourself."

"In those unregenerate days," said Mr. Pebble, "your body attracted my great hands like a magnet."

"Excuse please," a voice broke in behind them. "I catch sight of unfrocked bodies, so I bring towels."

With admirable presence of mind Spray Summers and Mr. Pebble snatched the towels from the Japanese and draped them about themselves to the best advantage. "You think of everything, don't you?" said Spray, in an evil voice. "If I wasn't so busy hiding my person I'd like to break your neck!"

"I not think of this," declared Nockashima. "This occasion too much for me. When I see boss and madam without stitch, I think naked lady come back and take clothes. I bring towels so not catch cold."

"I'm the only naked lady around here," said Spray Summers tartly. "Who's this person?"

"I beg your pardon," said a tall elderly gentleman, emerging from a clump of bushes. "I really wasn't going to make my presence known under the circumstances, but seeing you don't seem to mind——"

"Who told you that?" demanded Mr. Pebble. "I mind a lot."

"What were you doing in those bushes?" Spray Summers put in. "Do you happen to be a Peeping Thomas?"

"Far from it," replied the stranger. "I was merely trying to spare your feelings, but as I said, seeing you don't seem to mind——"

"I do wish you'd stop telling us we don't seem to mind," Spray interrupted impatiently. "If it wasn't for this towel I'd be groveling on my face in an agony of embarrassment."

"Will you be so good as to state your business," said Mr. Pebble, "and then clear out? This isn't a permanent exhibition, you know."

"Most assuredly," replied the gentleman politely. "An off moment, so to speak. It occurred to me in passing that you might be interested in some old and rare."

"Are you the man with the steak?" asked Spray Summers, out of a clear sky.

"I beg your pardon," said the old gentleman. "Where does steak come in?"

"I don't know that it does," replied Spray. "I just thought you might be trying to interest us in some old and rare steak. Mr. Henry ate ours all up."

"That was too bad of Mr. Henry," said the old gentleman with vague insincerity, looking reprovingly at Mr. Pebble.

"I didn't eat the steak," Mr. Pebble told him. "Mr. Henry is a bloodhound. That's a dog. Just who and what are you?"

"Look!" cried Nockashima. "Fifi, she come, too."

The group turned and watched the excited approach of Spray Summers' dangerously pretty French maid. What with her high-heeled shoes, her undulating hips, and the mincing steps she took, the girl was literally tripping across the grass.

"My word," observed the purveyor of old and rare. "This begins to look more and more like a musical comedy."

"All we need is a chorus of neighbors," said Mr. Pebble bitterly.

"Madam!" exclaimed Fifi. "What can one do? This is an affair of love. Privacy is most important at such times. These men are not amiable thus to delay your pleasure."

"°My God," breathed Mr. Pebble. "Are all women indecent? This maid of yours has put us on the spot."

"A thousand pardons!" cried the elderly gentleman. "I had no idea I was interrupting a——"

"Shut up!" shouted Mr. Pebble.

"It's quite all right, Fifi," said her mistress. "We can control ourselves. But I don't know what's come over everybody. Nockashima wants to keep us from catching cold; you want us to do something altogether different and better; this man keeps mouthing about old and rare, and we want to go swimming. Everything's all mixed up. Why don't you take them away and stop trying to memorize every joint in Mr. Pebble's enfeebled body?"

"Some are not present," said Fifi.

"That's just too bad," flung back Rex Pebble. "They're present but concealed."

"My word," murmured the Old and Rare. "This is better than a musical comedy. It's more like a burlesque."

"That monsieur I will take away," declared Fifi, "but not the unclean Japanese. He made a lewd suggestion a little while ago, then with a grip incroyable in one so small followed it up with a pinch." Here Fifi patted herself with a gentle but unabashed hand. "And, madam, I bruise so easily. There will be a spot on that place there."

"So do I," said Spray sympathetically. "I sometimes wonder if that isn't why we are built so large. You know —just to have room for the pinches of unclean men. And the more unclean they are the more pinches we get."

"A small pinch, yes," replied Fifi. "One can understand —one can even enjoy. That is a friendly thing and to be expected. But that man there, he has the fingers of steel. His clutch is like a trap. He makes me push a great cry even when Madam entertains."

"The wicked little beast," said Spray. "It seems to be a habit with him."

"It is, madam," replied Fifi, elevating her round tragic eyes. "It is a mania—a depravity. Pinch, pinch, pinch, all the time it's pinch. I get no rest, and sit down only with groans of distress. The small man with the talons, he is making my life miserable. I grow old from his fingers."

"If I not pinch," put in Nockashima, "Fifi get glum. Then she flaunt it and get it in way of work. I pinch and Fifi curse, then start sing so happily about la-

la-la.. Who is this la-la-la?"

"Not now, Nockashima," protested Mr. Pebble. "We will go into la-la-la later. Everything will be explained, including the technique of pinching evil-thinking French maids."

"I pinch baroness," replied Nocka. "She not cry. She giggle like girl."

"Then shoots your leg full of holes," put in Spray Summers.

"Ha!" cried Fifi, completely forgetting herself. "So the depraved one not content with mine also pinches those of others. He is a dirty cow and his mother never said no to a sailor. Upon the occasion of his next attempt, me, I will bite off his fingers."

With a flip toss of her pretty head Fifi, the fair product of France, swayed gracefully across the lawn, her flexible torso keeping rhythm with her emotions. Nockashima looked after her undecidedly, quite obviously disturbed by some inner conflict.

"Why should my mother say no to a sailor?" he asked Mr. Pebble. "That girl not know my mother. She crazy."

"Don't worry, Nocka," said Mr. Pebble. "I don't understand her either. There's no reason in the world why your mother should have said no to a sailor. There's no reason why your mother should have talked to a sailor at all."

"I go find out," replied Nockashima.

With an extra quick duck of his head the little Jap spell across the grass and overtook the French maid. Hurling the mangled remains of the English language at each other they disappeared from view behind the garden gate, from the other side of which Fifi promptly pushed a great cry.

"He's at it again," said Spray Summers darkly.

"At what?" asked Mr. Pebble.

"Do you want me to show you?" she demanded.

"You're showing the world already," he answered briskly, then addressed himself to the elderly gentleman. "They're all gone except you," he said. "When are you going?"

"As soon as we've settled this little business of the old and rare," replied the gentleman.

"Listen, mister," said Spray Summers. "I'm old, but I'm not so rare. If you don't clear out pronto I'm going to get tough as hell."

"You are," replied the elderly gentleman, but whether it was a question or a simple statement of fact neither Spray nor Mr. Pebble could decide.

"Couldn't you dignify this discussion," Mr. Pebble suggested rather hopelessly, "by giving yourself some sort of name?"

"Heaven strike me pink!" the old gentleman exclaimed. "I entirely forgot my letter. I have one, you know, but so much has been going on—what I mean to say is, I already feel a part of the family."

"Then don't," said Spray crudely.

The letter he gave to Mr. Pebble read as follows:

Dear Rex:

The individual who hands you this note seems to enjoy being known as Major Lynnhaven Jaffey. I doubt if he remembers his real name, having had occasion to change it so often. He has been everything from a soldier of fortune to a high-class swindler. I know he's a first-rate forger because he raised a check on me quite successfully.

However, he's a diverting rogue, and in view of his unique qualifications I thought he might be ideally fitted for the advertising profession. I am sure you will have much in common. He is all yours if the police don't get him first.

Most cordially,
Tom Pierce.

"That's very nice," said Mr. Pebble with a false laugh when he had finished reading the letter. "He speaks quite highly of you, Major Jaffey."

"He should," replied the Major enigmatically. "Now if you would care to give me a small check for a few items I should——"

"Skillfully make it a large one," Mr. Pebble finished for him. "Don't go on. I know all about it, Major. Why don't you toddle back to the house and call aloud for a long drink? We'll talk the matter over later."

For a fleeting moment the Major permitted himself to look slightly distressed; then the bland smile returned to his not unhandsome face.

"A thousand thanks," he replied. "A small drop of something would not be entirely unwelcome." Here he bowed gallantly to Spray Summers. "In the meantime," he continued, "I hope you enjoy your swim or whatever it was you were about to do."

He turned on his heel and strode across the lawn, which was just as well for all concerned, because Spray had it on the tip of her tongue to call the Major a big bum. Instead, she contented herself by sitting down on the flags and dipping her feet in the water. Rex Pebble sat down beside.

"That old man," she observed, "has a very bad mind."

"According to Tom's letter," said Mr. Pebble, "he's a very bad old man all over. I like bad old men."

"You should," commented Spray. "That's why you're so fond of yourself. What an odd sort of evening it's been. I wouldn't be a bit surprised if a couple of lions came bounding across the lawn and tearfully pleaded to be allowed to listen to Little Orphan Annie."

With the utmost conservatism Mr. Pebble lowered himself into the pool until he was standing on the bottom waist high in water. Turning to Spray he was surprised to see her examining her foot with an expression of profound astonishment.

"What's up now?" he inquired. "Feel any better?"

"Look at them!" Spray cried, holding out her feet to him. "And take a look at those legs. They couldn't be prettier if they belonged to a girl of twenty."

Mr. Pebble looked at the proffered legs and even went so far as to feel them.

"They look swell," he admitted, "and they feel even better. What's happened to them?"

"I don't know," replied the delighted Spray. "It just happened. Maybe it's the water. If it is, you should be fixed up fine by now. Are you?"

"What do you mean?" asked Mr. Pebble.

"Come here a second," said Spray.

"Nothing doing," replied Mr. Pebble. "I don't like the look in your eyes."

He turned his back to his mistress, peered eagerly down in the water, then took a quick jump. With an incoherent cry of exultation he flung himself on his face and began to swim the crawl with the vigor of a man far younger than his sixty years. Spray watched him with growing astonishment as his long arms cleft the water; then, breathing a silent prayer, she slipped into the pool. The moment the water closed over her head a feeling of buoyant happiness flooded through her. The blood in her veins grew strong with life, and weariness fled from her eyes. When Rex Pebble swam back to her from the other end of the pool he found a beautiful young woman looking down at him from the flags, a woman he had not seen for years save when memory had evoked her vision from the past.

"Hurry!" cried the woman. "Get out of that water quick, or you'll drop below the age of puberty."

"That would never do," said Mr. Pebble, springing from the pool.

It was a fine figure of a man who took the woman in his arms.

"What a kiss!" murmured Spray. "What a kiss. Do you remember how! Tell me, Rex, is my face burning? How old do you think I look?"

"Not a day over twenty-five," he declared. "Has anything happened to me?"

Spray inspected the length of the long, lean body, hesitated a brief moment, then politely averted her eyes.

"I should say it has," she announced decidedly. "Why, Rex Pebble, I haven't seen you like that for years." She paused for a moment, then added demurely, "I mean your white hair is all gone. You might be thirty-five, but I doubt it."

Mr. Pebble looked both proud and embarrassed.

"I say," he said, "what do you think has happened to us?"

"Darned if I know," replied Spray, eagerly examining various points of interest about her body. "I haven't had time to think. With a figure like mine I doubt if I ever will."

"I put it down to Baggage," said Mr. Pebble. "The contact of her body has fired this pool with vitality."

"Make it your business to see that her contact is confined to the pool," Spray Summers warned him, then added with a mocking smile, "Mr. Pebble, don't you think we are wasting a lot of time?"

"I think so," said Mr. Pebble.

Once more he took her in his arms and held her there for a long time.

"Thank God," murmured Spray piously, "it's quite dark now."

"Yes," replied Mr. Pebble, "it covers a multitude of sins."

"I could stand a multitude of sins," said Spray. "You see, I've been born again, and I have no sins left."

"Something should be done about that," said Rex Pebble, "or you'll fall into the error of self-righteousness. I wonder if the door to the pavilion is locked?"

"If it is you can break it down," replied Spray. "What does a small door mean in our young lives?"

"It might mean quite a lot," observed Mr. Pebble.

As they walked down the path in the direction of the pavilion Spray began to laugh softly to herself.

"What's it all about?" Mr. Pebble wanted to know.

"This," replied Spray, "is just about going to burn Sue up."

CHAPTER V

ALARUMS AND INCURSIONS

QUIET had returned to the garden. the grass and bushes were powdered with silver dust. Moonlight and starlight sifted through the air. A pale unearthly radiance lay over all things save where the tracery of trees tossed weirdly beautiful tapestries across the close-cut lawn. In a near-by bush a fastidious wing fluttered impatiently with a little drumming sound, momentarily ruffling the silence which was lulled again to tranquillity by the subdued chirps of drowsing birds. Far below in the dark oblivion slashed by the winding valley the lights of the little villages winked vaingloriously back at the stars. Lite an urgent summons from a lost world the rhythmic thrumming of a train rose on the still air, and the pain-edged voice of its whistle filled the night with a restless loneliness. Then silence again and enchantment, as the stars cast coins in the pool.

And into this silvery silence two white figures emerged from the small pavilion and mingled with the night. The silence was rudely shattered by the vulgar sound of a hand slapping bare flesh. No chance now for enchantment. They were back again, those two mortals, and with them they had brought a lusty love of life.

"Well, Dame Quickly," exclaimed Mr. Pebble with unwonted commonness as he briskly whacked his mistress on the flank, "there's life in the old mare yet—what?"

,"Ouch!" protested Dame Quickly. "Can't you ever learn when it's time to let a lady alone? What a way for a man to act."

"You should consider your self flattered," responded Rex Pebble.

"Flattened would be more like it," observed Spray Summers.

"You're upset," said Mr. Pebble with unruffled urbanity. "Listen, Spray, I can scarcely realize we're young again."

"If you can't realize that," Spray retorted with unnecessary significance, "I can't think of any new way to make the fact clear."

"Let's turn to athletics," Mr. Pebble hastily suggested. "Come on old darling, I'll race you to the other end of the pool."

"I will if you give me half a chance," Spray told him. "No monkey business in the water."

For a moment they stood poised on the edge of the Pool; then, like two living spears, cleanly sheathed themselves in its star-plunged depths. Behind them a trail of sparkling drops fell and twinkled in the moon-light. By the time the swimmers had reached the far end of the pool two years had been subtracted from their respective ages. And when Spray's gleaming body slipped sinuously from the wayer she stood revealed in the silvery light a beautiful girl of twenty-three. Although her figure was full blown and luxurious with all the approved pneumatic features, still it carried the speed and lith, sleek grace of a soft-footed cat of the jungle. An instinctive temptress was Spray, as are most women, which is just as well for the good of the species. Long lashes, wet from the pool, half veiled her large, dark eyes which were very wicked and charming. Her full lips, a trifle slack, were parted in an indolent smile. Hers was the fascination of youth made dangerous by a world of experience. There were two small ears, a short, selfish nose, and a wilderness of copper-colored hair, now matted to her head and spangled with drops of water.

The man who stood beside her was no mean companion, although it would never have occurred to an artist to single him out for a model for an epic advertisement of drawers, cigarettes, or motorcars. Ten years the senior of his mistress, he had an attractively knit body, long of limb and loosely jointed. And his muscles were not of the knobbily obtrusive variety, being of the sinewy pattern that told of a flowing continuity of endurance rather than brute strength. Yet in spite of his youthful appearance some traces of the man of sixty still lingered in his face. Unlike the more volatile Spray, he had not lightly cast aside the disillusioning knowledge of a past which had now so strangely become the future. His clear blue eyes were as wise and defensively skeptical as they had been, and the deep lines that cleft his cheeks gave an odd effect of maturity. His hair was rather silly, sandy colored and too finely spun. It did much to destroy the natural dignity of the man's expression. Beneath the eyes the cheek bones were harshly prominent, and the skin that slanted down to the chin had a firm, hungry leanness. His long thin face bore a stamp of distinction, a patrician type, the strong, aquiline nose made somewhat less formidable by the mouth beneath it, with the slow smiling lips a little bitter yet wholly pleasure-loving. It was a difficult face to read, so marked was it with conflicting characteristics—the face of a man who could scale the loftiest heights or else take a tremendous tumble down them with an equal thoroughness of purpose. One thing was fairly certain, Rex Pebble would never stand still in the same place long.

"You know," remarked the girl, lazily flexing her body, "if we keep fooling round this pool we'll be getting childish next."

"Even that," observed Mr. Pebble, "would be preferable to senile decay."

"I like us just as we are," declared Spray, "with a few cocktails tossed in just for good measure. Are there any left?"

Rex Pebble tested the shaker, then filled two glasses and extended one to Spray.

"Here's to that lush nymph, Baggage," he said, flooding his drink with moonlight, "a fair, virile wench with a bountiful disposition."

"You better lay off that supersexed wanton," Spray Summers warned him. "No one yet has ever accused me of being stingy. Furthermore, there's your old wife to be considered. What are you going to do about her?"

"Great guns!" exclaimed Mr. Pebble, suddenly concerned. "My wife! What is she going to do about me? is a lot more like it. I'll still carry on, of course. There's such a thing as loyalty. A chap can't very decently abandon a legitimately old wife simply because he happens to have suddenly grown backwards."

"Perhaps she'll die soon," said Spray consolingly. "It's almost time she did."

"God!" ejaculated Mr. Pebble in a shocked voice. "What a thing to suggest! Would you like to have me murder her, perhaps?"

"Not immediately," she replied calmly. "I want my revenge first. When she sees me all dolled up in the latest and most youthful styles she'll probably be glad to die."

"I hope you won't rub it in too much," Rex Pebble told her.

"Don't worry about me," said Spray. "You have quite enough to worry about as it is. There's your business connections, for example. Do you think people are going to believe you when you tell them you're Rex Pebble?"

"I don't care how passionate a woman may be," Mr. Pebble declared in a disgusted voice, "the practical side of her nature is sure to crop out at the wrong moment." Thoughtfully he sipped his cocktail, then resumed: "Indubitably there are going to be no end of embarrassing complications, but on this happy occasion I steadfastly refuse to anticipate them. Trouble can find its way about without my assistance."

"Here comes a compact little chunk of it now," observed Spray Summers, hastily snatching up a towel. "That runt of a heathen is running as if his heart would break, if he had one. Wonder what's taken possession now of his undeveloped mind?"

In a condition of mental and physical demoralization, Nockashima arrested his mad progress and stood scrutinizing the two nude figures, his small, rapidly blinking eyes generating hopeless bewilderment.

"This night," he announced at last, "the nakedest I recall. No clothes for anybody. Maybe I take off mine too."

"No," said Mr. Pebble hastily. "Don't do that. Someone must stay dressed."

"Perhaps yes," agreed the little Jap. "You see two other naked bodies knocking about? Old naked bodies—not so good."

"The parchment-faced little ape," muttered Spray Summers. "I like his nerve."

"Listen, Nocka," said Rex Pebble. "Those old bodies you referred to so offensively are new again. Here they are, standing right before you. Don't you recognize our voices?"

Nockashima received this startling information with truly admirable self-control.

"How nice," he said approvingly. "Hot stuff now."

"Just what does he mean by that?" inquired Spray. "Is there no bottom to his depravity?"

"Don't ask him to elaborate," replied Mr. Pebble.

"Voices just same," continued the grinning servant, "but bodies quite different. Very rapid improvement. Boss look similar to young nephew, Mist' Kippie. Madam some wow. Look like naked lady. Madam have every-thing. Pretty good, I think."

"Only pretty good," put in Spray tartly. "They don't come any better. I'm the swellest-looking naked lady you ever clapped an eye on, you squat myopic dreg."

"Madam look like naked lady on next lawn," declared the myopic dreg as if he had not heard. "You know, boss—pants snatcher."

The little man's eyes were not as myopic as Spray had told him. She did look remarkably like the nymph, Baggage. Her half-parted lips had the same provocative smile, and her body the same brazen challenge.

"You do look a lot like Baggage," remarked Mr. Pebble, regarding her curiously. "I knew there was something just a little different about you. Every now and then I've had a feeling she was looking out at me through your eyes. I hope it isn't a case of atavism. If she has merged her peculiar talents and disposition with yours there won't be a pair of trousers left in the countryside."

"How come you and Madam so much younger, boss?" Nockashima wanted to know. "Big surprise to me. Head take spin. Very strange thing, this. Very strange."

"It is," agreed Mr. Pebble. "And it has to do with magic. Some day, Nocka, I'll tell you all about it."

"Magic," repeated the Japanese. "You believe magic, boss?"

"I'm afraid there's no way of getting around it," replied Mr. Pebble.

"I know man who got around magic," declared Nockashima. "He Japanese fella, too."

"How do you mean?" asked Spray Summers, interested in spite of herself.

"By squeeze," replied the servant.

"What did he squeeze?" demanded Rex Pebble, then hastily added, "Think well before you answer."

"Well," vouchsafed Nocka, his eyes growing even more animated, "this man I know meet fox once. Fox suddenly turn into beautiful naked lady. By and by man and lady go sleep. When man wake up fox sleep on pillow beside him. Man nudge fox. 'Where my beautiful naked lady?' he ask. 'I that beautiful naked lady,' declare fox, much amused. 'Maybe yes to another fox,' say man all excited, 'but you great disappointment to me.' Here man squeeze down own throat of fox. Fox turn into big snake. 'Goodness gracious,' says man, 'this get worse and worse. This quite impossible now.' He keep on with squeeze, and snake turn into little flea. 'What idea?' demand man. 'Little flea not help matters any. Only small strand of patience remain.' Flea only giggle with rage-provoking mirth. 'You do that on other side of face,' grit man, and with both hands squeeze down on neck of little flea."

"How in God's name," demanded Spray in a thoroughly exasperated voice, "could that friend of yours squeeze down with both hands on the neck of a little flea? A flea hasn't got any neck to speak of—not even a big one. You're just telling us a long string of tiresome lies. How did it turn out?"

"Well," resumed Nockashima, drawing a deep breath, "flea make great moan and groan, then utter piercing scream and turn into lobster, and lobster turn into sheep. 'Getting close,' say man, 'but not quite.' He squeeze some more, and sheep turn into naked lady. 'Hullo,' say man. 'Where you been?' 'I been in trouble,' say naked lady, very hoarse. 'No more choke now, if please.' So man take hand from throat of naked lady and place elsewhere. Naked lady giggle just like flea. 'Suppose I turn into angry tiger?' she ask. 'If do,' say man, 'you have to hurry like hell.'"

"He did?" said Spray, now deeply interested. "And what did the naked lady do?"

"She not turn into angry tiger," replied Nockashima. "She give up."

"It was about time she did," declared Spray. "Just imagine, going through all that for no earthly reason. She should have given up in the first place. The man must have been frantic."

"That man my cousin," the small servant concluded proudly. "He quite fond of magic."

"He had every reason to be," said Mr. Pebble. "I'm quite fond of magic myself."

"Would you mind telling me," Spray Summers unamiably demanded of the little yellow man, "if you came streaking across that lawn like a bat out of hell for the express purpose of telling us a long, lying, and very dirty story about fleas, foxes, and naked ladies, not to mention your lecherous cousin?"

Nockashima's expression underwent a sudden and startling change. His features were twisted into lines of consternation.

"Goodness gracious!" he exclaimed. "So sorry, madam. Bad business back at house. We are all very deep in trouble."

"I knew it," declared Spray in tones of deep conviction. "I knew it from the moment he opened his lying mouth. That old and rare major has either walked off with all the silver or else set fire to the house. Which is it, Nocka?"

"You quite right, madam," said the servant, gazing with surprise upon his mistress. "House on fire all right, but not like you say."

"What do you mean?" demanded Rex Pebble quickly knotting the towel round his waist. "Speak up, you graven image."

"It was steak," spoke up the graven image obediently.

"I see it all now," said Spray with suppressed fury. "The steak got loose and went dashing about setting fire to the house. It's all very clear." She was silent a moment, then suddenly shouted at the startled Jap, "Be quick, weazened little liar of a man, what did the steak do this time?"

"Oh well," said Nockashima, a little sadly. "You know how it is, madam. Steak catch fire and burn oven up and oven catch fire and burn room up and room——"

"I know how it is," cried Spray in a wild voice. "And room catch fire and burn house up. We could play this game indefinitely. Come on, Rex, let's run like hell."

Following the example Mr. Pebble had set with his towel, Spray raced across the lawn, the sketchily draped Mr. Pebble at her heels, and the weazened little liar of a man, thoughtfully carrying the cocktail shaker, making scrambling noises in the rear while idly toying with the idea of suicide.

A few minutes later the three of them burst into the kitchen, which was filled with smoke and overflowing with firemen. Water applied with indiscriminate generosity composed the third and most disturbing element save one. That element was Fifi, the French maid. She was pushing both cries and firemen about with impartial zeal.

"Malheureuse!" she was lamenting as the group arrived. "This is conduct of the most furious. Madam will be decomposed. Allez-vous en, soiled cows! Vien vite."

"What kind of lingo is that broad gargling?" a fire-man was asking his chief when the voice of Spray Summers cut through the smoke and confusion.

"Nocka, you rat!" she cried. "What have you done with that steak? I'm going to have my dinner if I have to eat it on the lawn."

"Too crisp, madam," protested Nockashima. "Steak start all the trouble."

"Then fill that shaker," she snapped. "I'll drink my damn dinner. Where did all these silly-looking men come from? Tell them to clear out."

Fifi gave a small shriek that sounded more pleased than embarrassed.

"There are two nudes!" she exclaimed. "Regardez-la."

"Say, Chief," demanded the inquisitive fireman, "what kind of a house is this anyway? A sporting house?"

"You ask too many questions," retorted the chief. "Do you know where the fire is? I can't find a flame."

Upon the entrance of Spray and Mr. Pebble the business of fighting fire had been brought to a sudden and complete stop. The firemen were now standing about, their expressions registering emotions running from profound disapproval to open admiration, according to the characters of their individual owners.

"Say, sister," a voice sang out, "have you been playing strip poker?"

"Listen, lady," another voice called, "you're a big girl now. Why don't you hide your shame?"

"Hey, buddy," a third voice inquired. "Who do you think you are—Strangler Lewis?"

"Tell him for me," said another, "his cute little towel isn't on straight."

Nervously clutching his sole claim to decency, Mr. Pebble turned to confront his tormentors, then the hopelessness of the situation overcame him.

"Nockashima," he said wearily. "Are those cocktails finished yet?"

"Gord amighty!" observed a fireman in an awed voice. "With the house burning down around them all those two seem to care about is eating and drinking and carrying on foolish. I can't figure these society birds out."

"I could carry on foolish myself," contributed a brother-in-arms, regarding Spray Summers with unconcealed admiration. "That dame is making me downright silly."

At this point the chief decided it was high time to intervene.

"Say, lady," he said, stepping up to Spray. "You'd better run upstairs and put on some clothes. My men can't keep their minds on their work with you sticking around. I'm sort of slipping myself."

Spray laughed softly.

"What about the fire?" she asked.

"We're looking for that now," said the chief, scratching his sorely perplexed head. "There's got to be a fire somewhere, what with all this smoke, but damn me if I can find a single flame."

An anguished cry burst from Mr. Pebble, and the assembled firemen broke out into a chorus of coarse laughter. Spray turned quickly and looked at her companion in nudity, then added her voice to the chorus. Mr. Pebble's towel lay uselessly at his feet. Furiously he wheeled about and confronted the small French maid. This one, after a rapid survey, raised her wild eyes to heaven.

"This," she said in a voice choked with emotion, "is far more than I asked. M'sieu is too impulsive. We are not alone."

"Why did you take my towel off?" demanded Mr. Pebble.

"I wanted to fix him," exclaimed the maid. "It, as you say in your language."

The laughter of the firemen increased in volume. "It?" repeated Mr. Pebble, in a shocked whisper. "It? Just what do you mean, Fifi?"

"That!" cried Fifi, pointing, and Mr. Pebble shrank back from the unabashed finger. "The towel, m'sieu. Me, I want to fix that towel. It was about to descend."

Here she stooped suddenly and deftly flipped the towel. round Mr. Pebble's waist.

"Here! Here!" he exclaimed, seizing the towel with both hands. "Don't do that, Fifi. I can manage it." Thinking Mr. Pebble was endeavoring to toss the towel aside, Fifi struggled all the harder.

"But M'sieu should wear at least a little something," she protested. "These firemen, they have no appreciation."

"Take your hands away from that body," Spray Summers broke in angrily as she strode across the room. "Your appreciation is altogether too personal."

But the little French maid was not to be so easily turned from her purpose. Not recognizing her rejuvenated mistress, she clung gamely to her end of the towel while Spray snatched the other from Rex Pebble's nerveless grasp. Once more he was bereft of adornment.

"Oh, I say," he protested, dancing agilely after the hotly contested towel in the vain hope of obtaining some small degree of protection from it. "Can't you two women settle this matter amicably? Why not give me the towel? I'm still quite old enough to know what to do with it, and," he added earnestly, "I want to do it very badly."

"Assuredly, M'sieu has sufficient age," said Fifi. "I could see that at a glance."

"Did you hear that, Rex?" cried Spray. "This product of the Parisian boulevards has been giving you the once over."

"So has everyone else," said Rex Pebble in a hopeless voice. "Where the hell is Nockashima? Hey, Nocka, bring me a tablecloth or anything else that's handy. I'd be glad to get even a doily."

There was the sound of a great deal of china falling crashingly to the floor. This was almost immediately followed by the lurching entrance of the Japanese, negligently trailing a tablecloth. It was plain to see that the little man was far gone in drink.

"Here is, boss," he announced thickly. "I snatch off table plenty quick."

"So we heard," said Mr. Pebble dryly as he took the tablecloth and draped it round his body in a sketchy imitation of a Roman toga.

"That right, boss," said Nockashima approvingly. "All things concealed from prying eye now. You look so nice. Just like long-dead statue."

In the meantime, Spray, in trying to gain possession of Mr. Pebble's abandoned towel, stood in imminent peril of losing her own. Preferring to retain her dignity rather than to win a hollow victory, she suddenly relinquished her hold on the towel, with the result that Fifi was sent hurtling through space into the arms of the little Jap, who clung to her for a moment, then carried her with him to the floor from which she promptly began to push a series of frantic cries.

Upon this scene of utter confusion a third nude figure entered and stood peering down with polite interest on the two struggling bodies. This third nude figure was also draped in a large bath towel. And the figure, such as it was, belonged to Major Lynnhaven Jaffey.

"I was taking a bit of a shower," he explained to the room in general, "when, hearing a great commotion, I thought that possibly something might be wrong. Apparently there is."

"Everything is wrong," replied Spray Summers. "Every damn thing."

"I see," said the Major suavely. "This has all the ear-marks of a very low stag party. How I enjoyed them in my youth—the lower the better. I hope I'm not interrupting the entertainment."

"Not at all," Mr. Pebble assured him. "Nothing seems to be able to interrupt this entertainment. And in the meantime the house is afire."

"Great heavens!" exclaimed the Major, nervously fingering his towel. "My old and rare will burn."

"Your old and rare what?" demanded the chief in an uncompromising tone of voice.

"Never mind," said the Major firmly. "Never mind. I must protect my old and rare."

And with this he quickly departed,

"Damn me," said the chief, greatly puzzled, "if I can see why his old and rare should burn any faster than the rest of him. This is the craziest house I've ever been in. What's wrong with all you people, anyway?"

"I've got it, Chief," declared the inquisitive fireman. "We've been lured to a nudist colony."

"Oh, yeah?" cried Spray Summers in a nasty voice. "I wish someone would lure you to a graveyard! I'm getting sick of this. Come on, Rex, let's go upstairs." At the door she paused and looked back at the little Jap upon whose deflated chest Fifi was now sitting. "Nockashima," said Spray severely, "stop pinching that French trollop and snap to it with those cocktails. This smoke has made me thirsty."

"I not pinch French trollop," said Nocka, in a weak voice. "She sitting on it, madam, and me, too."

"Let the little drunkard up, Fifi," continued Spray.

"And give those dull-looking firemen something to drink. It might sharpen their wits a bit."

"Madam," said Fifi, looking curiously at the woman standing in the doorway, "who are you?"

"I'm your mistress," replied Spray coolly. "I've had my face lifted and everything else, too."

"And the M'sieu," asked the maid, "is he a new one, madam, or is he the old?"

"He is the old," answered Spray. "And was he lifted, too?"

"Entirely out of himself," said Spray, "but remember this, Fifi, just what was lifted should be no concern of yours."

CHAPTER VI

THE MAJOR'S OLD AND RARE

MR. HENRY, the non-smeller, felt nervously exhausted. By awkward leaps and bounds he was rapidly becoming a mental case. These leaps and bounds had carried him to the comparative seclusion of the front hall closet. Here he lay and considered the demolishment of his comfortable routine. The trying events of the evening had shot it full of holes. Mr. Henry seriously doubted if he would ever have the heart or the strength to reestablish it again.

From street corners the dog had hitherto been fearsomely impressed by fire engines and had vaguely wondered what devil's work they were about, but until to-night he had never had any dealings with the rough-and-ready gentlemen who clung to these moving vehicles on their terrific dashes through the streets. This one experience had been more than enough for Mr. Henry. Being a dog of delicate sensibilities, he had formed the lowest opinion of the swarm of heavy-handed ruffians that had so ruthlessly invaded the privacy of his home. The vast quantities of water they had brought with them, together with the alarming appearance of so much smoke, had forced the animal to retreat with streaming eyes and a wet hide to his present place of safety.

Here Mr. Pebble and his mistress discovered Mr. Henry on their way upstairs. For a moment they stopped to consider the fitfully trembling bloodhound; then Spray's lips slowly curved in scornful lines.

"Look at the recumbent coward," she said. "Look at him." She waved a hand disparagingly at the dog. "He lets the house burn down. He lets us all die in agony. He says, 'To hell with all that so long as I am safe and undisturbed.' And there he plops his great body down in that closet and reclines in a half swoon. If there ever was a pansy bloodhound that dog is it."

"Not necessarily a pansy, Spray." Mr. Pebble spoke up in defense of the dog. "That's a pretty hard term to apply to a bloodhound. Only a short time ago I would have swooned with the greatest relief in the nearest closet at hand. The poor beast is a little fastidious about firemen, perhaps. Can't say as I blame him for that."

"Well, I blame him for everything," retorted Spray. "If he hadn't eaten up our steak there wouldn't have been any fire, and if there hadn't been any fire there wouldn't have been any firemen. The dog deliberately got us into this jam. He couldn't have done any worse had he gone rushing through the streets screaming, 'Fire!' at the top of his lungs."

"You're beginning to talk like Nockashima," Rex Pebble warned her gently. "Don't do it, for my sake. I'm not even convinced there is a fire."

"Then you're just as dumb as those firemen," she retorted. "Never sure of anything. I suppose you'd have me believe there isn't a fire raging somewhere in this house? Don't be an ass. We're actually trembling on the brink of a volcano. It's terrific. And there that foolish sissy soul-fully luxuriates in the clutch of abject fear. No wonder he hasn't any girl friends. The poor mutt hasn't stayed away from this house a single night in his life. Does he expect us to carry him out in our arms? I'd like to torch-murder the beast."

"You're a little unfair to Mr. Henry," said Rex Pebble mildly. "I hope you wouldn't like the dog to become a debauched bloodhound. He's bashful about his nose, perhaps. I should imagine a smell-less nose would be a terrible handicap to a dog in his relations with the opposite sex. You must know what a high value a dog places on his nose."

"I neither know nor care what a dog places on his nose," she replied. "I'd like to place a price on that dog's head. I have my own nose to worry about, and it's fairly gushing out smoke. And another thing, Mr. Henry isn't atrophied in all his parts. He must be alive somewhere. Even if I were deaf, dumb, and blind I'd still find my man, believe me."

"I do, Spray," Mr. Pebble said with great sincerity. "I don't doubt it for a moment. You'd even find your men, but you shouldn't judge a clean-living bloodhound by your low standards."

Mr. Henry did not at all relish the situation in which he found himself placed. He strongly objected to having himself discussed by persons he believed to be perfect strangers. Unable to recognize his old friends by their respective smells, he could find no traces in their radically altered bodies to give him a clue to their real identities. One thing alone remained familiar, and that was the sound of their voices. But this strange phenomenon, instead of comforting the dog, disturbed him all the more. How could these apparently new bodies make noises exactly like the old ones? Furthermore, these strangers had succeeded in ascertaining his name. That looked bad. They were doubtless up to some mischief—probably trying to snatch him for ransom. Unwilling to give any cause for offense, he wagged a deprecating tail, twisted his back to his audience, and lay still, hoping against hope that his little yellow boy friend would stagger to his rescue.

"Mr. Henry's so lazy with his tail," Rex Pebble remarked sadly as he slowly mounted the stairs.

Mr. Pebble maintained a suite of rooms in his mistress's establishment. When things got too hot for him at his own home he frequently found it expedient thither to repair in search of mental tranquillity as well as bodily safety. Inasmuch as neither of these conditions lasted very long in the company of either woman, he was forced to do considerable traveling between the two houses. Mr. Pebble could not remember ever having been so fortunate as to find both of the ladies agreeably disposed towards him at one and the same time. Not infrequently in his endeavors to escape conflict he found himself leaping from the frying pan into the fire, both ladies being in their most hellish moods. In compensation he comforted himself with the thought that if Socrates achieved self-discipline by putting up with Xanthippe, he himself, by living with two shrews, might in the due course of time become twice as good as a philosopher—that is, if he did not crack under the strain. For the sake of convenience no less than cleanliness he found it helpful to maintain in each establishment a duplicate wardrobe and set of toilet accessories.

In the upper hall he took leave of his mistress and made his way to his own quarters. Here, for the good of his soul and the appeasement of his disgruntled poise, he poured himself a stiff drink and polished it off at a gulp. When both poise and soul were feeling somewhat bucked up, it occurred to him he might as well take a shower to dash off some of the wear and tear sustained by too long confinement in the smoke-filled kitchen. When this little matter had been safely put behind him, it again occurred to Mr. Pebble that it would be even a better idea to take still another drink for the purpose of keeping his soul and his poise in the pink of condition to which the first drink had jerked them.

It was while he was thus conscientiously employed that the sound of strange voices attracted his attention to the bedroom occupied by his mistress. Had that good lady been inhabiting the body she had possessed previous to her immersion in the pool, it would have mattered very little to Mr. Pebble if she had chosen to entertain the entire Marine Corps in her bedroom, but in her present rejuvenated condition he decided that such liberties smacked a trifle of immorality and were greatly to be deplored.

Tossing his soul and his poise to the four winds, but still retaining possession of his glass, Rex Pebble padded softly across the hall and bent an attentive ear to his mistress's door, sipping thoughtfully the while. It should be said for Rex Pebble that he was blissfully unconscious of the damning fact he was seriously involving himself in the low practice of eavesdropping. To make matters even, however, it should also be stated that had he been aware of the nature of his occupation it would have made very little difference to him. He had lived too long with two women not to know that the game was played without any rules. It was catch as catch can always. The great hother and pother which nice people felt themselves called upon to make about eavesdropping did not trouble Rex Pebble at all. While admitting the fact that the eaves-dropper seldom heard anything good about himself, experience had proved that he frequently gleaned some in-valuable sidelights about others. To him it was the logical and intelligent thing to do, especially when dealing with such an unreliable character as his self-dramatizing mistress. Therefore, with a placid conscience Rex Pebble addressed his lips to his drink and his ear to the door and eavesdropped for all he was worth. From the other side of the door Spray Summers' voice came to him in cold, dispassionate tones.

"For the second time," she was saying, "I ask you, Major Jaffey, to explain your remarkable conduct. What do you mean by taking a shower in a lady's bathroom?"

"I was told the house was on fire, madam," explained the apologetic voice of Major Jaffey, "so I thought I'd be less inflammable if I kept myself wet."

"If that was your brilliant idea," continued Spray, "why didn't you carry it out in Mr. Pebble's bathroom?"

"I didn't want to bother him with my old and rare,"
said the Major, as one who explains everything.

"And what, may I ask," she demanded, "have I ever done to make you think your old and rare would be warmly welcomed here?"

"It's still in tip-top condition," Major Jaffey replied hopefully. "I have it right with me."

"You have it with you," repeated Spray in a startled voice. "Quite naturally you would have. Where else could you keep it?"

"Oh, I sometimes forget it," the Major casually informed her. "Leave it knocking about, you know."

"I don't seem to understand all this," she declared, "and I'm afraid I should not be enlightened."

"But, madam," protested the Major, "it's very interesting, I assure you. You couldn't help being delighted."

"The mere thought of it even is revolting," she retorted. "What sort of a proposal are you trying to make, anyway?"

On the other side of the door Mr. Pebble's ear hinged forward in its anxiety to catch the Major's answer.

"I would welcome an opportunity," he told her, "to exhibit it to you and Mr. Pebble."

"Major," Spray Summers told the man, more in sorrow than in wrath, "I don't know why you haven't been run in long before this. Mr. Pebble is not the kind of man to be interested in your old and rare. He might be a bad man, but he's not morbid." She hesitated a moment, then added, "However, if it will make you feel any better I might take a little peek myself just to show you I'm broad-minded."

"What a woman!" Rex Pebble inwardly exclaimed. "Neither age nor youth teaches her any better."

"It's all wrapped up," said Major Jaffey, proudly. "No one can accuse me of not taking the best of care of it."

"Who would even think of it, I'd like to know?" retorted Spray Summers. "It seems to be the only thing in the world you give a tinker's damn about."

"It keeps the wolf from the door," observed the Major cheerfully.

"Does it?" replied the woman. "What a remarkable statement to make. I can't see the slightest connection between wolves and your old and rare."

"Madam," responded the Major, "I was speaking merely figuratively."

"Major," Spray said wearily, "I don't give a damn how you were speaking. Either produce this old and rare of which you seem so inordinately proud, or else have the grace to take it away. I want to put on some clothes."

"Very well, dear lady," said the Major. "I won't be half a minute."

Rex Pebble, on the other side of the door, was in a small flutter of excitement. He wanted to be in on this. His curiosity was only natural. He had heard too much about the Major's highly vaunted old and rare not to be interested on his own behalf. It must be something extra special, he reflected, as he removed his ear from the door and placed an eye to the keyhole. His vision was disappointingly limited. All he could see were small sections of two towels. Making the best of a trying situation he riveted his gaze on one of these and waited breathlessly. At last this remarkable old and rare was about to be revealed. But unfortunately it never was—that is, not on on this occasion. The three actors involved in this unedifying little drama were doomed to disappointment by the unexpected arrival of a fourth. A small protesting shriek from Spray greeted his arrival.

"What do you mean," Rex Pebble heard her demand, "by crawling in my window? Can't you see I'm nearly undressed?"

"Sorry, lady," said a bored voice. "Hope you don't think I'm blind. Nearly's not the word. You damn well are undressed. Why don't you put something on?"

"I've been much too busy," said the lady haughtily.

"So I see, lady," said the fireman, "but you'll have to cut all this funny business out for awhile. The house is on fire."

"This part of it isn't," objected Spray. "What are you doing up here?"

"I'm looking for the fire, lady," the voice explained patiently. "The boys downstairs are sick and tired of looking for it. And they're drinking something fierce. Say, lady, is that old bird your father or just a friend?"

"What's that to you?" snapped Spray.

"Not a thing, lady," replied the fireman. "Not a thing. I was just wondering what he was to you."

"That, also, is none of your business," Spray retorted, "but if you must know, the gentleman was just about to show me his old and rare."

"No shame," muttered Mr. Pebble sorrowfully. "No shame at all. Just a gregarious old moll."

"What was he going to show you, lady?" asked the fireman in an awed voice. "His old and rare, did you say? And you're telling me? Fire or no fire, I guess I'll go away."

"I didn't suggest it," Spray replied defensively, "but the man seems to be frantic to have someone look at his old and rare."

"Well, I won't be a party to this sort of thing," said the fireman. "I'm going to clear out."

"Don't go," said the Major politely. "Perhaps I could interest you. I make my living by it, you know."

"Not off guys like me you don't," proclaimed the fire-man with some show of heat. "We've got old and rares of our own. Why should I look at yours? Is there anything funny about it—you know—anything strange?"

"Of course, I can hardly say," replied the Major in a professional voice, "until I've looked yours over."

"You'll never get the chance to do that," said the fire-man stubbornly, "not unless you throw me down and hold me, the two of you."

"We could hardly bring ourselves to do that," declared the Major. "I merely thought you might be interested in comparing items, that's all."

"That's too much," retorted the fireman. "You have some paralyzing thoughts, mister."

"I'm getting sick and tired of all this talk," broke in Spray Summers. "Why don't you both toddle off with your old rares? They're no novelty in my young life. Here I come peacefully and decently into my own room to put on some clothes, and what do I find? I ask you that. What do I find? One man taking a shower and another one crawling in my window, and both of them trying to show me their old and rares. What chance has a poor girl got, anyway? I wouldn't be a bit surprised if that shrimp Nockashima came crawling out from under the bed."

"Listen, lady," put in the fireman in an injured voice, "I didn't climb up this ladder for the express purpose of showing you my old and rare. You've got me all wrong. I'm not like that, lady. I generally have to know a person a long time before I even think of such a thing. I know how to act. It's the old bird that started all this, him and his precious old and rare. What's he got to be so proud about, anyway?"

"I'm sure I can't tell you," Spray declared, "but he does seem to be just mad about it. That's all he's had on his mind since the moment I first set eyes on him."

"How they do run on," Rex Pebble mused, looking into his empty glass. "I wonder what it's all about?"

He was not long in learning. Major Lynnhaven Jaffey had been wondering the same thing himself. He now decided to take definite steps to bring the situation to a head.

"Aren't either of you fond of reading?" he asked, "because, if you're not, I might just as well call the whole thing off."

"Sure I'm fond of reading," retorted Spray, "but what has that to do with your old and rare?"

"Say, lady," suggested the fireman, seized by a sudden inspiration, "maybe the old guy is tattooed. That might explain everything."

"Will you please keep still!" cried Spray.

The suggestion of the fireman had so intrigued Mr. Pebble that he actually tried to worm his eye through the key-hole. Perhaps, after all, the man had hit upon the explanation of the Major's quaint obsession.

"I confess I am quite unable to follow this conversation," that gentleman announced in distant tones, "but I am referring to my collection of old and rare books. I have some exceptionally fine items, I assure you."

For a moment dead silence followed this revelation; then Spray Summers rallied her scattered faculties and made as women will—a courageous effort to save her own face at the expense of someone else's.

"Oh," she said a little flatly. "Why, of course. For goodness sake, Major, old boy, what did you think I was talking about? Address your remarks to this dumb fireman. He's balled everything all up. But don't be too severe with him, Major. He doesn't know any better. You know how firemen are. They are born with low instincts—all of them."

"Is that so?" retorted the fireman. "Trying to make me the goat, are you? Well, it won't wash. I had nothing to do with this old and rare party to begin with. And if you'd like to know the truth you're about the rummiest couple I've run into since I've been on the force. There you stand, the two of you, with only a pair of towels for protection, and acting as high and mighty as if you were clad in blinking ermine."

"What's a blinking ermine?" asked Spray, hoping to change the subject.

"Aw, it's some sort of a skin, muttered the fireman sulkily. "You should know, lady. They get it off animals—some sort of animals."

"Who do?" Major Jaffey wanted to know.

"Does," corrected Spray.

"How do I know?" exclaimed the fireman. "The guys what go after the blinking ermine, I suppose. Don't ask me, lady. I'm just a dumb fireman with low instincts like you said."

"You're all of that," replied Spray, "but I have to ask you questions. What makes these ermine blink?"

"Oh, let me alone!" cried the fireman peevishly. "I can't stand any more. Maybe the blinking ermine blink because they don't know any better. Maybe they blink because their eyes get all watery from looking out for trappers. There might be a hundred reasons, and," he concluded in a hoarse voice, "maybe they don't blink at all. This house is burning up, and there you stand trying to get me to tell you bedtime stories about cute little blinking ermine. To hell with ermine, I say!"

"And that's about the only sensible thing you have said," Spray told him coldly.

"Madam," declared the Major, "this fireman deserves to be pitied. It's plain to see he's in a state of nerves. He might even be a little mad. Not dangerous, you know, but still scarcely responsible. I have long believed that all firemen eventually become a trifle mental—like nurses and doctors and dentists; also butchers and judges."

Horrid, gasping noises from the window put an end to the Major's observations.

"Ugh!" mouthed the enraged fireman, and this was followed by a sound not unlike a long drawn out, "o-o-o,h."

Neither noise the man made was very pretty to hear. "Just wait till I get my hands on the old guy," he continued more coherently. "I'm going to tear his naked body to bits."

"Be quiet, my good man," said the Major, not unkindly; then, turning to Spray, he politely inquired, "Shall I show you my old and rare now, madam? I took the liberty of tucking the bundle in the bathroom where it would be quite safe."

"Then you also took the liberty of tucking your body under the shower," she commented caustically, "where it would be quite safe. Go on and produce your old and rare, even if it is an anticlimax."

"Say, lady," said the fireman plaintively, as soon as the Major had left the room, "I'm geting awful tired standing out here on this ladder. Can I come in now and adjust my nozzle?"

"Adjust your what?" gasped Spray a little hysterically, swinging quickly about. "You don't know what you're saying. You must be delirious."

"My nozzle, lady," went on the fireman in a dull, patient voice. "My nozzle needs fixing."

"Be still!" Spray scolded. "Don't go on about it. You're as confiding as a boy of five." She looked at the fireman rebukingly; then her heart softened at the sight of his worried face. "Oh, all right," she continued in a hopeless voice. "It's all too much for a single mind to bear. Come on in if you have to, but you've got to wait until the Major gets out of the bathroom. What with you and your nozzle, as you so childishly call it, and that one with his blooming old and rare, I'm beginning to think I'm going a little mad myself."

And so was Rex Pebble. Unable to stand the suspense any longer, he flung open the door and strode majestically into the room. He was just in time to see the fireman entering through the window, laboriously dragging after him a length of hose with a gleaming nozzle.

"Oh!" exclaimed Spray, looking at the hose. "Oh dear, how stupid of me. I didn't understand."

"And I still don't," said Mr. Pebble. "What goes on in here?"

"Gord!" muttered the fireman, gazing at Rex Pebble with round, wondering eyes. "Another old and rare. Don't anybody ever wear any clothes at all in this joint?"

CHAPTER VII

EXIT ON HOOK AND LADDER

"WHY should we wear clothes?" demanded Rex Pebble with an ill-advised swish of his toga as he stalked across the room. "this lady and myself have been born again. we have nothing to conceal."

"You've got enough and more," retorted the fireman. "I wouldn't go round like that in my own home."

"Fireman," replied Mr. Pebble, "yours is a mistrustful nature or a very bad home. At the moment, I can't say which. You should learn to forget your body—to dismiss it, so to speak."

"If I had a body like his," put in Spray, "I'd be only too glad to forget it. I'd chuck it through the window."

"What's so awful about my body, lady?" the man asked in hurt tones.

"Almost everything," declared Spray. "It's overdressed, to start with. You've got on a funny hat, and you've got on a funny coat, and your rubber boots are a fair scream. I don't know for certain, but I'd lay attractive odds you're wearing long drawers as well—red ones."

"I am," admitted the fireman. "I always wear 'em, but they are not red."

"As I thought," replied Spray. "They're not red, but he always wears them. That means he sleeps in the things, and probably in his shirt, also. Tell him to go away."

"But, lady," protested the fireman, "us boys just naturally have to sleep in our underwear."

"You couldn't sleep naturally in your underwear," said Spray. "Don't try to do it in this house."

"I'm not sleeping, lady."

"You might as well be," she told him, "for all the good you're doing."

"But, lady," began the fireman, then hopelessly abandoned all thought of speaking sensibly with anyone connected with this surprising establishment. "You've got me all confused," he finished moodily. "I can't seem to be able to think straight any more."

"Fireman," said Mr. Pebble, "sit down and tell us your story from the beginning. Take off your hat and coat and forget dull routine for a space. And please endeavor to stop bickering with that woman. You should have better sense."

"But this house is burning up somewhere," the fireman protested.

"But not here," replied Mr. Pebble calmly, "and we are all that matter. Anyway, fireman, if this house does burn down, I'll set fire to another one and let you put it out. Nockashima will do it for me."

"Ha!" exclaimed the voice of Major Jaffey as the man himself staggered from the bathroom with a large bundle in his arms. "Ha! How jolly everyone looks. Ha!"

"Will you stop making that foolish noise?" said Spray. "You talk like a radio announcer for little children."

"Forgive my enthusiasm, madam," apologized the Major. "I always get that way when exhibiting my old and rare."

Mr. Pebble groaned.

"I wish you would add `books'," he said, "when you refer to that bundle, Major. Although I know what's in it now, the shock still remains."

"Certainly, sir," agreed the Major readily enough, then paused and looked closely at Rex Pebble and his mistress. "Tell me," he continued, "are you the same couple I had the privilege of meeting near the pool? You seem so very much younger now, but, of course, I may be wrong. The light was failing then, and my eyes are not what they used to be. Also, owing to the circumstances, I imagine you must have been under a considerable strain at the moment."

"You can attribute your error to all three factors," replied Mr. Pebble, "although I will admit I haven't felt so young in years."

"I felt that way myself," remarked Spray, "before I got involved with these two idiots. They have aged me terribly."

"Considering your abundant beauty," replied the Major with questionable gallantry as he ran his eyes over the woman, "you are lucky you did not get yourself even more deeply involved. Had I been a few years younger——"

"Say it and I'll knock your block off," said Spray. "I've stood enough from you and your old and rare. Break out your items. Have you any real bad books in that bundle?"

"That's all I have," replied the Major proudly. "Frankly, I don't see how any one person could have written some of them. They seem more like a compilation—the dregs of the ages, you know. I've a few that are so exceptionally vile they have to be printed in Latin."

"Well, don't show us any of those," Spray told him. "I'm a patriotic woman, and I don't like foreign dirt. It must be made in America."

"Your country is quite capable of it," the Major assured her generously. "But most American women are still a little fanciful about pornography and husbands."

"Pornography and husbands," Spray interrupted, "mean exactly the same thing."

"Which is as it should be," replied the Major, "but as I was saying, my lady clients—they constitute the majority—seem to fall more readily for both men and books bearing foreign titles."

"They're more depraved," observed Spray, "and all women need a dash of depravity to round out their natures. Men are depraved always. Women only in spots."

"Lady," said the fireman unexpectedly, "you never seem to be able to get out of your spot."

"Hit him with something," said the lady composedly.

"I think I've been insulted, although it doesn't hurt any."

A perfunctory knock on the door heralded the arrival of Nockashima, carrying a tall shaker full of fresh cocktails and two glasses.

"Get two more glasses, Nocka," Spray commanded. "I'm celebrating this fire with the dregs of society. It's a regular slumming party."

"Very good, madam," grinned the little yellow man. "I go get. One glass for brute of fire fella, other for Old and Rare." At the mere mention of the name Nockashima seemed to become irresistably amused. He indulged in several inane giggles, then rapidly blinked his eyes. "Very funny name, that," he commented. "Always good for small giggle. Old and Rare. What is this old and rare he all time talk about? I fairly stream with mirth. Such elderly gentleman to go on so. Old, yes, but rare—I not think that, boss. What you think? Maybe I know. Maybe I not. I keep mouth shut. Not laughing matter, all this old and rare."

"You neither keep your mouth shut," Spray retorted scoldingly, "nor do you refrain from laughing. That's all you've been doing since you tainted the air with your presence—giggling and gibbering like an hysterical high-school girl with a case of yellow jaundice. Get out of here and fetch those glasses."

"I get," replied Nockashima. "I get, madam, plenty quick. I know man once with old and rare. He Japanese fella, too."

"No," said Mr. Pebble firmly but sympathetically. "No, Nocka. Not that one. You can tell it to Fifi after you've brought those glasses."

Nockashima was always at his highest efficiency when ministering to people's thirst, including his own. He was both generous and broad-minded about it. Something in his simple nature was soothed and filled with joy by having dealings with either a bottle or a cocktail shaker. He would never have lasted long in a bone-dry family. The quick little patter of his feet had hardly died away before he was back again with the glasses.

"Fire fellas all good and drunk," he announced as he filled the four glasses. "All wet, too. Unable to find small blaze they put themselves out with roars and drinks. Lots of fun down there. Fifi very busy with love and fury. I participate, madam, with tentatively. That right, boss?"

"Almost, Nocka," replied Mr. Pebble. "We'll take that up later. Is there still any smoke doing?"

"Plenty of all that," declared Nocka. "All come from oven where steak still smoulder. They not look into that. Shall I suggest, madam?"

"No," Spray told him. "I wouldn't go so far as that. They might think you officious. Firemen don't like to be told anything. Just let them romp around in their own oafish way. Perhaps they will go to sleep."

There was a knock on the door, and a fireman partially blinded by either smoke or liquor staggered into the room.

"Chief sends his compliments, lady," he said in a dazed voice. "He wants to know if we can set fire to your house in a couple of places—just little ones, you know. You see, lady, we've got to have some sort of a fire to give us boys an excuse for having stayed away so long. Can we?"

"Sure," replied Spray generously. "Go right ahead. Lend us your hook and ladder?"

"Help yourself," replied the fireman with a big-hearted wave of his hand.

"But don't hurt it. It's a good old hook and ladder. Hal, there, will help you. He swings a mean rear wheel."

"I do that," replied Hal modestly. "Glad to bear a hand." He paused and grinned at the other fireman, then added, "These are real nice people after you get to know them."

"That's mighty nice of you," Rex Pebble told the fireman. "It's a funny thing, but I've never been on a hook and ladder."

"You'll like it," said the Chief's emissary simply. "The corners are just great. They'll like the corners, won't they, Hal?"

"Yes," replied Hal. "They'll like the corners."

"May I be the bell ringer?" asked Spray Summers. "I never rang the bell on a hook and ladder."

"Go right ahead, lady," said the first fireman. "You can ring the bell just as much as you please. There's a siren, too."

"Isn't that dandy!" said Spray. "Empty that shaker, Nocka, and fill it up again. Listen, Hal, will you lend me your hat and coat?"

"Guess I better had," replied Hal, thoughtfully surveying the woman. "You don't seem to be willing to wear anything else."

"Then I'll drive," Mr. Pebble decided, "and the Major can hang on."

Nockashima giggled at this as if amused by some inner vision.

"Tough riding for Old and Rare," he said, "but what matter? All in fun. I come along with bottles."

"Must I go?" asked Major Jaffey. "I too have never been on a hook and ladder, and I'm not sure that I yearn to acquire the habit at my time of life."

"Oh, you've got to come," Spray assured him. "Our hook-and-ladder party wouldn't be complete without you, Major."

The Major sighed resignedly, then retired to the bath-room from which he presently emerged attired in a pair of trousers.

Several shakers later the five members of the improvised fire company, now no longer in their right minds, clung to the long vehicle for better support and peered unintelligently at its various mysterious parts.

"It's a wicked-looking thing," observed the Major skeptically. "Which is the front end of it, do you suppose?"

"Here wheel," exclaimed Nockashima. "Maybe that front end. I not sure. Maybe is, though."

"There are two wheels," declared Rex Pebble. "Two good excellent wheels. Both different. I'm looking for the front one."

"There's the front one," said Hal, the fireman. "That's your wheel. I'll take the back wheel and twist it clean off."

"I wouldn't do that," objected Major Jaffey. "We might need the thing for corners."

"There are not going to be any corners," said Rex Pebble. "I'm going to cut right through them."

"Oh, you take the front wheel and I'll take the back wheel," Spray sang in a high, plaintive voice, "and I'll be in wee bits before you."

"Don't," protested the Major, shivering in spite of him-self. "When your voice issues from under that helmet it sounds like a wind blowing from a cave. That's a very sad song. I have Scotch blood in my veins."

"And I have Japanese," Nockashima informed them. "Might not have too much of that very long. Where I stand, boss?"

"Stand on the running board," commanded Mr. Pebble, "so you'll be able to run back and forth with the bottles. I want some Scotch whisky in my veins. Pass me a bottle." He drank deeply, then surveyed his crew with a kindling eye. "A strange gathering," he murmured, "to be seen anywhere, but especially on a hook and ladder."

Rex Pebble had spoken no more than what was true.

For the first time in her life Spray Summers had allowed her personality to become completely submerged, although much of the rest of her was fully exposed. In place of the towel she wore the fireman's rubber coat, only the top button of which was in service. Her head, nose, and eyes were hidden from view within the helmet. Her legs and feet were bare save for the unhelpful addition of a pair of high-heeled mules.

"They ought to cut windows in these diving bells," she complained as she groped her way round the hook and ladder. "It's like playing with a prehistoric animal in the pitch dark. I'm not going to see much life in this darned thing."

"Why don't you take it off?" asked Mr. Pebble.

"I refuse," she retorted. "It must stay on. This helmet disguises my sex."

Major Jaffey laughed mirthlessly.

"I'm glad you think so," he said.

"Listen, lady," put in Hal, the fireman, "I don't like to say anything, seeing as how you all have been so nice to me, but if you're going happily about thinking your sex is disguised, someone's going to get an awful shock. That helmet just hides your head, and there's lots more to you than that. Why don't you button my coat? I always do."

"You button your mouth," said Spray. "I'm not going to suffocate for anybody. And, anyway, what's the great difference between us? You're naked from the waist up, and I'm naked from the waist down. It's a tie. And look at Gaius Cassius, there. He's just an animated tablecloth."

It was true. Rex Pebble was stalking about in the darkness very much in the manner of the last of the Romans. His feet were encased in a pair of soft-soled slippers. Major Lynnhaven Jaffey was dressed in the same fashion as the fireman, being content with a pair of trousers. The little yellow man was the best dressed member of the party. He was fully clad, and his white mess jacket gave a nautical touch to the outfit. However, it must be said that it would have been difficult to find five persons who looked less qualified to take a hook and ladder out for a spin.

"Yes," Mr. Pebble was saying to no one in particular, "it certainly is a bang-up hook and ladder. Never looked at one close before."

"Bang-up is an unfortunate term," replied Major Jaffey. "I greatly fear it's going to look even banger-up before this night is over."

"Have no fear," Mr. Pebble assured him. "Have no fear at all. This is going to be a runaway. I could drive the thing in my sleep. Come here with that pail, Nocka. I want a drink."

"We all want a drink, Nocka," said Spray. "We'll make it a stirrup cup."

The little yellow man set down his pail while the party gathered round it and selected bottles at random. Stars from a naked sky winked at their libations. It was a clear, still night. Occasionally a snatch of song or a burst of coarse laughter drifted from the house. Once the French maid, Fifi, was heard to push a perfunctory scream, after which the burst of laughter was, if anything, even coarser. The street was deserted. What few neighbors had been attracted to the spot by the noise of the fire apparatus had returned to their respective homes, their fond expectations unrealized. Few things are more disappointing to the normally constituted man or woman than a fire that fails to come off, especially when the fire belongs to someone else. Taking all things into consideration, Rex Pebble could not have chosen a better night for a hook-and-ladder ride.

"To your places, everyone," he commanded. "Hal, you know this hook and ladder very much better than we do, help them to climb aboard. Nockashima, look alert withthat bucket of bottles, and when anyone calls, scramble to him with a drink. I suspect he'll need it."

"Also she," commented Spray.

It is doubtful if the members of that oddly assorted group actually believed they were going through with the mad enterprise up to the moment Rex Pebble set the hook and ladder in motion with a violent and ominous lurch.

"It's a runaway," he called back over his shoulder. "I could drive this boat with my eyes shut."

"Hope not do," muttered Nockashima. "If boat run away already, what will be later? Mere scamper along, I fear, don't you, boss?"

"I fear nothing," Mr. Pebble shouted.

"So do I," sang out Spray. "Lend an ear to this one." Like a soul in torment the scream of the siren split through the night.

"Don't do that," protested the Major, who appeared at the moment to be chinning himself on a ladder. "It sounds so ostentatious. Why not glide smoothly along so we can all enjoy the scenery?"

"This crazy hook and ladder doesn't know any better," Mr. Pebble explained between lurches. "It seems to have only one speed, and that's high, like myself. Haven't found the foot brake yet."

"Well, hurry up and find it," shouted the firemen, his face streaming with perspiration. "If we don't brake together we'll damn well break apart."

"Sounds like a quotation to me," Rex Pebble observed above the racket. "Oh, here's the brake. Hold tight, everyone."

For an awful moment the hook and ladder seemed to be of at least two minds about what to do with itself. The front wheels came to a sudden stop while the rear ones appeared to be determined to continue forward to see what was going on up there. The middle section, after a passionate attempt to buck, compromised by slewing sidewise, thus giving to the hook and ladder the appearance of a sprawling Z. Mr. Pebble, looking back over his shoulder, found himself sitting almost face to face with the fireman in the rear seat.

"Good gracious!" exclaimed Mr. Pebble. "How did you get here? I've been under the impression there were yards and yards of sheer ladder between us."

"God!" grated the fireman. "What a thing to do! I'm disgusted."

"Mist' Old and Rare," proclaimed Nockashima, "seem to be disgust also. Hear funny noises he make."

"Dear me," ejaculated Rex Pebble, regarding the dangling body of Major Jaffey. "The poor chap. I think we've jerked him into a suicide. He's actually strangling to death between two ladders. Hurry, Nocka, and unhook his chin. I can't stand those noises."

"He not make them long," said the little yellow man. "All up soon with Old and Rare."

Giggling callously to himself at the prospect of the Major's approaching strangulation, Nockashima wormed his way through a jungle of ladders and laid hands on the dangling body. And that was literally what the Major had succeeded in doing with his body. In some strange way he had contrived to get his neck wedged between two ladders. The rest of the man was swinging free. Now, it does not improve a dangling body to be burdened with additional weight. The little yellow man burdened the Major's with his, or to put it clearly, he added his body to the Major's and clung on. Even in his agony an expression of sheer astonishment flickered in the old gentleman's bulging eyes before horror once more filled them.

"Come down," panted Nockashima. "You hear up above? Boss say not dangle. He not like whiffling noise. Squeeze hard through."

Every instinct in the Major's body cried out to have words with this maniacal Japanese, but those instincts were set at naught by his rapidly closing throat. Rex Pebble had climbed down from his lofty seat and now stood watching the efforts of the little servant with deep absorption. He was joined by Spray and the fireman.

"What's wrong now?" she wanted to know.

"The Major's dangling," Mr. Pebble told her briefly. "I can't drive a dangling body through the streets."

"Why doesn't that little Jap try to push the body up?" demanded the fireman. "He's swinging from the poor guy's legs just like they were a couple of ropes. That's not going to help his neck any."

"I'm afraid the neck is beyond redemption," Mr. Pebble observed. "However, there's no harm trying. Hey, Nocka! Stop playing Tarzan with the Major's legs and try to push him up. See if you can keep his head on. He'll be no good without it."

Nockashima reversed his tactics and pushed with all his might.

"You hear up there?" he grunted. "You hear what boss say? Push hard up. Altogether push." The Japanese took his own injunction so seriously that the Major's long body doubled up like a jackknife. This greatly perplexed Nockashima. "Can't squeeze shoulders through now, boss. What say I do—let body hang?"

"Spread the ladders," cried Hal, the fireman. "Here, let me at him."

He clawed his way through the ladders and quickly released the Major. That gentleman dropped to the street and refused to budge until he had been resuscitated by several drinks, after which he called Nockashima every vile name he could drag from the darkened recesses of his memory. This served only to amuse the little yellow man.

"Major better dead than live," he observed. "He make bad sounds either way."

"Is that so, you dope-fed flea?" growled the Major, seating himself on the curb. "Who did you think you were, anyway, the man on the flying trapeze? One would think my neck was a length of molasses candy, the way you wobbled it about."

"Let's try to forget all about it," Rex Pebble suggested, seating himself by the Major. "Sit down, everybody, and we'll have a bit of a drink before we try another spin."

It was while they were thus peacefully engaged that they became aware of a person behind them. Turning defensively, they confronted the presence. It turned out to be a hatless gentleman in evening clothes and a flushed face.

"Hello," said the well-dressed gentleman with childlike directness. "Give me some of that drink. I'm thirsty."

"Why should we give you some of this drink?" asked Spray Summers. "We're thirsty, too."

"But you've got such an awful lot of it," explained the man. "And I haven't any."

"We like a lot of it," Spray retorted.

"So do I," agreed the man. "Give me just a little sip."

"Give him a little sip," Mr. Pebble said, then addressed himself to the stranger. "Have you got a fire any-where that needs a little putting out?"

"I've got one inside me," said the man, "but nothing can put that out."

"You don't understand," said Mr. Pebble. "I mean a real one. We've got a hook and ladder we could use if you only had a fire."

"I've got a house," replied the man thoughtfully. "It would make a good fire. It's so big. But you might burn my family up. You don't want to do that, do you?"

"Not especially," said Rex Pebble. "We'll put your family out also."

"You mean, after it's caught fire?"

"Any old time," declared Mr. Pebble. "If and when your family catches fire."

"Why not put my family out first?" asked the gentleman.

"We might wake somebody up," said Mr. Pebble.

"That's right," agreed the gentleman, now thoroughly convinced. "We'll put them out after. Let's have some more drink, then we'll set fire to my house and family. Sure you can put them out?"

"No," declared Spray promptly. "We never put out any fires. My house is on fire right now, but we can't find out where."

"Maybe it's your family," suggested the man.

"No," replied Spray. "I don't think you're right. I haven't any family."

"Then it's burning elsewhere," commented Mr. Pebble.

"You never lose a chance, do you?" sneered the woman. "When I was a babe in arms I had a swell family."

"All right, sweetheart," said Mr. Pebble, hastily. "All right. Let's not start that again."

"I've put out lots of fires," Hal announced boastfully as he removed a bottle from his lips. "I've put out entire cities."

"That's all very well," put in Major Jaffey, "but what we need now is someone who knows how to build a fire."

"I know how to make fire," said Nockashima, "but I not know how to put it out. I break down in nerves."

"I can build 'em," bragged the fireman, "and I can put 'em out. Come on, show me this house."

Together the little party followed Hal across a smooth lawn in the direction of a magnificent residence.

"We'll set it afire in the back," he whispered, "because if we started it in the front someone might notice it before it had time to do any good."

"It's not going to do my family any good, no matter where you set it on fire," observed the gentleman. My name is Gibbs. What's yours? I'd like to know the name of the people I'm setting my house on fire with—it seems less impersonal that way."

"That man's name is Major Jaffey," Spray said with great presence of mind. "He'll do for the bunch of us. We're all Jaffeys except the opium eater, and he isn't human. The Major's our drunken father."

"He dresses you sort of funny," remarked Mr. Gibbs. "Haven't you enough clothes to go round?"

"Around what?" asked Spray.

"It doesn't matter," replied Mr. Gibbs. "Don't mention it. Sorry I spoke. What a lovely night for a fire. Thought you had no family."

"I don't count them," Spray told him.

"I couldn't tonight," said the man. "Not even if I tried, but I won't ever forget them."

This sort of conversation was enough to get them without mishap to the back of the house. Here they busied themselves collecting papers and bits of wood which, under the direction of Hal, the two-way fireman, they piled up in a corner of the back veranda.

"That should be enough to burn my house up," observed Mr. Gibbs, "not to mention my family."

The Major produced a box of matches, and soon the fire was merrily burning. Mr. Gibbs considered the blaze for a moment, then disgustedly snapped his fingers.

"There's been a mistake," he announced. "We've set fire to the wrong house. This one isn't mine."

"Don't you know your own home?" demanded Rex Pebble.

"Well, you see," explained Mr. Gibbs, "I live in the front of mine. Rarely get round to the back."

"Oh, I see," said Mr. Pebble. "That does make things different. What shall we do now?"

"We might put this fire out," replied Mr. Gibbs, "and then go over to my place. It's just next door. Or we might burn them both down. What do you think?"

"I think," said Major Jaffey, "that it's high time we were shoving off. It wouldn't look well for us to be seen setting fire to the house of perfect strangers."

"Oh, I know these people," declared Mr. Gibbs. "They are good friends of mine."

"You mean," put in Spray, "they were good friends of yours. I agree with Daddy for a change. Let's clear out."

"Wait a sec," said Mr. Gibbs. "I'd better let these people know their house is burning up, or they might burn up with it."

With this he started shouting in a loud voice and kept it up until a window flew open and a bald head was thrust out into the night. Mr. Pebble and his companions crept shyly out of sight behind some bushes.

"Oh, it's you, Gibbs," said the owner of the bald head. "Drunk as usual. What have you done this time—set fire to my house?"

"My mistake, Charlie," replied Gibbs. "I thought this house was mine. Sorry."

"No," answered Charlie, looking down at the blaze. "This isn't your house. Yours is next door. I've been living here for quite some time."

"Sure you have, Charlie," laughed Mr. Gibbs. "As if I didn't know that."

"But you didn't know it," said Charlie. "You just admitted you didn't."

"Not in the dark," explained Mr. Gibbs, "but now that it's burning down I recognize it distinctly. This is your house, Charlie, and I set fire to it. How am I ever going to make it up to you? Shall I set mine on fire, Charlie?"

"No," replied Charlie generously. "Don't do anything rash. Let me set it on fire for you."

"That's fair, Charlie," said Mr. Gibbs with every indication of sincere gratitude. "That's what I call meeting me more than halfway. But hadn't you better wake your folks up first? A spark might blow in, you know, and ignite one of them."

"I hope a spark ignites them all," declared Charlie with surprising ferocity. "If it did, I might be able to enjoy a little peace at home."

"But not if your home burns down," Mr. Gibbs re-minded him. "Not then, Charlie, because if your house burns down you won't have any home in which to enjoy your peace."

"That's well taken," said Charlie. "I'll be right down to help you put out this fire; then we'll see how your house burns."

Charlie's bald head was withdrawn from the night, and in a surprisingly short time the man appeared on the back veranda.

"It's a good fire," commented Mr. Gibbs modestly.

"Much too good for this house," replied Charlie. "A fire like that deserves far better material—something more institutional and centrally located. What's bad for fires?"

"Water," suggested Mr. Gibbs.

"I know," said the other impatiently, "but that's so old-fashioned. Couldn't we think up a new way?"

"You know something," said Mr. Pebble in a low voice to Spray. "The way they go on is almost making me sober. We've been listening to a conversation either between two exceedingly courteous lunatics or else two quietly plastered gentlemen with a quaint sense of fun."

"Perhaps they're drunk and insane too," suggested Spray. "These thoroughbred families can throw off some rare progeny every now and then. Let's clear out of this. We're really quite harmless compared with them."

But before they crept away through the shadows the members of the party were privileged to catch a last snatch of conversation between the two gentlemen.

"It entirely slipped my mind," Mr. Gibbs was saying. "Only a short time ago I invited a number of half-naked persons to take part in this fire. They had a dandy hook and ladder."

"That's too bad," was Charlie's sympathetic reply.

"They must have gone to some other house. I've had a swell hook and ladder up in the attic for years. Got it on my seventh birthday. Only trouble is, two wheels are missing and it hasn't any ladders."

"And anyway," said Mr. Gibbs, "it wouldn't be quite large enough. This fire's getting taller all the time."

"They do," observed Charlie wisely, "until they go out."

"That tears it!" exclaimed Spray. "Let's hurry. Those two men are as mad as a couple of hatters."

Mr. Pebble never did learn what the two gentlemen did with their fire. The amazing events of that evening and of many subsequent ones fully occupied his mind. In later years, however, he occasionally found himself wondering whether Mr. Gibbs and his friend Charlie were really as mad as they seemed or were merely passing the time away in idle banter. Probably he could have found out had he cared to, but it was one of those piquant little problems he preferred to leave unsolved. As it was, Rex Pebble learned far too many of the truths of life to make it a going concern. However, he succeeded in disguising this knowledge to himself as well as to others—that is, most of the time he did.

CHAPTER VIII

THE LOWER HALF'S A LADY

IT has been almost definitely established that no one hook and ladder ever succeeded in making more of a nuisance of itself than did the one so casually borrowed by Rex Pebble and his party.

After its departure from the slightly burning residence of Charlie, the various stages of its progress were reported more or less hysterically by outraged property owners of the surrounding community telephoning in to police headquarters.

The eccentric behavior of the hook and ladder could be attributed to several causes, all of which militated against the safety and best interests of those riding upon it as well as those innocent citizens who were so unfortunate as to have anything at all to do with it. Unfamiliarity with the operation of the attenuated vehicle was one of the main causes. Another one could be reasonably said to be the artificially stimulated condition of the members of its crew. A steady flow of gratuitous and irresponsible advice added to the general confusion, but by far the most influential factor was the preoccupied state of Rex Pebble's mind.

His thoughts still lingered with those two strange beings, Charlie and Mr. Gibbs. He was considerably puzzled by their philosophically discursive reactions to a deliberate act of incendiarism, which even at that moment was threatening the safety of one of their homes. Mingled with his doubts and speculations was a definite element of envy. Never before had Mr. Pebble encountered anyone outside of an institution whose conduct had been more calmly and consistently unbalanced than his own when once he had set his mind on it. If possible, he decided, those two gentlemen were even madder than Nockashima, and to Rex Pebble's way of thinking such a triumph of madness was well-nigh inconceivable. Therefore, with all these thoughts racing through his mind, there is small wonder that he drove the machine through the streets of that thriving surburban community with the capricious abandon of an enterprising child playing in a crowded room with an overgrown toy.

"Hey, Sergeant," a voice said over the telephone about ten minutes after the Pebble party had taken leave of Charlie and Mr. Gibbs, "a hook and ladder has just driven through my dog house."

"Eh?" muttered the somnolent policeman. "This isn't a dog house. It's worse. This is a police station."

"I know," came the patient reply. "This isn't a dog talking. I'm an owner, and I'm talking for my dog. A hook and ladder has just driven through his house."

"What's the dog doing now?" asked the sergeant, realizing something was expected of him.

"Does it matter?" demanded the voice. "But if you must know, the damn fool is sitting on the boards, and they're all full of nails."

"Why don't you whistle?" suggested the sergeant.

"Why should I whistle?" asked the voice. "I don't feel like whistling."

"I mean," said the officer heavily, "why don't you whistle to the dog?"

"Oh," replied the voice, "I see. Wait a moment." A shrill noise offended the sergeant's ears. "He won't come," the voice resumed in tones of discouragement. "Not a budge out of him. He looks sore as hell."

"He'll budge all right," said the officer, knowledgeably, "if he sits on one of those nails."

"Say, officer," continued the voice, "let's waive the dog for a moment."

"Don't see what good that's going to do," grumbled the sergeant. "It certainly won't help the dog any to go waving him about. He'd hate it more than sitting on a nail."

"I don't mean to wave the dog like a flag," protested the voice. "I mean, let's drop the dog."

"If you want to drop your dog," said the sergeant impatiently, "go right ahead and do it, but damn me if I'm going to help you."

"I don't want you to help me drop my dog," said the voice wearily. "I don't want you to do anything. Just hang up quietly and try to forget the whole unpleasant incident. Good-night!"

A vicious banging of the telephone on the other end of the line emphasized to the sergeant the speaker's desire to have nothing more to do with him. He was still puzzled some minutes later when the telephone rang again.

"Officer," cried an excited voice, "there's a hook and ladder full of murderers on my lawn."

"Funny place for a lot of murderers to be," commented the officer. "What are they doing on a hook and ladder?"

"It's what they are doing on my lawn that's burning me up," said the voice. "They're shouting and singing and flinging themselves about. You should see them."

"I don't want to see them," the sergeant answered truthfully. "But somehow that doesn't seem to be the way murderers are supposed to act."

"How are they supposed to act?" asked the voice.

"Oh, I don't know," the sergeant hedged. "Different ways, but they don't shout and sing and fling themselves about. Not murderers."

"Maybe they do after they've committed a pretty good murder," replied the voice. "Might make them sort of happy like."

"Murderers are never happy," said the sergeant, who had never seen one. "They slink along carrying blunt instruments."

"How awful of them," replied the voice admiringly. "Would you mind telling me if you happen to be a murderer?"

"I would be one, if you were here," snapped the exasperated policeman.

"You talk just like a murderer," went on the voice. "I mean, you seem to be so thoroughly familiar with their nasty ways—just how they walk and what they carry. It's wonderful. How about the murderers on my lawn? Do you want to come up and give them a little talk? I want to go to sleep."

"No!" shouted the sergeant. "Go out and throw yourself into their midst. I hope they cut you to ribbons."

"But, officer," objected the voice, "how could they, with a blunt instrument?"

This time it was the sergeant who viciously snapped down the earpiece. Before he had time even to think about cooling off, the bell once more chattered irritably in his flushed face. Seizing the telephone round the neck as if he were going to throttle it, he shoved the receiver against his ear with such force that he cursed bitterly into the mouthpiece.

"Damn it to hell!" he said.

"No," a timid voice faltered. "I don't want any of that. I want the police station."

"Lady," said the officer, "this is the police station. You're talking to it."

"Well, I must say," remarked the lady, "it doesn't talk like a police station. I mean to say, a police station shouldn't talk like that. Are you very busy?"

"Of course not," replied the sergeant with ponderous sarcasm. "Do you want me to come up and see you some time? Or would you rather bring your tatting down here?"

"I don't want to see you at any time," declared the voice decidedly. "I want to see a gentleman. A face just looked in at my window."

"What do you mean, a face looked in at your window?" demanded the officer. "Didn't it have any body?"

"Not at first it didn't," said the lady. "It was just a face, and it had queer little slanty eyes, and skin like an old, dried orange."

"What did it see?" asked the sergeant, growing interested.

"It saw me," said the lady. "And it spoke."

"It did?" replied the officer. "What did it say, lady?"

"Must I tell?" faltered the voice. "Must I?"

"Certainly," snapped the sergeant. "That's important."

"Well, officer," said the lady slowly, "this slanty-eyed little face said in the strangest voice, 'Night keep up all naked. This pretty good stuff.' That's what it said, officer."

"Why didn't you pull the shade down?" asked the sergeant.

"I was too busy crouching," replied the lady. "I got all scroggled up."

"You got all what, lady?" asked the sergeant in a shocked voice. "That sounds bad."

"Well, it wasn't any laughing matter," said the lady, "but it wasn't as bad as that. I got all scroggled up, you know—bent double and everything. And the face just giggled. 'He-he-he,' it went, just like that."

"Don't do it any more, lady," pleaded the sergeant. "It sounded awful at this end."

"It sounded even worse here," said the lady. "I'm way up on the sixth floor."

"I see it all, lady," replied the officer. "Don't worry your head any more. It must have been a bird. No one man is twelve stories high."

"No, officer," stated the lady most emphatically, "I know that. No one man is twelve stories high in his bare feet, but this man was standing on a ladder. I saw his body."

"Wasn't he even dressed?" asked the officer in a hoarse voice. "You really saw his body?"

"You're getting all mixed up," complained the lady.

"I was the one who wasn't dressed, but the man was. He had on pants and a white jacket."

"Thank God for that," breathed the sergeant. "Are you dressed now, lady?"

"What do you want to know for?" the voice asked suspiciously.

"Not for fun," replied the officer. "Suppose I send some of the boys along?"

"No," declared the voice, "don't send any boys. I want this handled by men."

The sergeant almost choked.

"What do you want handled by men?" he whispered over the wire.

"What do you think?" the voice demanded snappily.

"I don't know, lady," he replied helplessly, "but please don't say anything you wouldn't like used as evidence. Let's get back to your story. What happened next?"

"Well," the voice replied, "nothing much happened. I just stood there scroggling—bent double, you know—and those slanty eyes in that yellow face kept blinking at me like two jumping beans. 'You should see boss,' he said. 'Boss plenty naked, too. Only tablecloth. But he not have pain in belly. I go get.' Then——" "Have you a pain in your belly, madam?" asked the sergeant, growing a little tired. "I mean stomach," he added hastily.

"No," replied the voice quite cheerfully, "but that funny little yellow face made the same mistake, too. I'm all right."

"Good," said the sergeant, wishing the woman was in convulsions. "If you don't mind, will you please finish your story? I might have a murder or something at any moment."

"Oh, don't have a murder, sergeant," admonished the woman. "Try counting up to one hundred. Well, as I was saying, the yellow face disappeared, and before I had time to snatch a robe another one popped up in its place."

"Another yellow face?" gasped the officer. "Sure it wasn't the same one back?"

"You mean the back of the same yellow face?" came the voice.

"No, no, lady," said the officer, "I don't mean that. God!" he cried out in an exasperated aside, "this woman is worse than Gracie Allen."

"No, I'm not," retorted the woman. "I've heard her too, and she's ever so much worse than I am."

"All right, lady," agreed the sergeant. "Tell me the end of your story?"

"This new face was much better than the yellow one," the voice resumed. "A great improvement. In fact, it was a real nice face. Splendid eyes. I could feel myself getting red."

"How do you mean, lady?" asked the officer, hopelessly confused. "Where were you turning red?"

"All over," said the lady.

"All over?" the man slowly repeated. "Oh, I think I see. You were blushing, eh? Well, that was quite a blush, lady. Lots of ground to cover. Between yellow faces and red bodies I don't know where I'm standing. Kindly state only the important facts."

"This new face spoke English," the woman continued. "'Do you want to be saved?' it asked. 'What for?' I asked right back. 'I'm not so bad.' 'I should say not,' replied the face, but I wasn't having any of that, so I said, 'And furthermore, mister, this is no time and place to start preaching sermons to a lady.' 'No harm in asking,' he answered, 'but if I stay here much longer I'll be needing a little saving myself.' What do you think he meant by that, officer?"

"He probably wanted to strangle you to death," grated the officer, momentarily losing control of himself. "Sorry, lady. Is that face still there?"

"No," said the voice sadly, "but I don't think it wanted to strangle me. It didn't look like the face of a murderer. It isn't here any more, and when I looked out the window I saw a naked man in a towel chasing a hook and ladder down the street. I saw everything distinctly. The little man in the white jacket and yellow face was driving like mad. I couldn't have driven worse myself. And that's all I know, officer. Will you send some of your men around? I'm all upset."

"Me, too, lady," shrilled the sergeant, a maniacal light in his eyes. "I'll send around the firing squad."

"Then you'd better send that hook and ladder smack back with it," said the voice of the woman. "To put out the fire, you know."

Slowly and with the utmost care the sergeant lowered the receiver on its hook. He was too consumed with brute passion, too straining with evil intent, to trust himself to express his emotions either in word or deed.

The next time the telephone rang he turned the call over to a sleepy-eyed rookie.

"Hey, Pat!" called the sergeant with hypocritical heartiness. "Snap out of that chair and I'll give you a chance to take a call. It's a good thing to get the hang of. There's a knack in it."

Feeling as highly favored as his sluggard wits would over allow to him, the heavy-footed young son of Erin lumbered over to the telephone and made his hands into fists virtually all over it.

"Fine, Chief," he said gratefully. "This will do me good." Thrusting his mouth into the transmitter he began to do himself good at the top of his lungs. "Hello! Hello!" said Pat excitedly. "This is Murphy of the police force talking. Who are you?" A sudden pause. "Oh," he began again. "It's a drunken hook and ladder, did you say?" Another pause while Pat more deeply entrenched his ear. Then, "Hold the line, mister." Turning to the sergeant, Pat tried to impart his information. "It seems, Chief," he said, "that this guy has been dodging either a drunken hook and ladder or a hook and ladder driven by drunkards or maniacs escaped from the asylum. What shall I tell him?"

"That hook and ladder is going to drive me into my grave!" groaned the sergeant.

"That's what it's nearly done to this man," said Pat. "He says he can't keep up dodging it much longer. He's fair exhausted from being pursued by the hook and ladder."

"Ask him where it is," commanded the sergeant.

"Where is this hook and ladder?" Pat asked over the wire, then waited to be told. "Hang on," he said, and again turned to his superior. "I thought this was going to do me good," he complained, "but damned if I believe it will. Do all people go crazy when they telephone to us?"

"This is no time for idle questions," said the sergeant tartly. "I don't care whether or not it does you any good. That damn telephone has almost ruined me already. Where did the guy say it was?"

"He said it was all over," Pat replied. "Sometimes here and sometimes there. It sort of appears from all directions, then goes bounding in pursuit of him, no less."

"That guy must be drunk himself," muttered the sergeant. "A hook and ladder can't appear from all directions. Ask him if he is."

"Are you drunk, mister?" asked Pat of the man at the other end of the wire, then quickly removed the receiver from his ear. Even the sergeant, standing several feet away, could hear the incoherent protests tumbling from the mouth of the telephone. "He says he isn't, Chief," said Pat at last. "He seems to be sure about it. He says he is a public-spirited citizen, and unless something is done about that hook and ladder he is going to report the entire force. Do you want to talk to him? I'm dead certain this isn't going to do me any good at all."

"Are you afraid to talk to the man?" demanded the sergeant. "You started the conversation, go on and finish it."

"What shall I say now?"

"Ask him where he is—if he won't tell us where that hook and ladder is," replied the chief. "String him along somehow. Maybe he'll forget about it or the thing will go away."

"A bounding hook and ladder filled with maniacs would be a hard thing to forget," commented Pat, looking with distaste at the telephone. "All right, Chief. I'll take another chance." Once more he hid as much of his mouth as possible in the telephone and shouted what he hoped would be soothing words to the infuriated citizen at the other end. "Don't be like that, mister," said Pat. "We didn't mean it. The chief was just having some fun." Pause. "Oh, you're glad to know the chief is enjoying himself." Here Pat turned to the sergeant. "The guy says he's glad you're having a good time," he told his superior. "Says he wishes you were down there where he is."

"I heard! I heard!" cried the sergeant irritably. "Leave my name out of it. Ask him where he is."

After Pat had complied with this request he listened for a long time to the voice at the other end of the wire, an expression of profound astonishment on his face.

"What!" the sergeant heard him exclaim. "There's a woman on the hook and ladder? Yeah? Oh, half fireman and half woman, you say. Now, mister, how can that be? Hold on! I'm not calling you a liar. Sure, I know. Certainly. You can tell half of a woman when you see one. I never saw one that way. Of course, you're no baby. You could tell even less of a woman than that. Wait a minute. The chief ought to hear this." With wide blue eyes Pat stared his incredulity at the sergeant. "Golly," he said, "something's funny somewhere. I'm almost afraid to tell you what that guy told me. Shall I?"

"Go on!" cried the sergeant.

"Well," said Pat in a hushed voice, "he says there's a thing scrambling around that hook and ladder that's half fireman and half lady, and he claims the men are maniacs.

"Ask him which half is which," said the chief in a dead voice.

"Do you think I should?" asked Pat a little slyly. "I should think either half of a woman or a fireman scrambling over a hook and ladder would be enough to upset anybody. And when it comes to a half of each crawling after one another—my eye! I don't like to think about it."

"Go on and do as I say," said the chief. "It's important."

"Why?" asked Pat.

"Haven't you got sense enough to know that there's a lot of difference between the two halves of a woman?"

"I know there is," replied Pat, "but I don't see what good either half is going to do us now. Whatever half it is, the other one's a fireman, and that's not so good."

"What are you trying to get at?" the sergeant demanded.

"Nothing at all," Pat hastened to assure him. "I certainly don't want to get at that monster, no matter which half is which. Let's hang up, Chief."

"Go on and ask that question," commanded the sergeant.

"Listen, mister," said Pat diffidently. "The chief wants to know which half of the thing is which, a woman or a fireman?" As he listened his face grew pink. Finally he put his hand over the mouthpiece and addressed himself to the impatient sergeant. "It's the bottom half," said Pat in a hushed voice.

"The bottom half is which?" demanded the other.

"The bottom half is all lady," replied Pat. "Think of it, Chief, think of it. And on top there's a fireman. What a sight that must be!"

"It's as I thought," muttered the sergeant. "No wonder those men are maniacs. Did he say where this hook and ladder was?"

"Somewhere around Main and Spruce," replied Pat, "It's playing all about."

"Hey, boys!" the sergeant shouted with sudden decision in his voice. "Murphy, O'Brien, Samuels, and Schmidt, line up, the four of you." When the boys, languidly buttoning their tunics, were standing in front of the desk, the sergeant snapped out his instructions. "There's a wild hook and ladder raising hell all over this town. God only knows what it will do next. Go down to Main and Spruce and pick up the trail and——"

"Do you want us to shadow the thing?" Officer Samuels asked hopefully.

"Certainly not!" exploded the sergeant. "I want you to arrest that hook and ladder and drag back here either dead or alive. And everybody on it," he added.

"What about the half and half?" inquired Pat. "Shall we treat the thing as a lady or a fireman?"

"That depends upon which half gives you the most trouble," replied the chief.

"I don't like any part of the unholy body," answered Pat.

"You don't have to like it," the sergeant retorted, "Policemen ain't supposed to fall all over the people they arrest."

"Gord!" ejaculated Pat. "I wouldn't fall all over that thing if my life depended on it"

"What sort of a thing is it?" asked Officer O'Brien.

"It's a thing," Pat Murphy explained, that's one half fireman and another half woman."

"Yeah?" said O'Brien. "Who do you you think you're kidding? Which half is a woman?"

"The bottom half," said Pat.

"And how far up does it go?" asked Schmidt.

"That's none of your business," put in the Chief. "You clear out of here and bring both halves back."

"Divs on the south end," said Samuels as the policemen filed from the room.

"You're welcome to both ends of it," Pat Murphy told him.

The telephone tinkled merrily. Before he settled back in his chair the sergeant gently removed the receiver and placed it on the desk. Then he lighted a fat, black cigar and sighed a long pull of smoke into the still air. He had done his duty. Now he would rest and relax. He was still doing this when the head of the Fire Department strode in.

"I've lost my hook and ladder," he announced.

"You have?" said the sergeant mildly. "Well, that's just too bad. Every member of the community has found that hook and ladder with the exception of yourself. And," he added with swelling bitterness, "if you ever get the damn thing back, I hope to God you'll never let it out of your sight again. I'm dog tired of your hook and ladder."

"What do you mean?" demanded the other.

"Listen," replied the sergeant. "Have you a number on your force that's half fireman and half woman?"

"I don't know what you're talking about," said the owner of the lost hook and ladder. "Have you gone crazy?"

"I have," replied the sergeant quietly. "Stark, staring mad. Listen some more, Commissioner."

Then the sergeant told him all. And when he had finished, the Commissioner was just human enough to want. to know which half was which.

"I knew you were going to ask that question," the sergeant replied sorrowfully. "Commissioner, the lower half's a lady."

CHAPTER IX

CROWN'S COSMOPOLITAN

MEANWHILE, Mr. Pebble and party were steadfastly trying to mind their own business with a discouraging lack of success. For once in a blue moon the telephone reports of eyewitnesses had been substantially accurate, if a trifle irrelevant. One might even say those reports had been misleadingly conservative. No mention had been made of the incident of the demolished hothouse or of the mutilated ninth green on the local golf course. Also, several twisted lamp posts seem to have passed unnoticed. The desperate struggle caused by Nockashima inadvertently starting the hook and ladder during the temporary absence of Rex Pebble never became public knowledge, although it was long remembered by those directly concerned. Hal, the only professional present, was by far the most unhappy. He was firmly convinced he had lost not only his livelihood but also the need of having one, inasmuch as he would soon be losing his life as well. Nockashima's rendition of "The Last Round-up" in pidgin English went a long way toward making everything less pleasant. The Pebble party was now enjoying a brief breathing spell in a dimly lighted alley situated in the heart of the town. On their right rose the sheer walls of a large and enterprising department store. Throughout the surrounding countryside Crown's Cosmopolitan was jointly famous. No finer store existed outside of a large city. On the left of the little group the smooth, windowless side of a bank building offered scant hospitality. The end of the alley was uncompromisingly blocked by a formidable brick barrier. In other words, Rex Pebble and his companions would find themselves in a pretty kettle of fish should their present whereabouts be discovered by Pat Murphy and the rest of the boys. However, for a moment or so their peace remained undisturbed.

"It's pleasant here," Mr. Pebble observed. "A good place to stretch one's legs before hurtling forth on another spin."

My legs stretched from ear to ear already," Nokashima declared. "That seat too high for short Japanese body to attend pedals. Feet dangle on way."

"And if you try to monkey with the hook and ladder a second short Japanese body will be dangling at yellow end of a rope."

"Speaking of necks," remarked Major Jaffey, gently fingering his own, "mine has not settled back to its former position since that short Japanese body in question dangled on the end of my legs."

"Give me a cigarette, Major," said Spray Summers, "I'm dying for a smoke."

Courteously the Major passed a package of cigarettes among the members of the party. Soon five small red sparks were glowing in the darkness. It was these indications of life that first attracted the attention of the squad of searching policemen.

"Look!" cried Pat in a piercing whisper. "I'll bet they're down there. Be careful of an ambush."

"Did you hear that?" asked Hal in a low voice. "Somebody's betting we're down here."

"Then he wins," commented Rex Pebble. "We are."

"Not if I know it," flung back Hal. "They're cops, and they're after us. Nothing would please them more than to run in a fireman."

"How to get out?" soliloquized Nockashima in the manner of a Nipponese Hamlet. "That plenty vital question."

"We're not going to get out," said Rex Pebble. "We're going to get up and in. Bear a hand there, Hal. We'll raise a couple of ladders and escape through the Cosmopolitan. My wife has a charge account there."

"So have I," observed Spray Summers, "but any judge in his sober senses would think it an odd time to be seized with a sudden desire to make use of it."

Disregarding this somewhat depressing observation, the four men busied themselves setting up the ladders.

"Major," commanded Rex Pebble, "you and Hal go up first. Something seems to tell me that you are not without experience in the art of breaking and entering. Hal makes a regular business of it. Look lively, both of you. I hear the unmistakable sounds of flat feet flapping at our rear."

"I'd like to flop mine against theirs," grumbled Spray. "What have we done? Nothing!"

"Perhaps you're right," replied Rex Pebble, "but we've done it so damn thoroughly that it will be more than enough to lock us up for life if we trust entirely in our innocence."

"When I go, boss?" Nockashima asked eagerly.

"You can nip up at any old time," Mr. Pebble told him. "You're doing me no good here."

And that was exactly what Nockashima did. He nipped up the ladder with the agility of a monkey, which he closely resembled.

"Pist!" came the signal from somewhere in the darkness above their heads. "Pist! Pist!"

"What is it!" asked Mr. Pebble, lowering his voice.

"Pist!" was all he got for his trouble. "Pist! Hey, pist! Pis-s-s-t-t!"

"Stop it!" exclaimed Spray Summers. "Of all the asinine noises to make. And he keeps on doing it. Always makes me think of bum actors in long cloaks ducking in and out of the wings. Pist, up there yourself!"

Nockashima, who had been making no noise at all, evidently believing that something was expected of him, ducked his head over his shoulder and peered down into the darkness of the alley.

"Pist, madam!" he offered politely. "Am hell bent on escape. Pist! Pist!"

"Please stop pisting," shouted Rex Pebble. "There's no time for all that. It makes us nervous."

"Holy saints, will you listen to them?" Pat Murphy said to his brother officers. "It's lunatics they are. And it only makes the other two nervous. I'd get sore as hell."

Nockashima had disappeared into the blackness of an open window, and Spray and Rex Pebble were two thirds the way up by the time Pat and his boys had reached the foot of the ladders.

"Begord, it's true!" explained Pat, looking up at Spray. "It's half fireman and half lady."

"That lower half ain't no fireman," declared Officer Samuels with deep conviction.

"Well, it ain't no lady, either," put in the one called Schmidt. "Even in these-days a lady wears a little something."

"Hey, you in the helmet," shouted Murphy. "Stay where you are. I see everything."

As unconventional as Spray was, this gratuitous information made her feel decidedly uncomfortable. Clutching the awkward rubber coat around her, she took a quick, strained glance below.

"If you were a gentleman you'd bow your head," she called down, "and look at your ugly feet."

"And if you were a lady you'd take a pike at something else," retorted Pat. "What sort of a thing do you happen to be, anyway?"

"I thought you were seeing everything," she retorted.

"Not quite," said Officer Samuels. "It's still too dark."

"Well," replied Spray cuttingly, "you should have seen enough from where you're standing."

"I've seen almost too much," admitted Pat Murphy.

"One can't get enough of a good thing," Spray replied coolly, edging up a few more rungs. "That's what I always say."

"Will you come down, whatever you are?" demanded Pat Murphy.

"No, I won't," cried Spray. "Will you go away?"

"I'll come up there and lay hands on you," the exasperated policeman shouted.

"What a man!" she said to Mr. Pebble, perched semi-recumbent on the other ladder; then called tauntingly to the men below her, "Is that a threat or a promise?"

"You know," put in Mr. Pebble, "I'm finding it increasingly difficult to retain my poise. This ladder sways like a camel's back."

"I'm finding it damn near impossible to keep my modesty," she retorted, "and cimb the thing at the same time."

"Why trouble about modesty now?" he inquired. "After all, it's merely a matter of one's point of view." "That's just what I'm worrying about," said Spray. "Those coppers down there have the wrong point of view."

"Pist!" sounded suddenly in the darkness only a few feet away. "Pist!"

"He's at it again," grumbled Spray. "Will you tell me whether that noise is intended to repel or attract? I can't get the idea."

"Maybe the excitement has driven the Major mad," suggested Mr. Pebble, "and he thinks he's playing snake."

"I wish he'd stop playing it in my ears," she complained. "I'll never get up this ladder with all these interruptions."

"Look out, madam," Nockashima called excitedly from a window. "Officers make grade. Snatch at behind."

"What!" cried the startled Spray. "The horrid things! There is no time to stand on any further ceremony. Hurry

up, Rex." Hastily she scrambled up to the window, then added as an afterthought as she pulled herself through, "And no matter what those rude policemen snatch at, Nockashima, you should endeavor to select your words with a little more delicacy. I don't know which is the more objectionable, to be snatched at or to be told where."

"Madam," replied Nockashima pedantically, "there are two behinds. One is thing, other is place. I refer to latter."

"Say, lady," came the earnest but subdued voice of Hal, the renegade fireman, "you and that dopey laundryman are going to talk us all into jail if you don't dry up."

"I not wet yet," Nockashima announced proudly.

"Listen, little Fu Manchu," the fireman retorted. "Those flatties are about to chuck their dogs right in those windows. You'd better hide while you can."

"If dogs of flatties smell no better than Mist' Henry," replied the Jap complacently, "we remain in obscurity to end of days."

"Pardon the interruption," spoke up Major Jaffey in a calm, informative voice, "but from a brief investigation of our whereabouts I should say we are now in the furniture department. There is also a suggestion of toys at the far end. It's a jolly place for hiding. God only knows where we'll be cuter."

"Fine!" exclaimed Spray. "Lead me to a bed."

"Hot invitation, that," observed the voice of Nockashima. "Who you ask, madam?"

"Somebody hit that Jap," said Spray. "He's gone bad on our hands."

"Am on hands and upper joint of legs," the loquacious little yellow man informed them. "Like missionary fella, I progress amid encircling gloom."

"What's that!" exclaimed Spray as a violent commotion broke out near the windows.

"Flatties chucking in dogs," hazarded Nockashima,

"Dogs not amused, nor this wormlike son of honorable house. In silence I seek a huddle."

From the moment the little yellow man set forth to seek a huddle that floor of Crown's Cosmopolitan became the center of dark confusion, occasionally relieved by the flashing of electric torches, the flame of a match and the momentary switching on of overhead lights. Cries of consternation echoed through the vast department. There were the sounds of running feet, of pursuing grunts, of painful collisions with unseen objects, of unexpected giggles and scattered conversation. There were shouts of surprise and mortification and some of mortal fear. It was no floor at all for nervous people, yet every person on it was more or less that way. It is almost safe to say that no group of frenzied bargain hunters on sales day ever conducted themselves on that floor as unbecomingly as did the police and the Pebble party.

The opening signal of distress came from Spray Summers, who had thoughtlessly concealed herself in the first bed she could find. Her fool's paradise was suddenly and rudely shattered by the frantic arrival of two unknown figures caroming off her body from two different directions. They were received with a grunt of anguish which was the best the lady could offer at the moment. Painfully she reached out her left hand and felt a small semi-human face; then her fingers slipped down to the fabric of a starched jacket.

"Not that, madam," Nockashima whispered tragically. "Not that! If do I push loud cries like Fifi."

"You snake in the grass," gritted Spray. "Do you realize you're in bed with me?"

"Realization almost stupefying," breathed the little servant. "I feel just like it"

"You do?" Spray whispered. "Take this, then, and tell me what you feel like."

"Hardly can," gasped Nockashima, taking what Spray had given him in the pit of his stomach. "I feel like small cherry blossom beneath foot of great giant."

"This is no time to be talking about cherries," retorted Spray.

"Cherries my dish," the little man informed her. "I go mad for cherries."

"You've gone mad without them," Spray told him.

"Yes, madam," he admitted. "That why I go mad."

"Do you realize, small ounce of vileness, what a liberty you've taken?"

"If not take some liberty here," declared Nock, "I lose all liberty to dogs of flatties. Where are flatties' dogs, madam? I hear no sniff-sniff nor patter of bounding feet."

"One can't hear anything above the roar of those policemen," replied Spray. "Do you happen to know who belongs to this other body beside me?"

"Only vague surmise," admitted Nockashima. "Madam may have caught cowardly flattie. Squeeze down on neck. Maybe he turn to fox."

"I don't want to be in bed with a fox," declared Spray. "You're bad enough."

"If I turn into fox," mused Nockashima, "I lure dogs on pursuit of untamed goose, then I go home and. offer myself to nose of Mist' Henry. If he no smell, my broom droop with deep despond."

"Not broom," Spray corrected. "You mean your brush."

"Is that what I have, madam, if I turn to fox? Brush on the end of me. How nice."

"How awful," murmured Spray Summers. "Please be quiet, snake in the grass."

"One more thing done," the little servant pleaded. "I not snake in grass, madam. I not even so funny as fox. Just small little Japanese feller in bed with lady and unknown body, and contorted with alarm."

"I'm not altogether easy in my mind myself."

"Why not tentatively finger opposite body?" the yellow one inquired. "Maybe encounter familiar object."

In spite of herself, Spray laughed.

"What a fool you are, Nocka," she said, then turned to the other object behind her. "Who are you?" she demanded sharply. "Speak up!"

"Pist!" came so suddenly and explosively from the unknown body on her right that she jumped almost a foot from the bed. While she was up Nockashima frantically burrowed under her. When she settled back she felt very much like a person who had unexpectedly sat on a cat.

"Pist!" once more popped irritably from the man beside her. "Pist!"

"Unidentified must have been restraining those for long time," observed Nockashima in a muffled voice. "Your body, madam, is mutilating too many of my parts."

"And this body over here has got me completely baffled," replied Spray. "I don't know how to open a conversation with it if it keeps on making those noises."

"Pist!" uttered the body.

"Will you stop doing that!" cried Spray, blindly cuffing the body in the dark.

The pist was promptly turned to a grunt.

"My dear lady," expostulated the voice of Major Jaffey. "Never do that again. As it is, I doubt if it will be necessary. You should have better sense."

At this moment a light flashed blindingly in the eyes of the three occupants of the bed, and the voice of Pat Murphy cried loudly, "Here they are, boys! I've got 'em!"

From all parts of the floor heavy feet came crashing towards the center of attraction. The bodies on either side of Spray Summers were galvanized into desperate action as they melted into the darkness, their eager feet adding to the general din and confusion. Cursing all Japanese and majors from the bottom of her heart, Spray remained behind, struggling in the grasp of Pat Murphy. That lusty limb of the law unceremoniously dragged the furious woman from the bed, dropping his torch in so doing, then, with no definite object in mind, hurtled her along the floor.

"Say, Pat!" shouted a voice. "Where are you now, man? Is the lower half a lady?"

"Haven't been able to find hide nor hair of a fireman yet," Pat called back. "It seems to be all lady."

"Well, don't look any farther," Spray protested. "You're here to do your duty, not to amuse yourself."

"If you'd only tell me whether you're a lady or not," the policeman panted. "I might know what to do with you."

"And what would that be, may I ask?"

"Don't exactly know," said Pat, "but I wouldn't handle you so rough, maybe."

A body collided violently with the woman as a fresh pair of hands took hold of her.

"I'm with you, Pat," said the newcomer. "Which half do you want?"

"Will you two men stop trying arbitrarily to divide me," protested Spray.

"I'm one continuous body, and if there's any fireman about me I have yet to find it out."

"You mean, you're all lady?" breathed Pat.

"From head to toe," said Spray.

"The sergeant said you were some fireman, lady," said the other voice in disappointed tones.

"Well, you tell the sergeant," she retorted, "that I'm not going to switch my body about just to please him. Where are we going, anyway? Are we just taking a walk in the dark?"

"We don't know, lady," Pat Murphy replied. "Haven't had time to think. Hey, boys!" he shouted suddenly."Round up the rest of the gang. We've got one of them. Dig the others out."

From somewhere in the darkness came the quavering notes of "The Last Round-up." Nocka was at it again.

"I don't know where I've hidden myself," a voice complained, "much less where the rest of 'em are."

"Holy Saints!" breathed Pat. "What an awful sound! It's like a ghost wailing for its lost soul."

Spray felt herself suddenly seized from the rear and plucked from the grasp of her two astonished captors. She was dragged through an aperture, and a door slammed behind her.

"Who's got me now?" she inquired pessimistically. "Not that it makes much difference."

"You're in the model home," whispered the voice of Rex Pebble. "This is the bathroom."

"Thank God for that," said Spray. "How is it under the shower?"

"A bit stuffy," replied Rex Pebble, "but at least it's quiet and exclusive. You're a public scandal." -

"I'd be all of that," she admitted, "if I had a public."

"I say, old darling," asked Mr. Pebble conversationally from the shower, "doesn't this strike you as being rather an odd way to be spending the first night of our new lives?"

"It does. It does," she assured him. "It's one hell of a quaint way to be spending the first night of a new life or an old one. But we don't seem to learn any better."

"And," observed Mr. Pebble, "if those policemen have their way with us we'll be spending the last night of our new lives locked in the arms of the law."

"I've been locked in those arms already," said Spray.

"And you'd be locked in them still," Rex Pebble assured her, "had I known what use you were going to make of your freedom."

While this reunion of souls was progressing, Nockashima, that prince of Japanese house boys, had found his way by nervous fit after frantic start into the toy department, which was situated at the rear of the floor. Here it was his momentary bad luck to encounter the papier-mache head of an exceedingly dashing-looking lion, glorying in a pair of great malevolent eyes and a mane of tremendous vitality. It was a trying moment for the already hard-pushed little man. Although darkness saved him from savoring the full horror of the object con-fronting him, those parts of it which his groping hands had felt were more than enough to convince him he was standing unarmed in the presence of a deadly peril—possibly one of those dogs of the flatties, a strong, silent dog. Fortunately for himself as well as for others the little yellow man was too overcome by his emotions to push even so much as a squawk. Too terrified either to retreat or to advance, he remained static in the darkness, shuddering in all his Oriental limbs.

However, as time passed and no overtures of a hostile nature were manifested by the deadly peril, the inordinate curiosity which had made Nocka's life one continuous calamity reasserted itself to such an extent that before the lapse of many minutes he was cheek and jowl with this effigy of the king of the jungle. At last, with some vaguely formulated plan in his peculiar little mind, he slipped the head of the lion over his own and went circulating aimlessly through the darkness to discover what fate held in store for him in his radically altered appearance.

A short time later Officer Pat Murphy was indelicate enough to switch a light on the retreat occupied by Mr. Pebble and his mistress. Officer Pat Murphy was thereby a very much startled policeman.

"What's this?" he asked, for lack of anything better to say.

"A bathroom," replied Spray, springing up. "What does it look like to you?"

"Say, lady," he answered chidingly, when he had recovered a little from the shock of discovery, "you can think of the damnedest things to do when you're being chased by the cops. First you go to bed, then you find a bathroom. Haven't you got any better sense? This isn't a private home."

"It's the only private home I've got at the moment," the lady responded. "Be so good as to respect its privacy."

"The devil I will," said Pat. "I'm going to run you in.

"On what charge, may I ask?"

"On any one of fifty. You and your boy friends too. If I tell the judge what I just saw he'll put you away for good."

"Don't be childish, Pat," replied Spray. "How would you tell the judge that?"

"I'd whisper it to him," said Pat meanly. "In his ear, I would."

"Oh," retorted Spray, sparring for time. "Not in his eyes, like most people."

"Nobody whispers in other people's eyes," said Pat. "Don't be funny. Come on and snap out of this."

"I like it here," she told him.

"You certainly made yourself at home," he retorted. "Do you want me to put the bracelets on?"

"Do I have to look pretty to see the judge?"

"If he sees you the way you are, he's going to look awful," Pat assured her. "It might kill the old man." "Then you will be charged with murder," she said, "for showing me to the poor old man. Go away now and look for some of the boys."

"I will not," said Pat. "This is the nuttiest place to try to find anyone in. What did you want to come up here for?"

"I wanted to go shopping," she answered.

"You sure do need some clothes," he admitted. "All you've got on is a coat, and that isn't yours."

"How about fixing me up nice for the judge?" suggested Spray. "Slip downstairs and grab off a nice dress and a pair of passionate panties." - -

"Lady, you're bad," said Pat. "You shouldn't use such words. You're after asking me to compound a felony."

"You'll be compounding another one if you don't get me some clothes," she threatened. "I'm going to take the coat off."

"Don't, lady," Pat pleaded.

"Off comes the coat!" cried Spray.

"Button it up," he urged her. "What will the boys think if they find us together like this?"

"What do you think they'll think?"

"You know," he replied.

"I do not," retorted Spray. "I haven't an evil mind. And if I can make myself heard above the din the boys are making, I'm going to scream for help. Off comes the coat."

For the salvation of his own soul Pat Murphy sprang through the door and began to wrestle with the apparently furious woman. Unseen to the combatants, Rex Pebble thrust a curious head through the curtains and peered at the active scene, then hurriedly withdrew. To retain his poise he grasped the nearest tap, and a vicious deluge of icy water descended on his naked spine. A long, shuddering cry issued from the shower. The wrestlers immediately released each other and stood regarding the curtain with startled eyes.

"What's that?" Pat gasped. "It sounded like a poor soul being murdered in cold blood."

"Cold blood it is," complained the shower wetly. "The damn fools didn't have to make their confounded shower so all-fired realistic."

"Turn on the hot," suggested Spray, "and I'll come on in with you. I'm getting sick of this dumb policeman."

"You mustn't do that," admonished Murphy in a shocked voice. "You've gone far enough, lady. Who's the guy in the shower?"

"I'm the guy in the shower," the curtains announced. "And you're a gone cop. Stand where you are."

"What do you mean?" asked Pat.

"I've got you covered," said the shower.

"I wish you'd cover this lady," the officer answered moodily.

"Never mind the lady," snapped the shower. "You back out of this room."

At this moment a scream bearing all the earmarks of sincere distress came simultaneously from Spray and Pat Murphy. Popping his head through the curtains Rex Pebble made a scream of his own. Completely unstrung by this reception, Nockashima began to scream too, which made him all the worse. Three hurtling bodies bounded over his speedily flattened figure and became wedged in the door of the bathroom.

"Let me outta here!" gasped Murphy. "Holy Saint Patrick, the baleful eyes of the beast! Did you see them?"

"Shut up!" chattered Spray. "It might understand English."

"That monster's so awful," declared Pat, "it doesn't understand itself."

"If you two want to stand here and discuss the thing to its face," said Rex Pebble, "I don't want to be included. Give me a chance to run."

"Give me the strength," muttered Spray.

From all points of the floor lights were flashing on and off, and excited voices were bellowing through the darkness.

"Have you got one, Pat?" a colleague called out.

"I haven't," he shouted, "but one has almost got me. And what a one it is!"

"You mean the half fireman and half lady?"

"No," replied Pat. "It's half monster and half man. And it's all bad."

"Then don't arrest it," urged the voice.

"Arrest it!" cried Pat hysterically. "I'm trying to leave it miles behind. The baleful eyes of the beast. Let me through, the both of you."

As the deadlock was broken, Nockashima, bereft of his lion's head, rose from the floor and, still screaming at the top of his lungs, dashed after the retreating figures. The fireman known as Hal, on his way to no place in particular, spied the abandoned head lying in the light of the bathroom, and promptly placing it over his own, ran after Nockashima. Pat Murphy, looking back over his shoulder, caught a horrified glimpse of the oncoming figure.

"Begod!" he cried in amazement. "It's grown twice its size."

Nockashima, far too busy to realize his loss, followed the policeman's example, then turned his screams into speech.

"Dog of flattie," he told an uninterested world, "is fox of evil magic."

"Fox, me eye!" breathed Pat. "Take another look, you runt."

"Not need another look," Nocka assured him. "Didn't enjoy last. Wait till it turns to serpent. Then watch out."

"Don't talk like that," Pat scolded, "or I'll lock you up for baiting an officer."

"Please you do," replied Nockashima. "Lock me up from beast of monster when sure it not turn to beautiful naked lady. I know Japanese fella——"

"Shut up!" gasped Spray. "Would you tell dirty stories in the very jaws of death?"

"Not in jaws," murmured Nockashima. "I want but small how-do-you-do with jaws."

"It will soon be good-bye," said Spray.

Suddenly the overhead lights flashed up in all parts of the floor. Hal, who was passing a mirror at the moment, caught a glimpse of his unamiable reflection and jumped two feet from the ground, uttering hoarse cries the while.

"I'm worse than I expected," he mouthed hollowly. "I'm even scared of myself."

"Listen, he admits it," said Spray. "The damned thing's talking to itself."

"It's better than having it screaming at us," observed the philosophical Mr. Pebble, clinging to his dripping tablecloth. "Any fair-minded monster with eyes in its head would have to admit it isn't a hot number. That thing would be silly as hell if it considered itself a bathing beauty."

"Your sarcasm is about as labored as my legs," retorted Spray. "Heavens! What's that?"

It was the sound of several revolvers all talking at once. From various parts of the room excited policemen were taking pot shots at the fleeing monster. In self-defense Hal removed the lion's head from his and hurled it well before him. Cries of horror and stupefaction broke from all beholders of this ghastly act save Nockashima. That one was giggling knowingly.

"Very funny business, this," he managed to get out. "I fairly stream with mirth."

Spray blinked, then closed her lovely eyes, although running at full speed. "I wish it would chuck its legs away next," she wheezed; "then we might be able to give ours a bit of a rest."

"Never a dull moment," said Rex Pebble. "We got our youth and strength back just in time to become physical wrecks."

"Rex," cried Spray suddenly, "it's got me!" So saying she catapulted through the air, rolled over several times, then came to rest with Hal's helmet miraculously on her head and the lion's on her left foot. "Rex! Rex!" she sobbed. "The monster's swallowed my foot with his neck. Please do something about it."

"What do you want him to swallow it with?" Rex Pebble asked reasonably enough.

"I don't want him to swallow my foot at all," she complained rather pathetically, "especially since I've lost my corns. Come here and take it away."

Here she waved one slim, lion-capped leg aloft in a frantic effort to dislodge it. A carefully concealed police-man thrust his head from behind a pillar just in time to witness this odd spectacle.

"Hey, boys!" he shouted, quickly withdrawing his head. "It's one half fireman now, and the other half's a wild beast. And both ends are peering at each other."

The boys received this devastating bit of news in stunned silence. Presently a timid voice spoke up.

"Which half of the thing is wild beast?" it wanted to be told.

"I don't know," replied the policeman behind the pillar. "Both halves are heads and a lot of mouth."

"And what's become of that lower half of a lady?" the voice continued.

"Damned if I know that either," said the policeman. "I'm out of luck entirely."

"Why not take a shot at the wild beast?" suggested the voice. "That is, if you're sure no part of it is the lower half of a lady."

This suggestion paralyzed Spray. She strove so hard to get her leg as far away from the rest of her body as possible that she was lying on the back of her neck. A shot rang out, and the lion's head became merely a matter of record, its fragments flying through the air. They flew no faster than Spray. With one bound she was clear of the floor, and with another she was climbing up Rex Pebble's back.

"That ends all hope of poise," he bitterly observed. "What are we going to do with each other?"

"I don't know," she retorted wearily, "but I've been a half of this and a half of that for so long I might just as well pretend I'm a part of you. Run away somewhere and hide us. My foot still tingles."

"This way!" suddenly bellowed the parade-ground voice of Major Jaffey. "This way for the fire party. An exit. It is here!"

Although the good Major had not the vaguest idea as to what new dangers the exit led, he rightly assumed they could be no worse than those already confronting them. With the Pebble party at his heels, he dashed down several flights of stairs and at last emerged into the main floor of Crown's Cosmopolitan. Here, protected once more by darkness, the old business of hiding began all over again.

"Grab whatever clothes you can find and put them on," ordered the Major. "Thus we will be disguised for a later flight. If you insist on being honest we can charge them to Mrs. Pebble. Her husband will explain later."

"In detail," came the caustic voice of Rex Pebble through the darkness. "My wife will enjoy it."

For some minutes the darkness of the main floor was filled with the stealthy yet industrious sound of searching feet. Rex Pebble fortunately encountered the figure of a gentleman in evening clothes. This he promptly stripped of all garments and transferred them to his own person. He was completely attired in every detail, including a top hat. No sooner had he finished his toilet than he felt a pair of hands furtively investigating his body. Mr. Pebble froze in his tracks and tried to emulate the position of the figure he had just denuded. Suddenly his hat was deftly whisked from his head. Mr. Pebble made no remonstrance. The next minute one of his feet was lifted from the floor and the pump flipped from it. This happened to the other foot, and still Mr. Pebble made no demur. But when his trousers were firmly seized and neatly slipped down his legs he thought it was high time to take a little interest in himself.

"Whoever you are," he said in his most formal tones, "be so good as to put those trousers back where you found them. Also the shoes and hat."

"All right, boss," came the depressed voice of Nockashima. "You must look so nice. Not first time I undress you. He! He! Where I put pants?"

"Where I usually wear them, Nocka," replied Rex Pebble patiently. "On the legs and middle section." When the little servant had finished redressing him, Mr. Pebble patted him affectionately on the shoulder. "Sorry to have disappointed you. Better luck next time. Go find an outfit of your own."

"I go, boss," replied Nockashima. "I array myself like baron. All very fine."

But like many whose hearts are overflowing with the best intentions,

Nockashima soon became discouraged and finally desperate. This unsettled state of mind led to another contretemps.

Spray Summers, who had got herself into something rather good in the line of an evening gown, was at first a little flattered when she felt masculine hands laid upon her. However, she remained motionless and silent until she had assured herself that the hands were on friendly business. When her step-ins were seized and zipped from their place of repose she did not scream as would have some women, but merely satisfied her emotions by giving the unseen gentleman a playful little push. What was her surprise when she received a push back of such vigor that the breath was nearly knocked from her body. Staggeringback, she rallied her forces, shook her head like a dazed boxer, then gamely returned to the assault. No matter how friendly his intentions, this man must be taught a lesson. His advances had been satisfactorily direct. Those step-ins had been handled with the deftness of an expert. But the man's idea of playfulness was altogether too rough. He needed a little polishing to make him entirely acceptable. She would be forced to show the fellow that there was a right way and a wrong way to everything. In such affairs technique meant much to a lady. There was nothing to be gained in crippling a woman one intended to amuse later on. Therefore, when this time Spray Summers unleashed a blow in the darkness, she did so with a will. The flat of her swiftly traveling hand forcibly encountered a closely cropped head. There was a sudden gasp, the sound of a body operating out of control, then an alarming crash of glass as a show case was definitely and permanently put out of business. Spray smiled grimly but not for long. If he returned to her after that one, she reflected, he would be a determined chap indeed. And return he did, but in no soliciting mood. Spray felt herself grasped firmly round the knees, lifted from the floor, then violently deposited thereon. For a moment or so she sat moodily where she had landed and rubbed the spot of contact. Then she sighed. This last attack of her unseen admirer was sufficiently ruthless to convince her that no matter how agreeable he ultimately intended to be, he was certainly making a shambles of things at the present moment. In short, the ends failed to justify the means. The wear and tear was too terrific.

Heaving herself to her hands and knees, she was about to crawl from the field, using the better part of valor for an excuse, when she was seized from behind and the slippers—a size too large—dragged from her feet.

"What the hell!" she muttered, twisting her head back over her shoulder. "I say there, are you still playing, or are you mad at me?"

"Not each," came back the answer. "Striving to retain life in small body. Also to disguise same beneath alien garments."

Spray was appalled. The cool effrontery of this imp from some Japanese hell made her momentarily speech-less.

"Will you stop trying to disguise yourself beneath my garments?" she demanded at last. "Give me back my shoes and pants. You deliberately stole them from me."

"Not steal, madam," said Nockashima. "All charged up. Very sorry. Every figure I attempt to uncover turns into angry being. 'Go 'way, vile Jap,' all say. Night of vast frustration. Here things, madam. Want me to slip on?"

"You slip on through the darkness," replied Spray. "And don't come near me for years."

"As I thought," said Nocka, sorrowfully. "Once more driven round about. Don't angry, madam. Maybe I suicide in own blood. Not sure, though. Maybe dogs of flatties mangle first. Where are dogs of flatties? I not see one."

"Don't trouble to look for them," advised Spray a little more kindly. "They'll find us soon enough."

Nocka suddenly giggled.

"I thought you dog of flattie," he told her. "Fight grimly for life."

"Dogs don't wear pants, Nocka," she informed him.

"Dogs of flatties might," he argued. "How I know? Dogs of flatties adopt confusing disguise, maybe. I not surprise if do. What a romp we had. I almost repose in glass casket like famous Russian redman."

"Are you still drunk, Nockashima?"

"A mere pushover," replied Nocka. "I suspend, madam."

"I wish you could find a drink." Spray's voice sounded wistful.

"Wish could," said Nocka. "No disgrace in valiant endeavor. I worm in search, teeteringly. Excuse please, madam."

Spray listened to his quiet departure for a few minutes, then she no longer had to strain her ears. A great rumpus somewhere out in the black void apprised her of the fact that the little yellow man had once more established contact with an angry being.

"Take your hands off me, whoever you are," she heard Hal, the fireman, declaiming. "Neither man nor beast is going to handle me that way."

Seemingly the small creature was out of luck again. Feeling a little sorry for him and a lot more for herself, Spray rose slowly from the floor and rearranged her dress and things.

While she was thus engaged, several lights flooded on in various parts of the store. The darkness was decimated. She glanced quickly around, then froze in her tracks. Other than the invading policemen there seemed to be no sign of life. This was due to the fact that, like herself, each member of the Pebble party stood poised in a position of suspended animation. Major Jaffey was modishly attired in a checked cap and light raglan. Hal, the fire-man, looking like an example of what the well dressed man was not wearing, had rigged himself up in a cross between a yachting outfit and a riding costume, retaining the worst features of each. Of Nockashima there was no sign.

"They're hiding on us," said Pat Murphy in a low voice. "Spread out and comb the floor."

Looking tremendously impressive in his evening clothes, Mr. Pebble stepped forward and confronted Officer Murphy.

"Murphy," he said severely, "I would like to know just what you and your men mean by making a play-ground of this store? I am chairman of the board of directors and have a perfect right to be here. I was telephoned to during a party

I was giving and forced to hurry right down. If you haven't a satisfactory explanation, I'm afraid things are going to go very badly with you."

"Sorry, sir," said Murphy. "We were looking for a thing that was half fireman and half lady. One of the halves turned to a wild beast right before our eyes."

"I'm sorry, Murphy," said Rex Pebble regretfully. "When your buttons are popping off, just think of what you've been telling me."

"But this store was full of robbers and things," Pat desperately assured Mr. Pebble. "Ask any of the boys. We saw 'em and we heard 'em. Look, sir, that case is smashed a bit."

"True," admitted Rex Pebble. "I want to be fair and reasonable. We heard that disturbance. Perhaps robbers are in the store. If so, it is your duty to apprehend them. In the meantime have one of your men open a door and let us out."

With a stately stride Rex Pebble walked to the nearest door, a policeman preceding him. To the surprise and consternation of Pat Murphy and his brother officers the figures of a woman and two men suddenly came to life and followed their leader. Well in the rear glided the most surprising of all the figures. It was the stiff, lifeless form of a store model clad in the costume of a maid. This model had two pairs of feet, only one pair of which was moving.

"Look," cried Pat, pointing. "Look, for the love of God! It moves and it's not alive."

Major Jaffey, with great presence of mind, lifted the strange object in his arms and bore it to the door.

"It's the lady's maid," he explained over his shoulder. "The poor girl's scared stiff."

When the Pebble party was a safe distance from the store, the Major set his burden down, and the small body of the little yellow man was extracted with some difficulty, owing to the fact that various parts of him had become wedged within the hollow shell of his temporarily adopted habitation.

"Unable to disrobe one similar to Fifi in time," Nockashima explained blinkingly. "I attack from under. Amazed at own brilliance. What say, boss?"

"Ask that dimunitive Japanese maniac to say as little as possible to me for at least ten minutes," Rex Pebble said to Spray. "I will need all of that time to rehabilitate my poise. We are now going home—to my home, for a change."

"Look what I apprehend," announced Nocka, producing the lion's head from some recess within the shell of his recent disguise. "I bring home to Mist' Henry, and he bound with alarm."

Without a word Rex Pebble turned on his heel and led the way through the night.

Later that same night Officer Pat Murphy encountered the abandoned model of the maid leaning dejectedly against a wall. It was only after questioning it closely for some minutes that he discovered the object was not alive.

"I knew all along," he said to the fading stars, "there was some monkey business going on."

But when he gave his report to the sergeant he made no mention of his discovery. Things were bad enough to explain as they were, without adding another mystery to the list.

CHAPTER X

A WALK THROUGH TOWN

"NEVER mind about my excitable nature," remarked Spray Summers, as they turned into a particularly quiet and deserted street. "I never would have believed that being bottled up in a department store with so many men could make me so nervous, but I feel like jumping at every shadow. Can't we keep off these side streets? I expect to meet Frankenstein or Dracula any minute."

"After our recent experiences," said the Major gravely, "side streets are the thing for us. It was just about here, only one block down on the main thoroughfare, that we made that corner on two wheels."

The night was black. Black as ink. Black as pitch. Black as Egypt. Any one of the stand-by comparisons would have done, but the truth is that this particular alley looked like nothing so much as the inside of a stovepipe or a coal cellar in the dark. You felt as though something might be living in it, beyond eyesight, sneaking along, maybe tap-tapping with an invisible cane.

"Where are the stars?" asked Hal, the fireman, sleepily and innocently.

"Hasn't anybody told you?" returned Spray with kindly venom. "We're not using them since the Light and Gas Code was signed. They're on a strike. Wish they'd do some picketing, though," added the woman, shivering, as an afterthought. Rex Pebble, in the lead of the group, stepped into a doorway to light a cigarette. It seemed a shame to run the risk of having their trail again picked up by the police just for the sake of one little light. He opened a packet of matches and struck one. Nothing happened. He struck another match head, and this one, just as his companions caught up, ignited. Rex stepped out from the doorway.

"My God," screamed Spray at the top of her none too delicate lungs, "the place is alive with men!" She clutched the arm of Hal, who, stumbling along in his weariness, suddenly leaped forward like a fire horse at the sound of the bell. From the rear Hal tackled Major Lynnhaven Jaffey, who in turn whirled upon Nockashima. Spray Summers, seeing herself deserted, flung her lissom young form harshly against Rex Pebble.

"It's I!" cried Rex, pushing her away.

"Oh, yeah?" retorted the woman. "Well, plenty of women have gone wrong from believing men who said it's I in the dark." Spray landed a swift slap on Rex's right cheek, while Hal, the Major, and Nockashima, after banging one another around, recovered their wits sufficiently to rush to her defense. They all landed upon Rex full force. The poor fellow was sinking under their combined weight when Spray discovered their mistake.

"It's Rex!" she cried, and her friends, believing her to be hailing Rex's approach as a new champion, flattened the unfortunate man on the sidewalk. "I've got him," said Nockashima glibly, sitting on his boss's neck at the uncomfortable point where Adam's apple is the Gibraltar between Atlantic of body and Mediterranean of head.

"So I see," whispered a weak voice from beneath the human pile. "Now that you've had your fun, let me up, will you?"

"Very fresh for masher," returned Nocka, practically jumping up and down. "Teach good lesson."

"You let him up this minute, you wizened yellow idiot," said Spray. "Do you realize who you're sitting on?"

"Formal introduction not necessary," returned the Japanese,, who was proudly taking credit for the entire triumph of the onslaught. "Only that madam attacked."

"We do not care, my dear girl," said Major Jaffey with' great heroism and formality, "who the fellow is, so long as we have saved you from dishonor and disgrace."

"Let him up, Major," commented Spray. "You're too late. You should have met us in a dark street twenty years ago. That's my fate you have glued to the sidewalk there."

"Your fate?" inquired the Major, raising his eyebrows and looking round for Rex. "I was under the impression that I had been out with your fate all evening."

"Out with him and on top of him," returned Spray; "only, when you're through using his reconditioned chassis as a mattress, I think I'll wrap it up and take it home with me. In other words, gentlemen, you're sitting on Rex Pebble."

Three shadowy figures sprang up in the darkness, out-lined faintly in the pale wash of light that drifted through the street from the lamp on the corner. A fourth shadowy figure rose and seemed to creak as it rose. It also seemed to stretch its arms and legs, and from it issued a deep and satisfying groan.

"A good job," commented Rex. "I've never been so thoroughly mistaken for a gang of stick-up artists in my life. Something to add to my experience." While his three assailants continued to pour regrets and apologies upon him, Rex Pebble took Spray Summers' arm, and again the group moved down the street.

"First think we meet strange men and beat up," apologized Nockashima; "now only hope do not meet strange dogs or animals." He brandished his spoil, the lion's head. "May prove turning point in Mist' Henry's life. Very likely to arouse primitive passions. Either Mist' Henry overcome with superiority of imitation over nature, inspired to help self, or slink off coward-like." Nocka was genuinely worried. It was vital that Mr. Henry take to the lion's head.

"Never mind that bloody beast—I mean that bloodless beast," Spray spoke out of the blackness; "just let's get home before we massacre each other. Let me hold your arm too, Major. I don't feel too easy yet."

Spray Summers suited the prophecy to the moment, for, just then, from the dark triangle of a small doorway stepped a figure. The only thing visible about it was a white handkerchief across its face. The Pebble party felt its presence rather than saw it. They stopped short, arm in arm, with Nockashima in the rear pressing close against Major Jaffey and Hal.

"Stick 'em up!" said a voice, "or I'll fill your bellies full of lead!" Ten hands shot into the air.

"Now turn around and walk Indian file in front of me," continued the voice.

There was a peculiar note of hesitancy in the command. The voice seemed somehow to question its own judgment. It wavered. "Is that right, Joe?" it inquired of an unseen presence in the doorway.

"Yes and no," returned the presence. "Of course, you've got to vary your technique with the personalities concerned. However, I can't really sense these personalities, let alone see them. It's hardly a fair trial."

Rex Pebble felt that it was time to put in a word. "Are you predicting anything about a trial, or is that just part of your course in technique?"

"Just part of the course," said the presence in the doorway, which was male. "We're just a couple of young fellers working our way through school, and we're on the second story now, won't you help us out?" The presence seemed to be struggling with an old instinct for salesmanship, just as the actual robber appeared to be mentally thumbing the index of a book of directions on how to commit a robbery.

"Sure, glad to accommodate," answered Rex Pebble, "especially if you'll give us a receipt and let us go on home."

"Oh, no," said the first voice, quite shocked. "We can't let you go home alone. First we'll take your clothes—just come along now, strip them off—and then we'll be very glad to see you home."

"You'll see more than my home if you take these clothes off," remarked Spray, as she started to slip off her dress, "because I only had time to grab something for the outside. I'm practically nude inside, you know."

Both voices were silent. They seemed to be considering. What was the proper thing for a robber to do now? The romantic thing was to let the woman keep her clothes, reform yourself, and then marry her, but that seemed a little harsh for a young gentleman gangster just starting out.

Spray sensed the embarrassment that hung over the scene. "Oh, come now," she said, "we didn't mean to hurt your feelings. You're far too sensitive as it is. I just don't see how you could use clothes like mine in your business."

"Well," he said, "you'd better keep your clothes on. We want to keep this hold-up clean. No sex. It's against the Union now, anyhow." The fellow stuck a torch into Spray Summers' face.

"Oh, she's lovely," said the somewhat cold presence who came forward from his director's stand in the door-way. They both were engrossed; they spoke as though none of their victims could hear. "I could use that in my business."

"Look out now," said No. 1. "I may not know as much as you do about technique, but I can tell about some other things. You can't have love and a career, you know."

"Who do you think I am—Hitler?" inquired No. 2 icily. "I'm afraid that I'll just have to ask you to stick to your work. I think we might just try taking that dress off."

Rex Pebble realized that things were coming to a crisis. No. 2 was evidently a man of social grace, highly susceptible to feminine charm if, without even seeing Spray's face, he wished to take her dress off. Something had to be done quickly. Rex felt his adversary's weakness.

"You fellows might be interested in a little party we're throwing up at our place," he suggested. "It seems like an awful bad night in your line."

"Matter of fact, couldn't be worse," said No. 2 sociably. *"I never would have gone out at all if it hadn't been for* him." It appeared that he was pointing with scorn at his companion. "They didn't think he was getting along at all, and it was just my luck to have him come into my class. I always say that if you stay in a school as long as three years without progress, you'll never get out."

"Have you been in three years?" asked Spray Summers, following Rex's lead in hoping to keep the talk impersonal.

"In three years?" replied No. 1 viciously. "What does she mean, in three years?"

"Now, don't go getting on your high horse," warned No. 2, "because that's one of the main things that holds you back. She doesn't mean any offense. She merely means, have you been in *school* three years."

"Oh," said No. 1 with evident relief, "oh, that, sure. It isn't the work so much that holds me back as the social life. School is so much social life, nowadays."

"Which is all the more reason for you to come along and join us. When we left the house there was half a fire department and a French maid at play."

"See there," remarked No. 2, who apparently, after looking forward to a dull evening, saw things beginning to pick up. "What you ought to do is to get out and meet some of the customers."

"Can't mix business and play," No. 1 was murmuring stubbornly when Nockashima broke in with admirable tact.

"Perhaps," suggested the little man, whose knowing smile could not be seen in the deep night that surrounded them, "young men like nightcap?" No. 2 appeared to be utterly overwhelmed with this idea. He abandoned all attempt at a professional manner and frankly tugged at his companion's sleeve.

"Listen, pal," said Joe pleadingly, "these ain't the regular kind you'll find yourself sticking up. They're decent. They're worth meeting. Come to think of it, you ought to get used to finding your way around homes of hospitable people. It's knowledge that will come in handy some day. Go to the bathroom. Find how it lets out of the bed-room. Pardon me, folks," Joe interrupted himself, "I gotta tell him some of these things so's to sell him on the idea of coming along with us. It's the inside layout that counts. You got the approach. You can handle a ladder. I've seen you work: you're slick as a cat, you go through a place like greased lightning. The fellas all like to work with you. But what good does all this do you if you don't know the build-up of these places inside? Not often you get a chance like this. Come on, pal, I can't quit on you, but I want to go."

"That's right," said Rex Pebble, who would have been dubious about the whole proposition except for the fact that No. 1 could not be persuaded to lower his pistol, which was pointed directly at Rex, or so he imagined. "Why not settle the argument? You come along with us, Joe, and let your friend here bring up the tail end. He can keep on aiming his pistol at the last one in the line."

No sooner had Rex got the words out of his mouth than there was a mad scramble in the street, everyone striving to get first into line, with Major Lynnhaven Jaffey in the natural process of evolution coming out last, No. 1's unhesitating gun poked between his shoulder blades. The line proceeded up the street.

"Well, it's mighty funny to me," persisted No. 1 as the party moved along, "and I can't see why I should be still sticking you up when you're all on the move and on your way home, but I guess I know my duty when I see it. Get along there," he commanded the Major roughly.

"Could you possibly lower that thing just a bit?" inquired the Major, "because, while I may be an old man and not particularly interested in life, it tickles me when it bobs up and down. You might as well put it away, anyhow."

"What kind of drinks have you got?" asked Joe, coming to the point in a business-like manner. "Somebody remarked something about a nightcap. What's that?"

"Oh, that's a drink we give you before we put you to bed," answered Spray Summers, who had begun to won-der how these latest two additions to the party were going to fit into the group that might already be celebrating something or other at her house when they got home.

"Bed?" Joe packed a wealth of meaning into one small word. "Did you hear that, Elmer? Bed."

Rex, Spray, Hal, Nockashima, and Major Jaffey were swinging along in lockstep now, much more as though they were on their way to the workhouse than to Spray's comfortable home. .

"Why so surprised?" asked Spray. "Don't you boys ever go to bed?"

"Well, yes," admitted Joe. "But everything does seem pretty upset tonight. Not more than an hour ago I was back there"—he indicated somewhere behind them with a jerk of the thumb—"watching Elmer clean up his tool for the evening, and now here I am going home to bed with my prospects. I guess I'll never be a success. I think I must have an inferiority complex. Just ask me somewhere, and I'm a pushover."

"Well, you'll be all right when you get some of our drinks under your belt," Rex assured him. "I could use one myself. How long have you been in this game?" he asked the sociable young man who had directed the stick-up.

"Oh, say three years, off and on," returned Joe. "Long enough to get the feel of the thing. But I don't like it. I always wanted to be a banker."

"Well, now," spoke up Major Lynnhaven Jaffey, with interest, "just how much would you be interested in putting up, should the right opportunity present itself? I think I know of something most attractive to a chap of your background and bearing."

"Major, Major," warned Spray Summers, "remember he's only a boy."

"I could round up five or six thousand pretty easy," answered Joe, who in order to make the Major hear him had to raise his voice quite a bit. It was a strange procession. But it was making time, owing to the relentless pace set by Joe in the hopes that they could shake his accomplice or tire him out. "Five or six thousand, did you hear me?"

"That would do nicely," called back Major Jaffey, "this particular institution is out in Arkansas, near Pine Bluff."

"Neat," commented Spray. "An institution, is it?"

"What would five or six thousand get me?" asked Joe. "I want a white-collar job."

"Well, just look at me, my boy," admonished the Major. "You can hardly see me at the moment, but we'll remedy that later. I am a tall, distinguished, well-dressed man of sixty, and attribute my success solely to one thing: I never let anything worry me. You just let me have that five or six thousand, and neither of us will worry about anything."

"Could I stand behind a cage and pass out books?" asked Joe eagerly.

"I think you're confusing banks and public libraries," remarked Spray, "but you can do one thing for *me.*"

"What's that, lady?"

"Just sell your boy friend on the idea of dropping that gun. The Major, though a friend of mine, is pretty thin, and I've just been thinking that if your friend should shoot him, the bullet would probably push its way through him, on up here to me. And I don't want to die—not tonight."

"Listen, Elmer." Joe adopted a new tack. "If you'll put the gat away, I'll let you hold 'em up on the front steps of their own house when we get there. Think of what that would read like in the papers. I'll even have a flashlight picture made. Elmer Browne, snapped sticking up prominent West End residents. We might even get a spread in the society section. How's that?"

"How often," replied Elmer with ponderous dignity, "do I have to tell you that I take this profession seriously. If I stick somebody up, he stays stuck up, society section or not, even if I have to follow him home."

"That's it," cut in Spray, "we want to give you a break. We want you to have a fresh start right at our home. You're all tired out holding that gun. You'll feel a lot more like making a snappy hold-up if you'll just put it down for a while."

"And meet some nice girls," invited Rex.

"And have potent drink," added Nockashima.

"And take that damned pistol out of my shoulder blades," said the Major.

"Oh, all right," Elmer capitulated reluctantly. "But remember, when we get there?"

"When we get there," promised Rex.

"Speaking of there," suggested Spray Summers, her ear cocked in the direction in which they were walking, "I suspect that I hear music."

From the direction of the Summers menage there issued a medley of sound. It was as though a Negro band in collision with a load of milk cans were playing Gershwin. Somebody was evidently beating on a dish pan, and somebody else had manufactured a home-made comb cornet. The air was not easy to identify, as the singers themselves seemed uncertain, but one thing was sure, that Fifi, patriotic to the core, imagined herself to be leading in the less mentionable verses of "Mademoiselle from Armentieres."

"How nice," said Rex Pebble. "I think the Fire Department must have arranged a housewarming."

"Well, if they did," Spray came back, "I hope they left some of my extinguisher in the cellar. It sounds as though they must have drunk it all up."

"Do you take home gangs every night?" put in Elmer doubtfully, his fingers slipping over the handle of his pistol.

"Oh, no," said Spray; "these were just some fellows from the Fire Department who stopped in some hours ago to help extinguish a blaze. I think they stayed to entertain the maid, or vice versa. You'll like them. They're awfully jolly people—in for anything, at the drop of a hat."

"The drop of a fireman's hat is very important." Major Lynnhaven Jaffey cleared his throat and called ahead, "Don't forget, old man, that when we arrive at our host's I would like a few quiet words with you. A banker never forgets."

Turning from the side street abruptly brought the Pebble party suddenly before a small gate in the wall of Spray Summers' garden. Rex, as first in line, had been guiding the footsteps of that intrepid brigand Joe, a willing victim of victimized hospitality. There was a tiny ship's lamp alight above the gate, and in the diffused yellow glow from this the party drew up. Elmer, a tanned-face, black-eyed, sullen young man, regarded the company with distrust, wagging his head at Joe. Joe, on the other hand, wore an alert expression on his blond countenance. He turned a quizzical expression upon each face in turn. "Well," he said, "you're not a bad lot of yeggs at all. Who's the old codger?"

"That's your prospective banking associate, of whom you speak so flippantly," Rex Pebble informed him. "And be sure to lock the cash drawer nights," advised Spray.

"My friends here are being jocose with me," laughed the Major. "We'll just step inside and discuss the matter." The Major opened the little gate and stepped in. At once he stuck an astonished face back. "What's going in here?" he queried. "They've broken windows and knocked down doors."

"Still looking for a fire," said Spray disconsolately, "that's where our taxes go."

"Should think Mademoiselle Fifi provide plenty fire for boys," put in Nockashima.

"Well, you just go in and tell them to come out, Spray dear," suggested Mr. Pebble. "Tell them it's time to go home, that the chief wants them. And you might add that they'd better hurry, as we're arranging a little stick-up party on the front lawn."

"I will not," retorted the woman. "It's as much your house as it is mine. I'm damned if I'm going to get mixed up with any more municipal branches. I started out with the Fire Department, got in bed with the police, invited gangsters home, and now you want me to start all over. I may not be the same as I was this morning, but I know when my dogs are tired, even if I am restored to my youth, and they are tired now."

"Perhaps I'd better go in and fetch you the slippers Sue sent you for the anniversary of your seduction?" Rex insinuated, a teasing little smile curving his handsome mouth.

"You leave that huzzy of a wife of yours out of this," in a tone that rang through the night air. Both Elmer and Joe looked shocked. It was plain to see tha they felt that if the trend in robbery was towards the gentlemanly frisk, this was not the sort of company for them to be out with. From the house, however, came an inquiring voice that drew the attention of the company.

"Who's there?" it called in a deep bass.

"A friend," returned Spray Summers. "In fact, I'm the mistress of this house."

"Mistress?" questioned the voice. "Well, then, come on in," it continued with a show of determination.

"No, you come on out," returned the woman. "Let's play out in the yard."

"If you're really the mistress of this house, I'll give you a drink. I bet you'd like a drink, too. You must have been away a long time, because I've been here for hours and hours and hours, and I can't remember ever seeing you."

"Oh, you were young when I left this house. But don't let that worry you. I'll bet you know your way about now. Come on out and bring your friends."

"I haven't any friends. They've all deserted me. I'm all alone in the world. They're all out in the kitchen with Fifi, singing dirty songs."

"Why aren't you out in the kitchen with Fifi?"

"Because I don't know the words."

"That won't make any difference," called Spray. "Come on out; we want you for witness at a shooting."

"A shooting?" The word hung poised on air.

"Yes, and then we'll sing afterwards."

"Oh, but are you sure that **I'll** sing afterwards?"

"Well, what difference will it make? You can't sing now."

"That's right," agreed the voice. "You sound like a mighty sensible woman. I may be mad, but I think I'll take you up on that. Tell you what, I'll come out on one condition."

The Pebble party held its breath. Elmer was beginning to finger his pistol. It seemed like a shame to let the lad grow restive and really spoil things. Besides, he looked like an awfully good shot. Joe wore an apprehensive look, as though his period of influence with the hothead were rapidly drawing to an ending. Then there was the matter of ridding the house of firemen. This would take considerable strategy. A great deal depended on the answer of that unseen voice in the window.

"We'll do 'most anything to please *you.* " Spray Summers chose her words with care, as became the feat of dealing with a distant drunken fireman.

"I'll come down and I'll witness your shooting—or my shooting, if you must—but you've got to have a drink with me."

"Oh, that. That's easy." A sigh broke over the whole band, from the Major to Nockashima. "Hurry up, now, come on down and bring that drink. There're eight of us."

"*Eight* of you? What is this—a shooting gallery? Wait till I go where I started to go up here on the second floor hours and hours and hours ago." The voice trailed off like the Cheshire cat's head.

"What happens when he *does* come down?" demanded Elmer. "You told me when we got to the house we'd have the stick-up."

"Certainly," returned Rex, "but the idea is that you must accept of our hospitality first. One drink. One drink to a good haul and a better shot if necessary."

"That's fair," urged Joe, who in the soft light of the ship's lamp above the little garden gate was taking a keen interest in Spray Summers' lissom young form, and in those deep, burning brown eyes whose sparkle was heightened by her recent debate. Suddenly, while Elmer argued with himself, a hand was thrust through the gate, extending a quart bottle of liquid.

"Here," said the bass voice, "I'll be out in a minute. Don't you lose this, now, because it's all I've got, and you're all the friends I've got."

Nockashima took the bottle from the hand. Tut-tutting over it, the little yellow man bemoaned the lack of a cocktail shaker and equipment. "Gurgles from bottle grow tiresome," he murmured. "Anxious restore proper order to madam's bar. If any bar left." He gazed with rue toward the gate, when a bright idea seemed to attack him.

"Here, take," said Nockashima to his boss, handing him the bottle and at the same time donning himself the phony lion's head which he had lugged along as a trophy for Mr. Henry. "Scare burning daylights out of Fire Department."

Evidently the fireman with the conversational bass had returned to the house for glasses, for at this moment, as Nockashima poked his lion's head inside the gate, there was a crash as of many small glass objects dropped at once and a heavy pounding of feet on the lawn. "God help me!" the words tumbled through the night air, "if it isn't a menagerie." A door slammed.

CHAPTER XI

THE HOUSE BEAUTIFUL

WHEN the last sad sounds of the fleeing fireman had died on the night—or very early morning—air, Rex Pebble and his retinue still stood in front of the little garden gate of his mistress Spray Summers' house, wondering what next to do. A hold-up had to be arranged for the two mystified gentlemen gangsters who had accompanied the party home only on being promised that they might have their stick-up on the front lawn. That is, Elmer seemed adamant; Joe had really only come for the fun.

The party sadly lacked leadership. Its motives were many. Fascism was in urgent demand. Spray Summers' chief desire was to get home, and not far distant in her thoughts was a bed. Rex Pebble, to a not surprising degree, held similar notions, that is, if amended with a few last drinks. Major Lynnhaven Jaffey, after searching half the world around, suspected that at length he had found the ideal angel for his pet bank, in Joe the Brigand. Hal, a little ashamed of being away so long, rather hated to face his compatriot brothers-at-hose, though this dread was alleviated by the sounds of merriment that issued from the house. Nockashima, of the whole band, had the least complicated ideas: with a bottle of liquor in his hands, there was only one thing that really remained to be done, and that was to shake it up skillfully into tempting cocktails. Nockashima should have been house man to Jove, or Bacchus's bell boy: nothing delighted him so much as to relieve suffering mankind by the simple magic of alcohol.

Nockashima now addressed his mistress. "Early bird catch cocktail," the fellow put his thought axiomatically. "I go make same—providing sufficient glasses left in honorable establishment." Nocka vanished through the gate.

"You never have to worry about what to do next with that young Oriental around," breathed Spray with a sigh of relief and anticipation. "Shall we join the firemen?"

From Elmer there was a silence that, unseen, was a scowl. "I want to know——" began that young man.

"Yes, we know," returned Rex Pebble patiently. "But you can't start till you get inside. That's the first principle of burglaring. Haven't you even taught him that, Joe? You're a heck of a professor."

"He's persistent, Chief," replied Joe blithely. "Per-severance always wins. I'll bet you'll let him stick you up yet. Me for that nightgown that somebody mentioned."

"Nightcap," corrected Spray. "Remember, this is a nice house, and no monkey business."

Spray Summers, as hostess after her own peculiar fashion, led the way through the gate and down a pebble path to the veranda door. Off to the left of the party as they moved down the drive, the waters of the garden pool whispered in a slow night breeze. Their whisper was a dare to secret rendezvous, to something precious that few people would have suspected, for all the fresh lush summer loveliness of the garden and the clear deep beauty of the water. Spray Summers took Rex Pebble's hand in hers, in the dark. It was the first time they had been near the magic spot, the curious, kindly fountain of youth, since new strength and years came back to them. An evening had slipped by swiftly, on wings of adventure, and now, within the almost sacred precincts of the house again, Spray felt stirred as she had not in years. "We'll get rid of them all soon," she whispered. "If we don't, we'll let Elmer shoot them," Rex answered, pressing her hand tightly.

From within the house came continued noises of gayety and high joviality. "How shall we get them out?" asked Major Jaffey. "I'd like a quiet spot for a business conference."

"I must say, Major," declared Spray, "that you choose the damnedest moments for your multicolored activities that I ever heard of. First you appear out of the bushes minus clothes, stay with us all evening, appear to be on the verge of spending the night, and now you want me to drive out my favorite firemen so that you may have a conference in the house. Of all the brass." Spray laughed. "I think the best thing is just to spread ourselves here while we await Nockashima. Besides, the fire laddies may join us themselves at any moment."

"Can't you take it off?" asked Rex of Elmer, who was struggling to sit down on the stone terrace without entangling himself in his pistol.

"Never have yet," said Elmer doggedly.

"I should think it might be pretty uncomfortable at times," said Spray Summers with an evil look. "I can think of a couple of times, at least."

"Oh, he takes it off sometimes," Joe defended his true-blood comrade. "I think I know what you mean. Yes." Joe was subtle if not delicate.

A crystal tinkle of ice in tall glasses unmistakably heralded the approach of Nockashima, the tireless, the all-faithful. The drinks were long and cool and potent. From the first sip there was a deceptive charm to them, a suggestion that if you like me, don't hesitate to drink me, because I'm perfectly harmless, just a little drink trying to get along. They were matchless for good taste and for kick, the kind of thing one's palate remembers with the first fresh taste of surprise, in spite of what may follow after.

Nockashima had switched on a wall light on the veranda before departing again for the house, and in the glow of this Elmer seemed gingerly to be sipping at his glass. It was plain that he wanted it but hated to give in. "Go on, old man," urged Major Jaffey, whose glass was half empty and who feared that one slow drinker might slow up the tempo of the party. "Dive in—it won't hurt you. I hear that a good drink now and again improves marksmanship."

"Yeah," coaxed Joe, equally well along, "lift it up like this and take a great big swallow, like a man." Joe tossed off the remainder of his glass.

"Well," said Elmer with more determination than grace, "I'm a sport. I guess I can take it. Down the barrel!" He tilted his glass and drained it, wiping his mouth on his sleeve with a gusty "*Whew!*"

"So that's that," whispered Spray to Rex. "You can just hand me that gun."

From the house Nockashima came trotting with great excitement. "Mist' Henry delighted with head of lion," he announced proudly. "Expect great comedy when exhibit self to visiting firemen."

"The breaks seem to be coming our way," commented Rex Pebble. "Here, Nocka, fill up these gentlemen's glasses." Nocka, still trembling with excitement over the amazing courage of Mr. Henry, the smell-less bloodhound, poured gurglingly from a tall pitcher with frosted sides. Elmer, less scowling, reclined against a pillar of the stone porch, and Joe, blissful as a cherub, opened a quiet financial harangue with Major Jaffey.

"I think," Spray Summers' voice was low in her lover's ear, "that you and I might sneak out for a little anniversary. What do you say?"

"You bet!" responded Rex. "Look here, Nocka," he addressed the diminutive servant, suppose you take the responsibility of removing those raving hyenas in there before the police arrive. Will you do that?"

"Great pleasure, boss," grinned the Japanese. "Solicit help from Mist' Hal and others and make quick work of fire chasers. You beat it." Nockoshima's vocabulary strained at no gnats for delicay of expression. Elmer was staring thoughtfully into the cool green depths of his glass as Rex and Spray stole away in the dark toward the pool. His eyes were large and full of wonder. drink

Nockashima first helped himself to a generous drink and then clapped his hands sharply, like a miniature Eastern potentate summoning his slave. "Hi, Mist' Henry, hi!" he called. A creature crept out of the shadows, its tail drooping, and lifting large sorrowful eyes. He came up to Nockashima, plastering his small yellow hand with a bright red tongue of just about the same size.

"Do you know what's the matter with that dog?" asked Hal, the fireman, bluntly.

"Have suspicions but not plenty evidence for statement," said Nockashima. "However, Mist' Henry potentially very fine dog."

"That's just it," remarked Hal, "and that's exactly where I disagree. I don't think he's potentially anything. That is to say, I don't think he's got any potentials at all."

Nockashima sighed with the air of one who is reluctant to accept the truth. "If Mist' Henry only develop interest in other bloodhounds," he moaned. "Apparently very much one-dog dog. No interest in anyone but me."

"What did he do with the lion's head?" asked Hal. "Did he chew it up?"

"No," returned Nockashima more brightly. "Mist' Henry apparently very fond of mask. Must have known lion in this or former existence."

"Here's an idea," proposed Hal. "This dog has some kind of complex. You know. I could spell it for you, but it doesn't matter. It's something he lacks and keeps thinking about all the time. Like not being able to smell. I wouldn't go around with my tail like that if I couldn't smell. We got to show Mr. Henry how to be a poker face."

"That easy," agreed Nockashima eagerly. "Let Mr. Henry wear lion's head for some time, get to thinking self lion, maybe roar, certainly sniff, give nostrils work-out."

"That's right," said Hal, "but that ain't all." Hal cupped one hand over Nockashima's right ear and whispered, "This guy Elmer, he's like Mr. Henry. He wants to shoot somebody just to show how big he is. Suppose we get Mr. Henry and Elmer to get my pals out. That would be teaming 'em up!" Hal laughed softly. He was immensely pleased with his own idea.

"Gland idea," exclaimed Nockashima enthusiastically. "Combine good and bad points of situation. Great aid Mist' Henry and Mist' Elmer; big bounce for visiting firemen."

"I think that idea could be celebrated with a few more drinks, then," said Hal, quick to lose no quarter, or cocktail. "Or is there any left?"

"Always plenty in shakers of Summers house," returned the small fellow hospitably. "If no, can go out quickly for more." Nockashima poured liberally from the seemingly inexhaustible pitcher that served in place of the silver shakers now greatly in demand by the convention of heroes in the kitchen. In pouring, he did not spare Elmer, the reluctant drinker who had by this time become completely won over to the charms of blood-cheering alcohol and lay semiprone against the stone pillar, lost apparently in contemplation of some gigantic pilfery.

On nimble feet Nockashima sped into the house, pitcher in hand, returning in a split second with a fresh supply of drinks and the ferocious phony lion's head. Mr. Henry, as averred by his faithful friend the Japanese, may not have definitely feared the thing, but he certainly displayed no great affection for it. Nockashima placed the head on the veranda and urged the bloodhound to examine it. With slow, slouching, cautious steps, the lanky creature moved round it, drinking in its every repulsive feature with his sad, distrustful eyes, and making now and again a pathetic attempt to resuscitate his long-lost sense of smell, if such a sense had ever indeed thrilled those ponderous nostrils. Mr. Henry turned regretfully to the Japanese; he appeared in effect to shake his head. You may have imagined that I cared for it, his look seemed to say, and I don't want to disappoint you, but heaven knows I can't see why I should have anything whatever to do with it. What's it for?

"Tsch, tsch!" muttered the Oriental, chagrined. "Mist' Henry exhibit no distress, but also show no great pleasure."

"I could hardly say he seemed thrilled," said Hal scathingly. "It's what we say about some of the fire horses, there are more plugs than the iron ones on the corner. Try putting it on him."

Nockashima adjusted the grinning lion's head over Mr. Henry's drooping visage. Nothing happened. The figure stood still, a ridiculous blend of lion and bloodhound, the face looking pleased as Punch, the shaggy knees and legs of the brute sagging under its weather-beaten, bone-ridged body. The face swung slowly from side to side in a grotesque combination of radiant and dismal regard. Take it off, said Mr. Henry, it's no use. I can't smell, I have no emotions, as a bloodhound I'm a total wash-out. Nockashima seemed on the point of tears. Carefully and tenderly as though he were lifting back the shroud of a dear one recently passed away, he removed the lion's mask from the drooping bloodhound's shoulders. Mr. Henry had not changed his expression; he half stood, half sat, gazing at his proxy master with disconsolate incompetence.

"Here," said Hal, the fireman, "have a drink." He proffered his glass, out of sympathy and understanding, to the dog.

"That's a good idea," commented Joe, who, in his absorption with the unexpected delights of alcohol so freely dispensed, was beginning to tire of Major Lynnhaven Jaffey's steady quiet drone of sales talk on the merits of the proposed banking scheme. "And while you're at it, you might give me one—that is, if you can spare it from the cur."

"Him no cur," defended Nockashima, generously fillng Joe's extended glass. "Him bloodhound of noble blood greatly afflicted with multitude of sorrows of life. No blame for Mist' Henry. Suppose honorable stick-up man unable to stick up?"

"That's Elmer," admitted Joe readily. "Look at him. Dozing. Not doing a damned thing. Not even trying to get the lay of the land. I mean that in a clean way. Give him a drink too. Let Hal feed the hound a drink and I'll feed Elmer one." With none too gentle hands, Joe pried open Elmer's mouth and poured a glass of drink into it. Elmer gave no signs of feeling, other than a half absentminded air of gratitude.

Hal, too, was quick to take Mr. Henry in hand. "Here," said the young fireman, "drink this." Mr. Henry sidled over and obediently opened his cavernous jaws. The dog wrapped his great tongue around the glass—in fact, so recklessly that Hal clung to the stem with alarm lest he swallow glass and all.

"First time Mist' Henry ever take drink," murmured Nockashima, shaking his head as though his sense of morals, whatever they were in their obscure Oriental way, had been violated. If it was the first time the dog had taken to drink, however, he did not give indication of his inexperience. He lapped up the liquid and seemed to call for another round. "My God!" exclaimed Hal, examining the glass. "It's a good thing you didn't offer him the bottle. If you ask me, I think Mr. Henry's a silent drinker. Let's see what he'll do with another one. That one just wet his whistle."

"Beware drunken bloodhound," warned Nockashima. "Very much alarmed consequences Mist' Henry's heavy drink. Never can tell what happen." Hal ignored this sage advice. "Rats!" he said, "another drink will do the dog good. I think I'll have one with him. Here's to you, Henry, old boy, old boy," toasted his companion. The dog responded with what was the nearest approach to a smile of joy that anyone remembered to have seen written on his features. He gave a cross between a wheeze and a snort, ending in a low, melodious howl that brought Elmer's eyes open with a start, cut short the Major's monologue and caused a sharp, sudden quiet within the Spray Summers menage. With Mr. Henry's long last note lingering in the air, there was dramatic silence for a moment. The hubbub resumed, filling the dark, sweet-smelling garden and the veranda with a low buzz that might have been made by a ladies' aid society drinking spiked punch.

Mr. Henry, licking his lips monstrously, downed his second highball. Eyes focused on the creature. Stretching both front legs luxuriously, he wagged his head foolishly from side to side and glanced coyly at Hal, his benefactor, then at Nockashima, his future source of supply. With a new grace the dog ambled over to the Japanese and gazed into the depths of the silver pitcher in his hand. "No, no, Mist' Henry," remonstrated Nockashima, throwing Hal a reproachful look. "Now see, Mist' Henry practically confirmed drunkard. His fate in your hands now." The small yellow man appeared to waive all responsibility for the bloodhound, to wash his hands of the whole affair. "You put Mist' Henry to bed," he said to Hal.

"Leave him alone," returned that young man. "I think he's getting on fine. That's what's the matter with the brute. You've been sissifying him. What if he can't smell? He can drink, can't he? A dog's got to have some kind of fun."

But it was at this point that Mr. Henry really became alarming in behavior. With the pitcher upright in Nockashima's hand, it seemed impossible to get a drop of liquid out. The dog realized this and made a sudden lunge which landed Nockashima, amazed beyond words, in a sitting position on the lawn. The pitcher was now on the ground. Mr. Henry tentatively put forth one paw to tilt it over. With admirable dispatch Nockashima recovered his bearing. He snatched the pitcher off the ground, stubbornly folding his arms about it. Mr. Henry seemed to consider, then, with great deliberation, as though he wished to injure no one, but was equally determined to have his way, the bloodhound laid a ponderous paw on either of the little man's shoulders and pressed him to the earth. Just to make his intentions clear, that he bore no ill feeling, he swiped his great red tongue twice across the man's face and, standing on Nocka's chest, sank his mouth into the pitcher. There was a deep gulping sound, like the noise of an old-fashioned cistern when the bucket reaches the surface and begins to imbibe water for its return voyage.

Hal rose hastily and rushed to Nockashima's aid. He was too late. The man was not hurt, though stunned. Mr. Henry, having cleaned up the pitcher, calmly moved off Nocka's chest and began, first lumberingly, then with a sort of childish gayety, to cavort about the lawn. Not since he was a pup, if even then, had the bloodhound appeared so full of pep. He tore off apparently in pursuit of imaginary bones that had been pitched to him, cutting great circles about the lawn and then lunging into the circle of light like a locomotive out of a tunnel. With a tremendous bound he leaped across the huddled figures of Major Lynnhaven Jaffey and Joe, who were practically embracing one another in their panic. Elmer rubbed his eyes as the bounding creature stopped long enough to place a thick alcoholic tongue on his cheek.

"Great Fujiyama!" exclaimed Nockashima, giving way to his tallest expletive. "Mist' Henry mad with drink. How will ever explain to boss unusual behavior of pet?"

"I don't think you need to worry about that," said Hal as he dodged an affectionate forward pass. "Mr. Henry's not anybody's pet now. The world's Mr. Henry's pet."

What to do with a stewed bloodhound? Nockashima called and wheedled. It was no use. The creature knew the pitcher was empty, and that was that. Elmer was the first member of the party to suffer from serious attack.

Some instinct—could it have been a reviving sense of smell?—led the beast to rush the stick-up artist, languishing on the veranda, and, pinning him down, to lap up what remained of drink in his glass. It was some time before the print of importunate claws smoothed out of Elmer's face.

"Damn you, Joe!" sang out the attacked one. "You not only stop me from my work, but you get me into a dog-fight. What did he do to me, sting me or bite me?"

Mr. Henry sprang happily here and there, racing off into the shadows of the garden, only to tear back in search of companions. He would whirl first up to one, then to another, until Hal, realizing his desire, timidly ran away with the dog. When they emerged a second later from the dark, Hal was limping in apparent agony. "He plays too rough," the fireman complained. "I never met such a dog. Whose bloodhound is he, anyhow?"

"Mist' Rex' bloodhound," returned Nockashima, "and he going to be plenty sore when he sees condition of pet. Heaven knows what Miss Spray say!"

"The thing to worry about is what we'll do," said Hal, a victim, "because this has got to stop. He's a regular lion." Hal stopped short. "Say, that's an idea," he exclaimed, "why not put the lion's head on Mr. Henry now? Hell's bells, what a lion he'd make!"

Nockashima was in a quandary. He didn't want to take Mr. Henry indoors in this shameful condition, nor did he wish to call for help. The suggestion was not a bad one. It would cut off Mr. Henry's sight, and there was no telling what might happen. It couldn't be worse than having a mad dog at large on the premises. "Here, Mist' Henry, hi, come, nice bloodhound," lured the deceptive Japanese, pretending to produce a flask from his pocket. Mr. Henry slowed up in a whirling circle, bewildered with doubt. He didn't really know whether he should have another drink or not. Enough was enough; he had lost all sense of inferiority, and he was certainly the center of attention, if not of alarm. Mr. Henry's life long ambition had been to be a catastrophe, and this seemed his big chance—only if he didn't get too tight. One li'l' drink. The dog hesitated. He moved cautiously to Nockashima's side.

Suddenly, from behind, the lion's head was clapped over his shoulders. Mr. Henry emitted a long, soul-rending protest that again brought complete blanketing silence to the house and its environs. No heart could have heard that anguished howl in the night without missing a beat.

Mr. Henry had put his whole being into it, a magnificent, ravishing cry of outraged merriment, but it did not produce results. The lion's head stayed on. Fortunately for Mr. Henry, though he could not see, he could breathe through the lion's nostrils. He snorted and uttered a second howl. There was silence. Mr. Henry felt a grey surge of disgust sweep over him. What bad sports humans were! Here they go and get a bloodhound tight and then they wouldn't play. It wasn't fair. Everything began to seem muddled and confused; Mr. Henry's canine values were completely upset. He felt like running right out of the garden gate and never coming back. By gosh, thought Mr. Henry, he would—and forthwith he started at a gallop in the direction of what he imagined must be the gate.

In all fairness to his human playmates, or drunken associates, it must be said that Mr. Henry was properly warned. As the hound leaped off into the darkness, it is possible that Nockashima, spiritually psychic to the demands of inebriated characters, canine or human, may have guessed his intention. That is, to make off with himself, out into the great wide world, where no bloodhound is obliged to drink white man's liquor and not have white man's fun.

"Be careful," shouted the house man to the rapidly retreating figure. "If wish long sprint in woods, do not head for fountain."

"God knows what that crazy mutt will do next," complained Hal, rubbing his thigh. "He certainly stepped all over me."

"What you expect?" demanded the Japanese man curtly. "You kennel snatcher! Go feed nice dog all gin—best Tom Collins Nockashima made in three summers—and expect him to behave as in Book of Etiquette. I only uneasy about Mist' Henry's whereabouts now."

"The dog has had three drinks or more," put in Major Jaffey. The confusion had been a great break for Joe, for in the midst of the clamor he had been able to remove himself somewhat from the Major's wave length and no longer had drilled into him comparative bank earnings for the last ten years. "I've only had four, and I'm not nearly so well behaved. If I had my youth back again, I'd scamper around the yard and do somersaults myself."

At this moment there was a loud splash. It was the sort of sound that could only be made by the unexpected contact of a whirling object with a large expanse of water. The splash was quickly followed by a loud and terrible howl.

"Something dreadfully wrong now," remarked Nockashima with fatalistic philosophy. "No ordinary dive. That accident of two bodies—water and other body."

"Could that poor hound have jumped into the——" Joe left his question unanswered. It was quite clear what had happened: Mr. Henry had taken the wrong direction. He had headed straight into the garden pool.

"The poor brute," commiserated Major Jaffey. "I do hope that he has not drowned himself."

"Poor brute more likely drowned if stayed in present company than in pool," commented Nockashima dryly. "Other people's liquor flow freely."

"That was a crack," interposed Joe, "which I have no idea of hearing. Consider it erased, rubbed out. Wiped off."

From the direction of the pool came another howl, this howl curiously less distinct. There were no further splashings. Nockashima and Hal were collecting themselves with an idea of stopping this bloodhound suicide, if that was his idea, when an object emerged from the darkness that would have stopped a magician in Baghdad. Half lion, half pup, it pranced up, wagging its stubby tail and begging for affection.

"You can't tell me," said Joe rubbing his eyes, "that bloodhounds breed that fast. And even if I believed that, I wouldn't believe they'd be born with fake lions' heads on. What a nightmare!" Joe hid his eyes.

The joyous malformation, which seemed utterly delighted with life, was undoubtedly the old Mr. Henry, now become a new Mr. Henry. His small sleek backsides wiggled mischievously, and his tail stood up as pert and emphatic as an exclamation point. His body was thin, like a colt's, but there was youth in it, and a careless abandon that was completely new to Mr. Henry.

"Only one thing do now," said Nockashima, as the first to recover his wits, "and that, use Mist' Henry to help scare away firemen."

"I want to be in on this." Hal rose and followed Nockashima, who was leading Mr. Henry toward the house. "I've always felt some of the fellows needed stirring up, and now I want to see how they'll take it."

"Bring Elmer," Major Jaffey instructed Joe, "because we want to let him see how a real stick-up is staged, and after that, if there's anything left, we'll let him play with that pistol of his." Joe, practically shouldering Elmer, staggered in the rear of the procession.

To firemen, absent from the station for hours in search of a blaze that never appeared, and lured away from the gentle art of fire-fighting by such odd-pursuits as blotting up a few drinks and playing around with a French maid, the sudden sight of a Japanese face is not calculated to improve public confidence. And if, in addition to all these things, the face be accompanied by a bounding half-dog, half-lion affair, the effect is likely to be quite upsetting. Such was the combined effect of Nockashima and Mr. Henry when Elmer, pressing jealously to the fore, produced his gun and brandished it in the doorway. The place was cleared instantly. There were several hurried words of protest, but for the most part the kitchen and the premises were clean-swept of firemen.

"Holy mackerel!" whispered the station lieutenant, "if that isn't Hal with them!"

"The house is screwy, Lieutenant," advised another, who helped to lead in the disorderly retreat of the department. "I've known that ever since that girl Fifi got started."

"Got started what?" Even in his haste the lieutenant could not suppress his curiosity.

"Oh, surprising a fellow with pretty intimate business now and then, especially as a fellow goes to sit down."

"Oh, that," said the lieutenant. "Come on, we'll never get away if we start to talk about the monkey business of this house, including that gal."

"What have we been drinking?" asked one fellow in consternation, as he peered from his hiding place behind the large electric stove. "I thought there was something wrong about getting this whole joint free, including the French one."

"That was wrong to begin with," whispered the lieutenant, who crouched beside the man. "What is the creature? I seem to remember having seen the Jap before."

"I'd say it's half and half," was the answer. "Half beast and half pet. That is, if it's real."

Mr. Henry, filled with drink and the glamour of youth, roped about the kitchen, practically dragging Nockashima after him. Fifi, still preoccupied with the cocktail shaker, over which, in the absence of Nockashima, she had been mistress, had not noticed the uproar. Firemen are apt to do anything, Fifi had learned, and they seemed al-ways ready to start off at the sound of a gong. Something came nosing at her back. "Go 'way," said the girl. "Now, now, go 'way." She reached behind her, intending to slap the playful fireman, when her hand encountered something new and strange. It was somewhat bearded, it had an unusually large mouth, even for a fireman. Fifi raised her hand a bit. No fireman that she knew had such heavy brows. There was a loud sniff, a sniff like a dog. Fifi thought with scorn of Mr. Henry and his lack of smelling ability; at least, if the house was beset with firemen, there weren't any dogs around. The girl helped herself to a small drink and looked around, charitably intending to give the playful fellow a taste of her highball.

"Oh, mon dieu!" the cry rang throughout the building. Rex Pebble and Spray Summers, blissfully resting beside the pool, heard it and started for the house. They could hardly believe it, but it seemed that something was either happening or about to happen which they had never imagined possible with a Frenchwoman.

"Take eet away," cried the girl. "Eet is hor-ri-ble. You feelthy man!" she screeched at Nockashima. Mr. Henry was delighted with this show of attention. He bounded about the prostrate girl, quite out of control, and in touching the corners of the room, caused the heroes of many fires to cower in their hiding places. For the first time in her experience Fifi willingly embraced a Japanese. With a quick motion she grabbed the little man and clung to him in terror.

Rex and Spray at this moment appeared in the door-way. The room was a wreck. Glasses graced the floor, over which Mr. Henry tore in ecstasy, tail waggling, lion's head tossing. Fifi hid her eyes on Nockashima's shoulder.

There was hardly a sign of a fireman, except for stray helmets here and there, and a coat or two piled on the stove.

With amazement the mistress of the house gazed on the scene of recent revelry, and at the creature which romped about the room.

"If I didn't recognize the symptoms," said Spray, "I wouldn't know what it was."

Mr. Henry paused for a second to whiff generously at his mistress's feet. It was a new sensation for the creature. He drew enormous breaths and smelled rapturously. It was as though a man long blind for the first time beheld the sunlight. Mr. Henry, restored to puppydom, had regained his sense of smell. And he meant to use it.

"Well, he seems to be shaking a mean nostril at your feet," said Rex. "You lose your corns, and Mr. Henry regains his smell. That's fair."

"Let's forget my corns," retorted Spray, "and see what can be done to clear up this bacchanale. Here, Henry old fellow," she said, picking up a fireman's helmet, "smell this out."

The bloodhound took an eager whiff and reeled off. From corners firemen emerged.

"Not that I don't want to be hospitable," called Spray as they poured forth into the night, "but it's time all good firemen got to bed."

"Is this Elmer's cue?" inquired Joe enthusiastically from the doorway. "Can he hold up the Fire Department? He's rarin' to go."

Nockashima, pushing the weeping Fifi away, hastened after the exiting firemen. "That our idea, madam," he said over his shoulder. "Mist' Elmer devote pistol to fleeing figures."

Elmer leered in the doorway, a face in the night. In trembling fingers he held a revolver. "Can I now?" he asked. "Can I let 'em have it?"

"I think that would be a very fitting climax to the party," remarked Rex Pebble. "Yes, let 'em have it." Elmer whirled about unsteadily. There were loud reports on the night air, and in the distance much shouting of unmentionable words.

"Mist' Henry like March," philosophized Nockashima, "come in like lamb, go out like lion." For mingled with Elmer's shots was a clamor like the far-off baying of the hounds in a posse pursuit of escaping convicts.

Spray Summers calmly, with hands on slim, alluring hips, surveyed the scene of hilarity. It was anything but a house beautiful, but it never lacked for excitement.

CHAPTER XII

SUE TURNS

SUE PEBBLE was Rex Pebble's wife. She had been that for twenty-one years. Obdurately, determinedly, Rex Pebble's wife. There had been times, in those years, when Sue's patience had been strained to the breaking point, but she never gave up. Start a thing, you must finish it, was Sue's philosophy, even if in name only. She liked being Mrs. Rex Pebble, she liked the house she lived in, she was not blind to her husband's faults, and best of all, she was not blind to her own. Mrs. Pebble liked her fun and could take it. Though her heart line may have somewhat resembled the twisting course of the Snake River during the years of her marriage with Rex, she had at least pursued a tangent of tacit honesty, and she had made Rex a good home.

Mrs. Pebble glanced about the spacious, well-appointed living room. Violently addicted to change in a great many different things, perhaps her best expression of this attitude had been in the quick adoption and equally rapid scrapping of various modes of house furnishings. This room, like Mrs. Pebble's emotions, had gone through regimes of horsehair, mission, antique, and Colonial. The room was now modern. It was hard but not harsh, with its pleasing tubular curves of gleaming metal and its soft, downy corduroy upholstery. Mrs. Pebble looked about her with evident satisfaction, while in a small mirror that she held in her hand she proceeded to make up her race. There was some contrast here. There were few modern lines in Sue Pebble's face. Sue had reached fifty-five years of age, and despite her often frantic efforts to deceive, on close observation she looked it.

For instance, there was her hair. It was blond. It had been blond originally, but it was a white blond now. If Sue had not developed so watertight a system for regular visits to her hairdresser's her hair would probably have showed more white than blond. As it was, she out-Harlowed Harlow. And the mouth. There was a certain tense, fierce expression about it, as though Sue Pebble hardly dared laugh out loud for fear something might crack or chip. She wore a high collar that flared around the upper reaches of her throat. Her lips were carefully outlined with sharp bright scarlet. Sue spent a great many hours a day in the huntress's passionate pursuit of beauty.

It was with no pleasure that she gazed into the little mirror. Damn it, thought Sue, you can do wonders with your figure, but what can you do with your face? Considering everything, her face was about the best it could be, but it was not exactly satisfactory from any standpoint.

With pent-up resentment, Sue Pebble thought of her husband. Rex was older than she, but he carried his years with a great deal more ease and grace. He was a distinguished old devil, she thought, and he certainly didn't deserve the break the years were giving him. These considerations led inevitably to a question that always lay smoldering, not to say blazing cheerily, in Sue's mind. How did that woman Spray Summers, the huzzy, keep her hold on Rex Pebble?

Sue thought of Spray with very little envy, so she imagined, but with an amazing amount of curious respect. Simply out of professional regard, she was constantly pricked with amazement at this phenomenon. There had been quite a few men in Sue Pebble's married life, but, drat them, she thought, they had always folded their tents and silently stolen away. Spray was only a few years younger than Sue, yet she held a firm grip on the woman's husband. What in heaven's name, Sue wondered, did they do all the time—all those long evenings on which, with the poorest excuses, Rex Pebble stole away to be with his mistress?

Sue's questions and her little game of make-up were suddenly interrupted by the sound of the doorbell. Pretty late, she considered, as she rose to go to the door, but one could never tell what doorbells at late hours might produce.

It was just Kippie, Rex Pebble's twenty-three-year-old nephew, who looked so much like his uncle at the same age that Sue almost started with surprise every time she saw the boy.

"Well, what do you want at this hour?" the woman demanded. "You know very well where your uncle is!"

"I don't," lied Kippie glibly, "and besides, might I not sometimes wish to see my charming aunt?"

"Stop it, stop it," said Sue glumly. "I can't listen to any such words as those after the inventory I've just been giving myself."

"What, scoring up your lines again, you old witch?" said the young devil. "You ought to go out with me some time. I'll bet I could add a few curves of surprise to your collection."

"Oh, no, you couldn't," retorted Sue. "You look too darned much like your uncle to add a thing to my experience. I could keep one jump ahead of you in anything you did."

"I don't think that sounds very nice," said Kippie, "but I'll give you credit for the best sort of meaning. By the way, what do you mean, I should know where Rex, that old fox, is at this hour?"

"It's the children's hour, isn't it?" demanded Sue Pebble. "And besides that, it's an occasion. Twenty years ago tonight my husband seduced his lifelong mistress. You can imagine with what misgivings I sit alone at home. I'm glad you came: we might have some fun."

Kippie's young face, so disturbingly handsome to the woman, was puckered with doubt.

"Well, I don't care what the occasion is," he remarked with a curious note of concern, "but I've got to see the old codger. Something's up on the market. We might be wiped out. You know, stranded at the bread line."

Sue Pebble's nose showed that she had caught the scent. Only one thing could give her quite the look of quiet determination that was printed on her features. She rose from her chair and started toward the telephone. "I know the number," she said. "In crises, whenever I've had to get that man in a hurry, I've imitated everything from a Negro maid to a taxi driver. I only hope I don't get that slant-eyed Japanese master of lies on the phone, as I did one night."

"Here," said Kippie, catching up with her and detaining her. "Don't do that.

Phoning won't do any good. I've got to talk with Uncle Rex in person. This is serious."

"Well," returned Sue, "what did you come here for?"

Kippie ran his fingers through glossy brown hair. "The truth is," he said, "I saw the light as I drove past, and I just wondered what you were doing. I thought you might be in for a little adventure."

"Adventure?" inquired Sue, pricking up her ears. "Precisely what kind of adventure? Are there men involved?"

"Well, I've got to see Uncle Rex, and we know where he is, and this is sort of an anniversary"—Kippie told the story in one breath—"and I thought it might be a lot of fun just to drop by and pay our respects—that is, your respects."

"Well, I'll be damned," said his aunt. "I think that calls for a drink." She started for the pantry. "And I don't know but that I'll take you up on that," her words floated back from the door.

So it was that several shakers later Sue Pebble, accompanied by a young man strangely resembling the youthful Rex Pebble, set forth for the home of Spray Summers. The ride, due to their condition of heightened gayety, was a fairly hilarious one, over a course that wove perilously around corners and through red lights that continued to blink their reproach at the fast retreating car.

"So this is the love nest?" said Sue Pebble as they drew up with a shriek of brakes in front of the house with the garden and the pool in which her enterprising husband had installed his mistress. "I think they ought to have Japanese lanterns out, or flags in front, or a band playing." She added, "How do you suppose they're celebrating?"

"I'm too young to answer that one, Auntie," said Kippie, "but I can use my imagination, or should I?"

"Never mind," answered Sue. "I see lights, and I think I hear music. There must be other guests. I hope I shan't have the pleasure of meeting his other wives calling on my husband's mistress, or is that too confusing?"

"The morals of this family would tax the English language," said Kippie, "and I haven't even begun to tell you about mine."

"Take it from one who knows," advised his aunt, "and stay single. Rex has been going along for years under the false impression that three can live as cheaply as one."

"All I hope is," Kippie said wistfully, "that they have as good liquor as the old girl had the last time I was here."

"Am I the other old girl when not present?" asked his aunt sternly.

"Nope," answered Kippie blithely, "I just call you old soak and let it go at that."

The woman and her youthful escort stole quietly through the little garden gate that so lately had been the scene of a near hold-up and an impromptu cocktail party. The gravel of the walk crunched under their feet as they neared the door. "Shall we ring," inquired Rex Pebble's wife, "or just break in? I seem to lack the proper etiquette for calling on the mistress of one's husband, particularly on the anniversary of her seduction. I daresay I won't be any more welcome for the anniversary present I sent, either." Sue tittered with mirth. "Bedroom slippers—for her corns. Best wishes from Sue Pebble."

"Come on," said Kippie, who was familiar with the house. "Let's just slip in the side door." They entered a reception hall, from which a stairway ran up to the second floor. It was dark and smelled strongly of whisky and burned clothing. There was a faint whiff of dog about the place, also. "There's been a party," observed the young man, "and someone got burned."

"I hope it was that wench," returned Sue Pebble uncharitably. "I can hardly wait to see her in her bedroom slippers, sitting by the fire."

"They're upstairs," remarked Kippie. "Let's go on up."

"Don't be a fool. I may be the man's wife, but I know when I'm not wanted."

"Oh, come on, we'll surprise them."

"I should think so."

"Wouldn't you like to be surprised?"

"I have been. That's why I'm a wife in name only."

"Well," said Kippie, taking Sue Pebble's hand and urging her up the stairs, "turn about's fair play."

They tiptoed up the stairs in a spirit of jovial fun, hoping that the upper floor would yield the highballs of which it seemed to smell so generously. Suddenly a door was thrust open and a small dark form padded toward them along the dimly lit hall. At its heels followed a creature of jagged outline, which appeared to be a misfit head on a very gay animal body of four legs and a joyously wagging tail. Still in the rear were two figures with locked arms. The leader of this miniature parade bore what was unmistakably a cocktail shaker. The figure hesitated; so did the procession. A light switched on.

"Hi!" Nockashima greeted the newcomers. "Unaccustomed to receive guests on upper story, but this pleasant surprise. How do, Mist' Kippie." The years had only added to Nockashima's stolid Eastern philosophy. If people wished to keep coming to call all night, that was too bad but unavoidable; and if they wished to insinuate themselves into the more intimate apartments of the house, they might hold themselves responsible for shock, not him.

"I think, in view of your perpetual rudeness and deceit over the telephone," said Sue, advancing on the diminutive figure, "that you may just pass over that shaker."

Nockashima clung to the object. "Very special property, this," he returned. "Never allow out of personal hands."

"I'll get personal with your hands," cried Sue, snatching the shaker. "That's right, Auntie," cheered Kippie, "let her have it, Nocka. I think Mrs. Pebble should be given the run of the house."

"Come, come, my good woman!" remonstrated Major Jaffey, stepping forward, "and who may you be?" A slight tussle over the shaker seemed imminent.

"I might ask the same of you," returned the woman, "if I didn't think it would be wasting good breath. I haven't the slightest idea who you are, but I would suggest that you just pick up your feet and carry them on downstairs. I'm going to have a good big highball and then take a look around for my husband. I want to congratulate him."

Major Jaffey was visibly taken back. So were Rex Pebble and Spray Summers, who stood only a few feet distant from Sue Pebble, just on the inside of a studio door. Spray called the room a studio: it was where she kept a choice assortment of spirits, vinous and alcoholic.

"In that case," the Major was humbled, "I suppose I'll just breeze along downstairs. Coming, Hal?" The fireman and the Major pressed past Mrs. Pebble somewhat fearfully, while Nockashima hurried off for glasses.

"Back in a minute, Auntie," said Kippie. "I think I'll see that we get the proper size of highball. They're a little backward sometimes around here."

Sue seemed torn between a desire to investigate the home of her husband's mistress and an appetite for the contents of the shaker. She reached for the nearest door-knob and turned it slightly. Rex Pebble and Spray Summers, on the other side of the door, hastily retreated. "I think I'd better go and see what I can do about her," whispered Rex.

"Get rid of the old hag as soon as you can," returned Spray. "What poor taste to come at this hour!" Spray drew her lace gown about her lovely young form. "I wish she could have come with the milkman."

"I'm surprised that she didn't," said Rex knowingly.

Spray stood back of the door, and Rex slipped into the hall. The man was quite unprepared for the reception that greeted him.

"Hello!" remarked Sue Pebble sharply. "No tricks, now. Quit jumping in and out of doors."

"I'm not jumping in and out of doors," the woman's husband answered in an astonished voice. He was astonished both at her remark and at the apparent calm with which she greeted him. Rex had been ready to weather a tempest of wrath.

"Well, what did you go in there for"—Sue pointed to the door through which Kippie had vanished—"and then come out here? Don't think I've had that many."

"I wouldn't put it past you," answered Rex, both vexed and mystified at his wife's behavior.

"Something's come over you since you came in this house, young man," remarked Sue Pebble sternly, "and I just want to warn you not to get fresh. You brought me here, it was your idea—be a gentleman."

"I never said a word about your coming here. In fact, I hoped you never would come here," said Rex.

"Look here, this has gone far enough. Did you or didn't you suggest that we come to see that huzzy, Spray Summers?"

"Of course I didn't. What makes you think I did?"

"Nothing more nor less than my ears," snapped Sue. "You may think I'm older than you, but I'm not deaf."

"I have no reason whatever to think that you're deaf. But I could show you a thing or two."

"What are you driving at?" asked Sue acidly. "I'm beginning to think that I'm loose with a madman. After all the things that I've done for you, that you should lure me to this evil place and then begin to play practical jokes on me." Sue Pebble was approaching the point of tears. Looking at this attractive young male, she could only think of her husband as she had first met him, and it was a pleasurably poignant memory.

"In addition to jumping in and out of doors," Sue reproached, "you have to go around without any clothes on. Whose pajamas are those?"

A light of realization began to dawn in Rex Pebble's eyes. So Sue thought he was Kippie. For the first time during the whole adventurous evening he could see himself in someone else's eyes, as he must really look, though Spray's point of view, it must be admitted, was a bit colored by prejudice and emotion.

"Look here," said Rex in a kindly tone, "I think there's a mistake been made. Come with me into the bedroom." Rex started toward a door across the hall.

"That would make two mistakes," Sue's voice was tart, "and I want to tell you that, broad-minded as I am, I'll brook no incest, even by marriage."

"Come in here and I'll tell you a secret," coaxed Rex.

"Not on your life," returned Sue, "and I think the quicker you stop this foolishness, young man, the better it will be for you. Just wait till I find your uncle, or did he put you up to this?"

Something slipped a cog in Rex Pebble's mind. He was overwhelmed with mirth at the oddity of the situation. Rex laughed loudly. "He certainly did, the old devil," he exclaimed, snatching Sue off her feet and bearing herthrough the bedroom door. There were screams in the hall which the closing door muffled.

Young Kippie, from where he stood matching glasses with Nockashima, heard the screams and came running into the hall. Spray Summers heard them too and also rushed into the hall. The two bumped into each other, then stopped in surprise. Before him Kippie saw a lovely creature in a thin lace gown, ready for bed. His eyes swept her; he was moved to speech.

"Oh, I say," remarked the young man, "this is a pleasure."

"I think you're getting too accustomed to things," said the young woman. "What did the old hag say?" "What old hag?" asked the puzzled Kippie.

"Sue, you fool, your wife," said Spray Summers.

"I have no wife," Kippie returned. Then, after glancing up and down the lovely, appealing figure, he said abruptly, "I want to come in with you. May I?"

"What for?" snapped back Spray. "Are you mad or am I?"

"Just for fun," answered the very forward young-man. "Oh, that." A pause. "Come on in." Spray's graceful hand stretched toward him.

"Just a minute, if you please," said the voice of Rex Pebble, issuing from the opposite bedroom door.

"Good gracious!" said Spray, staring at Rex and realizing her mistake. "I thought he was you. How careless of me. I'll have to watch my step. You look so much alike."

"Hold on," said the disappointed Kippie. "I thought I was myself, but apparently I'm that guy. Who are we, anyway?"

"Believe it or not," answered Spray, "he's your darling uncle Rex, and I am the mistress known as Spray. A miracle has given us back our youth, and we are preparing to make the best of it."

"No, you're not, huzzy," Sue Pebble chimed in, appearing behind her husband in the doorway. "If I have to tear his body limb from limb, I'll get the secret of this rejuvenation out of him, and use it myself." The woman threw Rex Pebble a fierce look. "Then I'll make the best of it!"

"You may have the secret, my dear," said the woman's husband, "if I can give it to you. I'm beginning to think it's more of a curse than a blessing. Particularly to be sane and yet young. The two don't mix."

"Oh, they don't, don't they?" interrupted Spray Summers hotly. "Well, fancy that! Only two minutes ago you were standing on the other side of that door—a *bedroom* door—suggesting things to me that I hadn't considered for years, and now here you are—telling your wife—the old cow—that you're cursed with youth. It wasn't youth you were cursed with two minutes ago."

"Well, if he wasn't cursed with youth, just what was he cursed with?" inquired Sue Pebble. Her tone had that icy cordiality which women hold in reserve for their most bitterly detested rivals. "Just what *was* he cursed with?"

"For my part," said Spray, raising her voice, "I wouldn't say that he was *cursed* with anything. But whatever it was, it was something you haven't known about for a long, long time."

"I suppose you know everything that goes on in our home?" Sue shot back at her rival.

"I certainly know everything that does not go on in your home. And I do know what goes on in my home."

"Make up your minds, girls," Kippie cut in genially. "Decide between you where something does go on. It's important."

"You keep your trap shut, you young whippersnapper," Sue hissed. "I'll thank you to keep out of what you've gotten me into. As for you, Rex Pebble," the woman flung at him, "I should think you'd be ashamed to go around jazzing up your body like that! You should be content to grow old gracefully."

"Like whom?" Spray's quiet young voice bit into the controversy.

"Like me," Sue snapped back. "I've had my fun and I don't go around like a chameleon, changing colors all the time."

"I don't suppose you put that red on your lips, either, or were just threatening to tear Rex Pebble limb from limb unless you could discover the secret of youth?"

"Since I've seen how young blood goes to old heads, I've learned a lesson." Sue spat out the words, but they deceived no one. With wonder and envy she looked upon Spray's body that glowed with beauty and vitality. There they stood, elderly blonde and young brunette, Rex Pebble's public and private life, his lost world and his world regained, while the man gazed from one to the other in silent bewilderment. Never could there have been a greater contrast between two women, yet their behavior was strikingly alike. Both wanted the man and were ready to do battle for him, even to his chagrin and embarrassment. Rex glanced at Kippie. Surprise and a little horror were written on the young man's face.

"Listen," Rex whispered. "Let's skip the tournament and get a drink." The two stole away downstairs, Nockashima following in awed silence. A few minutes later they were comfortably ensconced in the kitchen, scene of late merriment, all thoughts of the battle lost to mind. Hal and the Major toasted the new arrivals.

Upstairs Spray Summers had the parting shot as she prepared to retire into her bedroom and close the door temporarily upon this disconcerting woman.

"Incidentally," Spray remarked, "you might just drop that cocktail shaker. No wonder some people get such queer ideas in their heads. I'm sorry for anyone who can't take his drinks." The door closed none too gently.

"I'll see you later," promised Sue Pebble between clenched teeth, "and when I do, you won't know me, even if I have to cut my hair."

For the second time that evening Sue was on the verge of tears. It was all so bewildering, and she felt so left out of things. What was the secret? How had they done it? Did she have a chance in the world of catching up with this curious parade of youth? Sue felt very sorry for herself. It was extraordinary, too, how possessive she had become about Rex. She was wondering at the whole state of affairs and, in desperation, considering a drink out of the shaker which she still held when a soft hand slipped its fingers into hers.

"I heard the whole thing, my dear," murmured a pleasant feminine voice, "and I don't blame you a bit. For fifteen years I was shut up in stone and never had a chance. It's terrible."

Sue Pebble turned and stared. The girl beside her was young and beautiful in a classic, glowing sort of way. She had long hair, wound about her head, and she moved with a flowing rhythm that was unlike anything Sue had ever seen. However, Sue winced at the expression "shut up in stone."

"Don't tell me," she admonished, "that you've been shut up in a tomb and have just come to life. I couldn't stand it. Too many awful things have been happening around here."

"Very interesting, if you ask me," said Baggage, the garden piece. "That is, if you like firemen. It just happened that I brought one upstairs with me. He wasn't run out with the rest. He's gone to sleep in there." She indicated a door.

"Of course, nothing that you say makes the slightest sense to me," remarked Sue, "but then I'm getting used to that. I don't understand about the fireman or the stone or anything," she faltered.

"Come with me," suggested this unusual girl, "and I'll tell you a story that will curl your hair. Besides, if you're a good listener I'll give you a secret you'd very much like to know." Baggage led the way downstairs and out into the garden, meanwhile telling the tale of her sudden overpowering impulse to leap into the glorious pool, and its consequences.

They drew near the pool. Sue stared with envious fascination at the calm water, gently ruffled by the breeze.

"If you want to be as young as that other bi—I mean wench—you see your husband told me not to say `bitch'—why, just swim across the pool, and you'll have it."

"Have what?" Sue inquired.

"It," repeated Baggage. "Isn't that what you were wishing for just now? Youth, beauty, sex appeal, or what have you these days. Anyway, you'll be like the other one in there." This she said with a wave of her slim white hand toward the house.

Sue was skeptical but interested. Between the lines of the girl's story, which recounted so many years of gazing wistfully out at men from a cold beautiful stone face, and of watching the playful antics of couples on this very lawn, she could read genuine longing and convincing desire. She was inclined to believe the fantastic tale, if for no other reason than that the creature seemed to tell it out of such a wistful sort of memory.

"Why are you telling me this?" she asked.

"The gods only know, perhaps," said Baggage. "But I think I'm jealous. And, anyway, you're his wife, and it will even things up a bit if you both are young together. Not only even things up, but make them much livelier, and I love excitement!"

"Maybe it was what was in the shaker, but whatever it was, or is, I'm diving in that pool," said Mrs. Pebble. "The only thing I can get is a cold in the head and my clothes wet, if your recipe doesn't work, and if it does—well—let the fireworks fly!"

So saying, Sue Pebble, who had not swum with such enthusiasm in years, plunged into the silvery water. For a moment she stood poised, as though experiencing a new sensation. A delighted smile began to spread over her features, which even in the dusky light of the garden appeared magically to take on new attractions. The woman dipped her head beneath the surface and came up beaming.

"Something's happening," she shouted with joy, as with new life and vigor she began to streak across the pool. An inscrutable Mona Lisa expression grew on the lips of Baggage. For soon, on the other side of the pool, stood a girl who, even in the wet baggy clothes of a middle-aged woman, was a creature of infinite blond beauty.

CHAPTER XIII

MAN INTO CHILD

THE new and lovely edition of Sue, Mrs. Rex Pebble, stood beside the magic pool, rinsing her soaked garments and regretting not a whit the miraculous plunge that had caused her to ruin one of her favorite gowns. Sue ran admiring hands over her hips. They were beautifully rounded, svelte but well filled, the kind of hips that make cotton look like silk and $17.75 resemble a straight $75. No more lying awake nights planning how to infuse youth into her clothes; no more anguished early mornings of strenuous exercise, or evenings of denying herself the fatal sweets that add weight.

"Look," called Sue Pebble in a voice so musical that it surprised herself, "did you ever see anything neater?"

She indicated her bust with a proud gesture.

"Very good," commented Baggage across the water,

"but I think I'm pretty neat myself." The girl abruptly lifted her skirts, revealing ankles and limbs of graceful beauty. They were, however, somewhat on the classical mold, while Sue Pebble's rejuvenated form was nothing more nor less than the lusciously appealing, smoothly curved figure of a girl in the deceptive neighborhood of twenty.

"No wonder," returned Sue; "You ought to be beautiful. You've been in this pool all your life."

"A hell of a lot of good it did me," came back the sharp answer. "I'd like to know what fun the Venus de Milo ever had. All that ever happened to her was to have her block knocked off." Baggage, out of bitter experience, was deeply scornful of the ways of art.

"I wonder, my dear," said Sue, in the voice of half-abstraction which a beautiful woman uses while she is engaged in examining her figure, "whether you have ever looked at the Venus closely enough?"

"Oh, I've been chipped myself," said Baggage, "but that's just by curiosity-seekers, people you'd meet in any museum. It's no more damaging than riding in a taxi—I should say less so, on the whole. What I mean is, there I was locked up in stone for fifteen years, watching everyone else have fun, while some of them actually used to laugh at me."

"They did?" inquired Sue, but her tone revealed only perfunctory interest. Sue preened here and there, removing wet garments from time to time to get as much look at her new-found loveliness as she possibly could.

She began to wish desperately for a full-length mirror.

"They used to snicker and say, 'Wonder what that old gal would do if she could get down off her pedestal?'"

"Well, my dear, wasn't that just what you were thinking yourself?"

"It certainly was," answered Baggage, "but it was the way they used to say it that burned me up. Of course, my clothes were old-fashioned, but, after all, you can't keep up with the styles if no one will send a sculptor around. Besides, those men do have the most awfully phooey ideas. A sash here and a bow there, and they call it class. Personally, I think clothes are heaven's greatest gift to man. I'd rather tantalize any day than give away the whole show the first time I see a man."

This bit of philosophy seemed to give Mrs. Pebble pause. She shook out her tousled golden curls and a strange light came into her china-blue eyes.

"You know," said Sue, "you start me to thinking. I believe I'll actually have to borrow some of that brazen huzzy's clothes."

"Borrow them?" mocked Baggage. "I've been changing dresses every two hours since I jumped off that rock." She pointed with distaste to the plinth that stood in the center of the pool, lonely and deserted without the adornment of her classical beauty. "When I get through with a dress, I just touch a match to it. I've always wanted clothes to burn."

"How do you get them?" inquired Sue. "Do you know where the clothes closet is?"

"Do I?" asked Baggage. "That's where I parked that red-hot fire-eater I was out with when I first met you in the hall. He's lying under a blanket and two or three old suitcases and some shoes. I thought I'd cover him up so nobody'd take him away till I saw whether I could use him again."

"What's the matter with the poor fellow? Is he ill? Was he overcome?"

"He's just tired," returned Baggage. I thought he needed a good nap, so I just handed him a little poke in the nose."

"I see that I can learn things from you," remarked Sue Pebble, walking around the edge of the pool toward Baggage, who stood nearest the house. "Just now I can't think of anything that would give me greater satisfaction than a small theft from Miss Spray Summers' wardrobe. I hate that woman cordially."

"Oh, I know," answered the girl. "And I do too. She's so damned confident. No woman ought to be as confident of a damned man as she is of your husband. And she has been for years."

"You're telling me," said Sue. "Personally, I don't give a hang much one way or another, but I hate to see the bi—wench have such smooth sailing."

"The nights I've stood out there and watched them," Baggage's words seemed torn out of a searing memory. "At least you would have thought they'd have the decency to keep from in front of me. But no, sir, they seemed proud as pie about it. They hadn't been out in the garden much of late, though."

"You liked my husband, didn't you?" asked Sue Pebble, drawing close to Baggage.

"You mean, I *like* your husband, responded the girl with determination, "but I don't seem able to get near him with that woman around."

"Well," said Sue, "we're both out after the same scalp. You've helped me a lot, and now I'm going to do something for you. Just come this way and show me that clothes closet."

"We want to be careful not to wake up Bill," Baggage observed, "because if we did he'd probably raise a heck of a squawk and the whole house would come running."

At the precise moment that these two eye-filling figures were moving across the Summers' lawn toward the house, Rex Pebble, inside, reached a decision. He was in no cheerful mood. To have a mistress restored to her pristine beauty and an elderly wife dropped on your hands in a rage of jealousy, perhaps quite justified, is something to add iron-gray hairs to the head. This was one situation in which Rex, an inventor of sorts, could think of nothing to relieve the tension of the situation. And on top of this here was young Kippie telling him the most monstrous kind of ill luck at the office. It appeared that the Rex Pebble fortune was on the eve of being rubbed out. It was horrible to think what both Sue and Spray would have to say, after all these years, in a jam like that. Rex's new-young brows were furrowed with care.

The group on the whole was a congenial one. There was Major Jaffey, who since the dramatic departure of Joe, his banking prospect, with Elmer, had no one but Rex to whom he could confide his world-shaking ideas. There was Hal, the faithful fireman, who had stayed on after his fellows had gone. Nockashima, feeling the call for food, was busily preparing a steak on the capable-looking electric stove, at the same time feeding Mr. Henry from a baby's bottle. Mr. Henry had doffed his ferocious king of the jungle headdress and was now nothing more or less than a playful bloodhound puppy, who frisked about the kitchen, exhilarated by his brand-new sense of smell. There was plenty to smell in that room. Steak, highballs, toasting bread, and the various alluring scents of Spray, Sue, and Fifi, not to mention Baggage, who had passed to and fro through the place.

"I could make a suggestion or two," Kippie was saying, "only I'm afraid of getting my head snapped off."

His uncle turned on the youth, though actually to an outsider it would have looked as though one youth were turning viciously on another.

"None of your funny ideas," said Rex Pebble, shaking a vigorous forefinger in an elderly way that was quite incongruous with his dapper appearance. "I suppose you don't think it's enough to have imported your dear aunt into this madhouse? That idea ought to last you for about a month."

"But this is a dandy thought, Uncle Rex," explained Kippie. "I wish you'd give me a chance to tell you about it. It's about an invention."

"Oh, yeah?" Rex's tone was bitter. I suppose you want me to start a nudist colony or a health-giving springs resort founded on that blasted pool."

"Not at all," returned Kippie. "All I'd like to see you do is get back the blueprint of the mouse trap that fellow got away from you."

"Rats!" said Rex appropriately. "I hoped I'd forgotten that. There may have been money in it, but I was gypped, and the fellow got away with the plans, and that's that." He dismissed the subject.

"Wouldn't you get it back if you could sell it and save us on margin?" Young Kippie's tone was sly.

"Nocka, when you're through torturing that piece of meat," Mr. Pebble addressed his small servant, "I think it would be a good idea to open up a bottle of brandy for Mr. Kippie. I can't think of anything but brandy and women that will keep him quiet, and of these two, drink is the lesser evil."

"O.K., O.K.!" Kippie was quick to jump at whatever came his way, "but if I ever get a chance myself, I'm going to get that mouse trap back, and the world will beat a path to my door."

"I don't seem to need mouse traps to get the world to my door." Rex glanced around the room, which seemed wilted in its state of disarray. No one had bothered to pick up the glasses of the late firemen's ball. In fact, the only difference in the room was that other glasses had been added by the more recent inhabitants.

"Down, Mist' Henry, down!" Nockashima pushed the eager bloodhound away from the sizzling skillet and hastened to produce the bottle of brandy. It was old and mellow, and it had the look of belonging in an inn in Normandy on a cold midnight, when the innkeeper, maids, and attendants gathered round the kitchen.

"What's Spray doing?" inquired Kippie eagerly. "I thought she liked brandy too."

"She does, you young hound," responded his uncle, "which is all the more reason for you to confine your thoughts to yourself. I'd hate to think of letting you loose with Spray Summers in her present state. As though I hadn't enough troubles. Did you ever think, young man, that you ought to get married and settle down?"

"What brings that up?" asked Kippie. "You got married, but I never noticed that you settled down. The fact is, I suspect there's been a lot more going on around here tonight than anyone knows."

"We haven't been around here much tonight," Major Jaffey defended his host. "We've been out riding and all sorts of things."

"Yeah," said Hal, "you'd be surprised if you knew all the places we've been and the things we've done."

Kippie preferred the main line of discourse. He accepted a brandy from Nockashima, who passed drinks to the others as well.

"Suppose, then," the young man countered, "if you want me to settle down, that I ask you for Spray Summers' hand?"

"That would be a hell of a note," rejoined his uncle.

"Seems perfectly proper to me. She's a lifelong acquaintance of yours, sort of a friend of the family, as it were. You could give her away."

"How could she tell us apart?" parried the older man.

"There're ways—we're not twins."

"You don't know that."

"I hope we're not. You could just as well be your own nephew. That would make you completely backwards."

"I am now, but what I want to know is, why should you think you'd like to marry Spray Summers?"

"Because she's a nice girl."

"I can see that everything's different," objected Rex. "That was certainly never the reason I was attracted to her."

"Oh, well, she's changed."

"She couldn't change that much. Besides, I have reason to believe differently."

"Supposing I were to get older, could I marry her then?"

"Not without my consent."

"But if you're where you were twenty years ago, you don't know whether I have your consent or not. You aren't yourself. You're what you used to be."

Rex Pebble saw that it was time to put a stop to this harangue. "I can see that you're where you be, and apparently always will be—standing beside a bottle. Don't try confuse me any more than I am. That is, unless you can relieve my mind of that overdraft account."

"That's the great disadvantage, remarked Kippie sagely, "that you grow backwards in everything but difficulties. Maybe you can find a pool that turns bonds into gold."

"Give Mr. Kippie some hot food, Nockashima," instructed the young man's uncle, "and let's see if we can't stop the flow of his thoughts. I'm going out for some air."

Rex Pebble strode out onto the veranda. It was queer, he thought, that one's necessities should be so insatiable. Here, by a gentle miracle of a prankish and beneficent stone figure, the one person dearest to him in the world was restored to her youth and the ripe physical beauty that had caught him up in passion in his younger years, and yet he wasn't satisfied. First there was in his mind the vision of Sue Pebble, his wife, as she looked at the lovely Spray with jealous envy in her eyes. Sue had not been a bad wife to him, in spite of her frequent flirtations and her stormy temperament. Certainly Rex had lived for more than twenty years in the same house with Sue, and that was something he had not done with Spray, for all her charm. It worked both ways. Seeing Spray in the evenings, when women are able by artificial charms and the conspiracy of nature to appear most glamorous, had added to her attractions, kept them perennially stirring to the man. Seeing Sue in the daylight, with the white glaring atmosphere of practicality about her, had taken away from her feminine appeal and had added to her reassuring stability. He felt sorry for Sue that she should be so unfortunately placed in the all too penetrating spotlight of everyday life. She had been robbed of a part of her woman's heritage. Rex Pebble felt on the point of tears. He felt sorry for himself too. For here, with Spray restored to him, and himself, too, young again, and with a new feeling toward Sue, the unhappy business of money had shown its ugly head.

It was at moments like this, when the world seemed pitch black and without point, that Nockashima seldom failed to appear to comfort his boss. The Japanese appeared now.

"Mist' Kippie and Mist' Henry fed and bottled," he announced. "Good idea catch breath of air on lawn. Just hear noise in upper story also—feel safer outdoors."

"You're right," agreed Rex Pebble, "I was afraid of that. It's much safer outdoors. What are they doing?" Rex glanced toward the upper floors of his mistress's home. Something very queer was going on. Lights were flashing here and there, as though someone were running from room to room, switching them on and off. "Is somebody playing tag?" asked Rex.

"Sounds as of great whoopee. Loud manly answered screams. Have idea Miss Baggage on loose," answered the wise little man. "Also Miss Spray and honorable wife up to old tricks."

"You mean they're having an argument over, me?"

"Cannot tell subject, but quite plenty redhot, boss. It appear much hair-pulling."

"Well, I think I'll just take a little pull at that bottle you so thoughtfully brought along, my good fellow," said Rex, relieving Nockashima of his pet. "This is good stuff, indoors or out, with wife or mistress, at home or abroad." Rex, who had not indulged deeply during the entire adventurous evening, took a long drag and smacked his lips. "We ought to think of a nice game ourselves," he suggested. "You and I ought to get together and play something. We never have."

"What shall it be, boss?" asked Nockashima, whose chief charm, perhaps, was the complete readiness with which he embraced any new suggestion of adventure or diversion. "Leapfrog?"

"I'm afraid I might hurt you," said Rex, "and then again you might hurt me. I don't trust that ju-jutsu."

"Me no ju-jutsu artist," Nockashima declared, "just humble Japanese fellow anxious to play. Suppose call Mist' Henry. He always ready to play, too."

"O.K.!" said Rex Pebble, "get the hound. One bloodhound more or less can't hurt." Rex chased his first brandy with another quick one. The tempo and warmth of his s blood was pleasantly speedy. "Here, Nocka, let's see you toss one off. That's the first requirement for a really good game of any kind."

"Here goes!" Nocka held up the brandy bottle. A shiver raced over his small, sturdy frame. "Hot stuff that. Make plenty warm belly. Very comforting. Hi, Mist' Henry," the man called in his peculiar way, ending in a low, tempting whistle that could not have been duplicated by another human being. His mouth was large and usually fixed in an irrepressible grin that produced in the whistle a quality of escaping steam, which wound up in a surprisingly sharp note of command. A racing figure hesitated uncertainly just outside the door to the veranda, while a screen door slammed shut.

"Mist' Henry very smart dog, even when honorable battery recharged. Not silly. Very sensible bloodhound with new acquired smell."

"Let's hide from him," proposed Rex boyishly. "I think I can get behind that tree."

Let it be said for Rex that he tried to get behind the tree. The trouble was' that the tree would not get in front of Rex. It wobbled and wavered and behaved in a fashion totally unprecedented in Rex's memory. Mr. Henry, entering gayly into the spirit of the chase, was dangerously near, seeming to prefer the scent of Rex to Nockashima's more obvious smell, lurking beside the stone veranda steps. Rex Pebble helped himself to a short choke of brandy before attempting again to cope with the tree. Hoping to appease the thing and make an ally of it, he offered the tree a swallow of brandy in a low tone. The tree continued to dance but refused to accept the man's hospitality. Wherewith Rex dashed a small slosh of brandy against its trunk and silently christened it the Sally Rand. "Stop it, Sally," whispered the husky male voice, "you make me dizzy, and how can you expect me to find coverage in a game of hide-and-seek behind such a whirling dervish?"

The tree was utterly obstinate. It would not hold still. Rex grew quickly disgusted, as Mr. Henry appeared to get hotter and hotter on the scent. The man lunged from behind the tree and sought the protection of some near-by bushes. These two were addicted to the dance, but in a much smoother, more classic sort of way. They held hands gracefully and loped about like the figures of a Greek frieze. It was not so hard to conceal oneself behind them or in them. The bushes, however, did have very sticky fingers, and they kept pricking Rex here and there most irritatingly. "Behave," growled the man fiercely, "or I'll not give you a drop of brandy, not a single little drop. I won't even baptize you, and how you'd like to go all your life unbaptized? Just imagine, no name, no nothing. By the way, are you all sisters, or am I seeing more of one family than there really is? To think that I've been in and out of here all these years and never knew what charming neighbors we had."

Mr. Henry, dashing up and enthusiastically licking Mr. Pebble's hands and face, cut short this monologue, while Nokashima stepped forth rather unsteadily from hiding and suggested that another game would not be amiss.

"You it," he told Rex.

"Don't be cryptic," replied his playmate. "I it—what do you mean?"

"Just that—you it."

"Haven't you any verbs?" Rex interrogated sharply. "Can't explain," said Nockashima thickly. "You tell him, Mist' Henry. Tell him he it."

"Stop it!" commanded Mr. Pebble. "This is the worst language I have ever heard. I'm surprised at you. You could curse me out with words like that, and I wouldn't know the difference. What are your antecedents?"

"Got no ant'cedents, however, nevertheless," said Nocka. "Very simple. We play game now."

"Not till I get it straight. Explain it this way: Suppose there were four of us playing?"

"Me tell him tell them tell you you it."

"Impossible!" exploded Rex. "You're either a genius or rapidly descending into the moronic stage. Do you always go after the pronouns when you have drinks, Nocka?"

"If good-looking," admitted Nockashima, "especially fond just plain she. No it. Lady them best of all."

Rex sighed heavily. More and more it seemed useless to try to understand; yet the man evidently had something in his mind. "Well, supposing I consent, what do we do next?"

"Absorb small drink," said Nockashima quickly, his eyes gleaming. "Very intoxicating evening. Stimulating to all concerned. Most enjoyable part of evening now in progress for unspeakable Japanese man. Great fun at games." Nockashima interrupted his flow of bouquets long enough to take a good firm hold on the brandy and pour a fiery trickle down his throat. "Hot dog, let's go!" he cried.

"What shall we play now, you insatiable Oriental athlete?" asked Rex Pebble of the diminutive man, who danced round him in glee, rubbing his stomach happily with both hands.

"Now we skip steps," said Nocka.

"Yes, Nocka, I know," answered Rex sympathetically, "I've skipped steps too, but I never tried it as a pastime. However, nothing ventured, nothing learned." He followed Nockashima to the steps.

"Oh, infinite more humor, boss, to skip steps. I begin," and with a pleased expression in his tiny eyes Nockashima flew up and down the steps on nimble feet, skipping to the tune of a very weird chant that only Nocka, and maybe God, knew.

To Rex Pebble this demonstration of the crazy little fellow was the last straw. He felt himself slipping, his poise seemed to have vanished, and with a last effort he pulled himself together to call for a drink. As always, the magic word brought Nockashima to his senses and his shaker, in this case a brandy bottle.

"Watch me," said Rex, standing on the top step of four, "with a running start I bet I can stop before I get to the water. Wait, though," the man added, "suppose you go get a watch and we'll time each other. We'll have races. Mr. Henry can hold the watch."

"O.K.," said Nocka agreeably. I go get timepiece." Nockashima hurried on unsteady legs into the house. Left alone, Rex Pebble felt the gayety of the games slipping away from him. His forehead was warm and moist. Instead of four steps there seemed to be eight, instead of one tree there seemed to be two. It was nice, anyway, he calculated, that things worked out so evenly. Just double of everything. That was fine. He wondered if there were two bottles of brandy instead of one, and indeed there were. Not only two bottles, but just twice the amount of brandy as in the one bottle. Rex began to speculate as to how this other bottle of brandy might taste. Would it be different, or would it taste the same, and if he drank out of the one, would it reduce the amount in the other? It waa a charming speculation that left room for a great many discoveries. If there were one Spray Summers now, that would mean two—only the disadvantage would be that his wife, Sue Pebble, also would be multiplied by two. Which would mean that the fight between the two women would be twice as fierce and, also, alas, if Rex's overdraft were now $25,000, under the present system of computation, that would mean a deficit of $50,000.

It was all very distressing. Rex began to feel that he couldn't stand it. If under normal conditions it would take Nockashima two minutes to find a watch, this would mean four minutes before he could return and the happy games be resumed. Rex began greatly to feel the need of water on his forehead. He decided to take a chance on reducing the amount of brandy, which was now double, and lifting the two bottles with both hands, drank with both mouths.

Well, at least it was consoling to think that he had four legs to walk on. This happy thought produced a decision. Rex looked toward the inviting waters of the pool. A little dip would do him good, he thought. On all four legs he began to gallop to the edge. His forefeet were over the side and touching the water before he remembered that there was something strange and magic about this small body of water, something that had brought him new youth and vigor and that might very likely handle him roughly if indulged in too liberally. It was too late, however, to stop. He plunged into the gratefully cooling waters and waited curiously to see what might happen.

What did happen was most shocking. A contracting sensation overtook the man, shook his frame with short spasms as though he were being pushed bodily into a hot-water bottle that was too tight for him. He underwent a brief siege of choking, his eyes blurred as though with fever.

With rapidly diminishing strength Rex beat back the water. He tried breast and crawl strokes and then a general sort of floundering, but it was easy to perceive that something very unusual was taking place within him. Either he was losing his strength altogether to some unknown inner tax of power, or else, perhaps, the magic pool was busy doing its stuff again. Rex Pebble began to grow alarmed. With the greatest difficulty he managed to keep his head above the surface of the water. He raised his voice to call Nockashima, but nothing happened. Rex had yelled, and he had heard nothing. He cleared his throat and took a fresh start.

"Nockashima," he screamed, and as though from afar, strange and unfamiliar as the voice of a babe, he caught a minute sound: *Nockashima!* Rex was very quiet. This was terrible. He couldn't make a sound. Suppose he should drown? But the water couldn't be that deep; no one could possibly drown in Spray Summers' handsomely landscaped garden pool. A man would have to be an utter fool, holding his head under, to do that. Rex looked down at the glistening surface.

What he observed, floating like jelly beneath the silver surface, was something to startle a city editor. This time Rex could not believe his eyes. The brandy was no good. Too bad to spoil a nice evening this way; it had started out so glamorously, so memorably, and now here he was, whisky and highballs and gin and brandy, imagining the oddest things about his own silly body reflected in a garden pool. Rex summoned his courage and endeavored to take a realistic view of the whole matter. He glanced down into the water, and what he saw this time made him start in amazement and chagrin. Eyes may be bad reporters the first time you send them out, but the second, they have to tell the truth; and the truth was cruel. Rex Pebble put all the lung command into one mighty screech for Nockashima. Across the lawn came the piercing cry of an infant. There was no doubt of the horrifying truth; Rex Pebble ducked his head under water. It popped up again in shame and mortification. Where only a few moments before had been the whipcord, vigorous, handsome form of a young man was now the sprawling body of a baby. "Oh, my God!" murmured the strange infant, then howled aloud again for its faithful Japanese follower.

Nockashima, hastening on nimble but uncertain feet into the garden with a watch for the impending races, was bewildered at the disappearance of his employer. There was not a sign of the man in sight. No bottle, no coat, no trace of him anywhere. Even Mr. Henry had vanished. Nocka unsteadily beat around the bushes, and then, remembering Rex's penchant for hiding behind trees, began to startle imaginary playmates by dodging around and crying *hi!* wherever he went. Anyone watching the fellow would have thought him utterly stark, raving mad. Liquor has its novel effects, but the game which Nockashima seemed to be playing with himself was gone about in a spirit of absolutely logical insanity.

Nevertheless, no tree yielded Rex Pebble. Nocka grew uneasy. What could boss have done with self? He cogitated. Nocka felt sure the master had been having a very fine time when he had left only a few minutes before, and it was totally out of keeping with his character for him entirely to abandon an object while in his cups. Nocka counted off on his fingers various improbabilities: Rex had not run away; he had not hidden playfully anywhere on the lawn; he certainly had not gone indoors, for Nocka had just come from the house through the only door that opened onto the veranda. The Japanese was genuinely disturbed and puzzled.

Then he heard the cry. It was a baby's importunate yell to be tended to, and at first Nocka imagined that the long-awaited heir had at last arrived next door. The little fellow was feeling rather fine, and he felt glad that the anxious parents had finally been blessed. Complacently he went on to enumerate the possibilities of the whereabouts of his boss.

The baby cried again. There's really very little to consider deeply about a baby's cry unless it comes late at night and keeps one awake, or unless one is the father of the infant and has to walk the floor with it. Nockashima, however, pricked up his ears sharply the second time he heard this particular baby cry. It was not the tone exactly that electrified his small Oriental being: it was what the baby said. Nocka was standing fairly near the water from which the cry seemed to emanate; he could not have been mistaken.

"Goddamn it, you dopey Jap," said the high falsetto, speaking, however, in crisp, careful enunciation, "come here this minute and drag me out of this pool before I shrivel up to nothing. Quick, I tell you—I'm on my way!"

Nockashima had seen a lot of queer things in his life, but now he was dumbfounded. Horror rendered him speechless. He dreaded to turn his eyes to the pool because of the sight which he was sure would greet him. And it did.

For there, struggling and breasting the surface as best it could, was a babe of perhaps one year old, greatly impeded by long trousers, a dress shirt, and a tuxedo coat.

"Well," said the mind of Rex Pebble through the voice of the babe-in-arms, "don't stand there all night. That is, unless you want to lose the best boss you ever had. I'll be subtracted to zero if you don't hurry. I think I must be down to about one year now. Only a year left to go, and I'm going backward fast."

The startled house man recovered sufficiently to rush to his employer's rescue. With tender care he reached down and lifted the squirming form from the water. Nockashima felt an almost fatherly pride as he cupped the infant in his arms. Life had its compensations. He had never dreamed that he would hold Rex Pebble in this fashion. The quaint fellow began to croon what he imagined was a lullaby as he started toward the house, rocking his impromptu cradle back and forth to the melody. It wasn't hard for Nockashima to rock, not in his condition.

"Stop that!" remarked the baby harshly. "Don't you think it's bad enough to have to endure this final mortification, without being sung to? Get me a brandy-and-soda, and make it snappy!"

Seldom had Nockashima heard such commands from the sweet mouth of a new-born. Seldom, either, had he observed so ludicrous a costume as Rex Pebble wore, the long trousers drooping and dripping far beyond the tender pink toes they concealed.

With a curious mixture of feelings and a very unsteady walk, the little yellow man crossed the lawn with his new charge to the home of Rex Pebble's mistress.

CHAPTER XIV

OF HUMAN BADINAGE

WHEN Sue Pebble, accompanied by that lush garden piece, Baggage, emerged freshly trim and twenty from the wonder-working waters, she made straight for Spray Summers' home with the evil intent of lifting a new gown to take the place of the one which she carried, dripping, on her arm. Sue was attired solely in step-ins, and a sweet sight she was, too. The garment fitted her appealing form like a pair of mittens, showing off its lovely contours to the best and most dangerous advantage, depending upon the point of view.

"Here," directed Baggage, "we'll just slip in the bar and have a little snifter to celebrate before we go on upstairs."

At first Sue was reluctant to enter the kitchen-bar, not because the men of the house were collected there, but because, before she took another step, she had a vain desire to observe her new build in a full-length mirror. The idea of a highball, none the less, overcame her pulsing vanity, and Sue went into the room with Baggage.

Kippie, Major Jaffey, and Hal sat in the kitchen, steeping themselves in the beneficent fumes of alcohol. Kippie had had quite a few. Robbed of the brandy bottle which Nockashima had carried out into the garden, he had laid siege to the cellar and from it taken a choice array of old Irish whiskies. Kippie knew the secret of Spray Summers' cellar, which was that, because of Sue Pebble's scruples, Rex did most of his really professional drinking away from home. Kippie was so-high with his Irish whiskies-and-waters, and was holding forth with great gusto on the vices and virtues of blondes versus brunettes when Sue and Baggage entered.

The three men, lifting their eyes through a haze, stared at the newcomers. Sue Pebble, clad in step-ins, showed not the slightest embarrassment. Temporarily Sue had lost sight of the magic of her transformation.

"Which one of you men would like to lend a girl a drink?" demanded Baggage. "You seem to be pretty well stocked."

"Both inside and outside," admitted the handsome young Kippie, "but not too much so to know a pretty girl when we see one, eh, fellows?" The Major and Hal murmured hearty approval.

"Well, I like that," remarked Baggage, since all eyes seemed to center on the charming Mrs. Pebble. "No accounting for tastes. However, you may pass that bottle around, and we'll toast your good taste." Baggage was a generous-hearted girl.

There was a general clinking of glasses.

From Sue's arm hung the dripping clothes which she had just taken off.

"Have you been immersed in a lake or something, madam?" asked the Major, by way of opening a conversation.

"I'll say I have," smiled back Sue, "and what an immersion it was, old son."

"Major Lynnhaven Jaffey, at your service, madam." This with a dignified bow.

"I'll be calling on you, probably," said Sue.

"I'm usually in bed by eleven," returned the Major, misunderstanding.

"You're one up on me, Uncle Jaffey," said Mrs. Pebble, "but you do look like an exceptionally decent sort."

At the moment Hal, the fireman, who out of the entire household had probably made the steadiest, least spectacular alcoholic progress throughout the evening, broke in, gazing at Sue earnestly.

"Say, lady," inquired Hal, "is this guy really your uncle?"

"No, I have no uncle," Sue replied. "I did have, but he's dead."

"Dead?"

"Quite."

"Your uncle is quite dead, lady?"

"He should be. He was a fine fellow."

"You seem to take his passing rather calmly." Hal shook his head sorrowfully.

"He didn't pass. He was murdered." Sue looked intently at Hal.

"Don't look at me like that, lady. I didn't murder your uncle. Did I?" asked the anxious Hal.

"How could you murder my uncle?" calculated the lovely Mrs. Pebble, drinking.

"Offhand I can think of five different ways to murder people. I've been considering them for years," said Hal.

Kippie, through his bewildered point of view, had been trying to make something of this hit-and-run conversation. Apparently there was nothing to be made, only a vague doubt assailed him. He glanced sharply at the wet garments hanging on Sue's arm. Surely somewhere he had seen those clothes before. There was something very familiar about them which he couldn't quite place.

"Speaking of murder," Kippie tried a shot in the dark, "where did you get those clothes?"

"They're my clothes," returned Sue defensively. "I bought them—that is, my husband bought them for me."

"Who are you, anyway?"

"You ought to know who I am."

"Maybe I ought to, but I don't, and that's what's worrying me. You're pretty, I like you, I could be very fond of you, but I don't know you." Kippie shook his head sadly.

"Maybe I know somebody you know," said Sue Pebble teasingly. "Maybe I know an aunt of yours or something."

So that was it! A small charge of recognition went off in young Kippie's head. The woman had his aunt Sue's clothes. A murderess! She had done away with his aunt and taken her clothes.

"That's right," Kippie agreed cautiously, "maybe I might have an aunt or something. By the way, when did you see my aunt last?"

"Oh," responded Mrs. Pebble coyly, "I haven't really seen her since I put on these step-ins."

Aha—check! flashed through Kippie's mind.

"How was she?" asked the woman's nephew shrewdly. "I had a hard time with her, but I finally got her to agree to do as I said."

"What did you say?"

"I told her it was time she passed on."

The foul, heartless cruelty of it! Kippie thrilled to the scent of violent death. He almost whistled for Mr. Henry, the bloodhound, then considered how much more a hero he would be if the whole discovery of the deed devolved upon himself.

"Didn't you care for my aunt?" asked Kippie craftily. "Why did you tell her it was time she passed on?"

"For one thing," answered Sue Pebble enigmatically, "her batteries needed recharging. Then there were other things wrong with her—her husband, for instance."

"It seems to me that that's off the point," cut in Sue Pebble's self-appointed cross-examiner, helping himself to another whisky-and-soda and blinking at his aunt through heavy-lidded eyes. "I asked if you had no emotional feeling toward my aunt, no affection for her."

"But I am on the point," protested Sue. "I say that the worst thing wrong with her was her husband. He was an old fossil."

"*Was* an old fossil?" inquired the young man sharply, wondering dimly when it was he had last seen his uncle. He looked around the room. No Rex Pebble in sight. He tried to find his way back in memory through a tangle of uplifted glasses to the last time he had seen the man. Very darkly, as though from a great distance, he seemed to catch a glimpse of Rex Pebble leaving this room with a bottle of brandy under his arm and some most disturbing ideas in his head—something about an overdraft. That was it! Kippie had brought the news from the office himself. And Rex had gone off into the garden in a distressed state of mind. It was very evident that this beautiful creature in step-ins, who sat beside him gracefully tossing off liquors and enjoying herself, was a first-class criminal character, fit for the line-up.

"If you ask me," confided Sue Pebble, "I think your uncle was an awful fool to marry that woman in the first place. Imagine being cooped up in a house for twenty years with a person like that."

The crassness of the woman, talking about the person, or perhaps the two people, with whom she had done away, shocked Kippie to the core of his soul.

"Don't you think my uncle and my aunt got along well?" asked the young man.

Sue Pebble was enjoying herself to the fullest. To be young again and unrecognized and on her own. Besides, this handsome Kippie was a distressingly accurate replica of her own Rex when she had first married him. Sue smoothed her golden curls with a graceful hand.

"They got on well enough for a couple of old dodos," she returned, "but I can't see why you're so interested in old people and the past."

"I'm interested in justice," flashed the young man. "I won't see innocent people foully murdered and not lift a voice in protest."

"So you think I'm the murderess, do you? Well, I want you to know that your uncle had just as much to do with killing his wife as I did. Besides, if the truth were known, there's a brazen challenge who lives around here named Spray Summers, that had as much to do with it as anyone."

Things were moving entirely too fast for Kippie. He was delighted to uncover one murder, but a widespread net of crime was more than he could comprehend. It smacked too much of mass production.

Kippie's one-man investigation of the foul deeds which he suspected had been going on outside, on Spray Summers' lawn, was destined to get away from him. At this moment Spray Summers herself came into the bar. Her dark beauty was contrasted sharply with the blond loveliness of Sue Pebble. The women stared at one another, held rigid by a long bond of fascination. Spray Summers had seen Mrs. Pebble years before, when the woman was Rex Pebble's lovely young wife, and she could not forget that memory. With a jealous pang she realized that Sue, too, had discovered the secret of the pool. She coolly sized up the appealing girlish figure in the cream-colored pants. What would Rex think? Spray wondered. But Rex Pebble's nephew was not to be detoured from his criminal exposures. In Spray he sensed an ally.

"This is the murderess of your husband," he calmly introduced Mrs. Pebble. "I suspect that she may have got rid of the old lady too."

"I think she did," commented Spray thoughtfully. "She got rid of the old lady all right, and I distinctly remember hearing her say that she would also tear Rex Pebble limb from limb if he didn't give her the secret of youth that he had. Why, the poor man's probably lying all over the garden this very minute in small bits. Let's go and see."

"No, wait," Kippie directed. "We want to hear her whole confession."

"Well, if you must know, I fell in love with a younger man."

"What," said Kippie, greatly surprised, "I don't see how you could have fallen in love with a younger man. That is, without falling in love with a man who was too young."

Baggage, who had been preoccupied with Hal, having a penchant for firemen, interrupted. "Well, say a man about your age," she hazarded to Kippie. "I understand what she means. I think you're just about right. I could use you." Baggage advanced upon the young man; there was meaning in her eyes. But Major Jaffey, interested in the outcome of the inquest, detained her with a hand on her arm. "Won't you sit here, my dear?" he suggested, offering a knee. Such offers come with disconcerting infrequency in the life of a girl like Baggage. Like a drowning man, in a flash she recalled her years in stone. No one had ever offered her a knee. She sat down abruptly, but her mind was still on young Kippie, so tantalizingly like the Rex Pebble she had watched grow out of magnetic young manhood into distinguished though dapper age.

"It's a long story," continued Sue Pebble, "and I shan't burden you with it here, but, in short, this young chap was my husband's nephew."

Kippie whistled between his teeth. Things were moving around in a whirling circle. Kippie took a drink.

"Come clean, my dear," said Spray Summers icily to her rival as Kippie's expression grew darker and more bewildered.

"This, Kippie dear, is your charming Aunt Sue. But I still believe she may have murdered her husband for the secret of youth she was raving about."

"By the way," said Sue sweetly, ignoring Kippie's chagrined amazement, "where is that dirty, low-down husband of mine? He's not in the garden, I assure you. I generally imagine that you have him in tow when he's missing, my love, but I see that something or somebody else must have got the lock and key tonight. If you'll pardon me, I think I'll just go in search of some dry clothes." Sue Pebble swept from the room, a fuming Spray after her.

"God, this is too much for one fireman to bear! It would take more than a seven-alarm fire to make me feel this bad," said Hal, dropping his head on his arms.

"Quite more thrilling than any of my adventures have ever been," murmured Major Jaffey from beneath the lissom weight of Baggage. "One does not know what to expect next."

"It's a good thing I'm not a mind-reader, Grandpop," said Baggage impudently. "I've always had the idea that this was the way to start things." Baggage bounced up and down on the old gentleman's knee.

"I don't understand what you mean by things," remarked the Major, "but the drift of your inference is very bad indeed. You should keep such ideas to yourself."

"Not after fifteen years on a marble column, I shouldn't. I have every intention of telling the world exactly what I expect to do. Even if I get disappointed," added the girl bravely.

"Well, there's always the danger of trial and error," the Major told her sagely, "but I should imagine you would bat a fairly high percentage."

"Take that one," said Baggage pointing at Kippie. "I think I'll drag him out into the garden with me. For years I watched his uncle and this Summers woman behave in the most scandalous way in the night on the lawn. This one's a pretty good imitation of the original. I believe we should get along swell." The girl slid off Major Jaffey's lap and approached Kippie with determination.

"Come with me," she commanded.

"What for?" inquired the befuddled youth.

"That you should ask!" exclaimed the girl.

"It's better to ask first and get things clearly understood. I may be risking a lot."

"Don't be so old-fashioned. Come right out with it. I can't imagine what your generation is coming to if it gets so inoculated with decency that it has to hedge like that."

"I don't want to go," said Kippie stubbornly.

"Something's wrong with you, then, or else you're not Rex Pebble's nephew. He never said that to anyone."

"It's certainly time someone in this family called a halt."

"I'm not going to lower my womanhood," stated Baggage, "to stand here all night arguing about a little detail. You come with me or I'll scream. I'll scream so bloody loud they'll hear me at the police station, and then wouldn't you be ashamed? Imagine what you'd have to tell the officers when they came. Denied a little girl, just feature that—what the coppers would say!"

"I think you're disgusting—you're too plain spoken. Can't you veil a few things?"

"Veil them?" Baggage glanced down at herself with evident astonishment. "I believe in solid cloth and no veils. I'm darned sick and tired of veils. You would be too if you'd caught cold as many nights from draughty wrappings as I have. Yes, sir, I believe in good honest whole cloth, or the human hide. There's only two ways to tempt, by sleight of hand or by slight of eye."

Here the girl gave way to her emotions. "Come on, now, and listen to my story. I was the one that put your uncle and the Summers creature and Sue Pebble up to their tricks. I'm the cause of this whole evening. If I hadn't slipped off the pedestal, Rex Pebble would never have regained his youth, but I admit that if I'd thought I could have found you here, I'd have stayed down there in the garden and waited."

There was a loud infantile wail from the direction of the upper floor.

"Hurry up," said Baggage, "they're in the second generation upstairs." Kippie let his dark, fiery young eyes wander over the appealing girl. He debated. There was too much going on to go out, and yet...

"Hurry," urged Baggage, "I think we're on the point of something."

"I think we are," answered Kippie, taking her arm and moving toward the door. "I think they're bringing a baby downstairs."

They were bringing a baby downstairs. The child was Rex Pebble, who screamed and protested above the din made by the two women and by Nockashima. The devoted little man still clung to his charge, in spite of frantic snatches at the poor manhandled body of Mr. Pebble. Across the man's loins, in lieu of diapers, Nockashima had rigged up a heavy towel and a large safety pin of such a size as to make it look more like an instrument of combat than a method of holding on one's clothing. Both Rex's hands and feet were in a perpetual wriggle, while he screwed fists into his eyes, bawling at the top of his high falsetto voice. On either side Sue Pebble and Spray Summers besieged the harassed Nockashima.

"You let me have that thing this minute," shouted Sue. "He would play a trick like this on me just when I get in form. Give the brat to me, you slant-eyed Fu Manchu, and I'll do something about it."

"Nonsense," said Spray harshly. "Give it to me. It's in pain. It needs bicarbonate of soda."

"Ridiculous," cried Mrs. Pebble. "Give a baby bicarbonate of soda!"

"It isn't a baby," Spray retorted. "It's a full-grown man."

"I don't dispute you there," said the wife. "You have plenty of basis for your statement, I daresay. But it's not a full-grown man at this moment. Not unless this deceptive Oriental is a magician with bath towels."

"It's ill, just the same," Spray Summers contended loudly, above Rex Pebble's long-continuous wailing. "It does need soda or ginger or catnip or something."

"Catnip, indeed!" screamed the baby. "You get me a whisky-and-soda. How long do I have to yell for one simple little thing? Isn't it bad enough to be in this condition without having you two women pulling me about like a fishing worm?"

"Worm, ha, that's good!" cried Sue. "Worm, that you are. Do you realize that I'm a young woman, hale and hearty, and that here you maliciously have yourself changed by a supersexed wanton into a mere babe-in-arms?"

"I'm sure I'm not finding it an experience to treasure in memory," said Rex bitterly, "but the least you could do would be to get me that drink."

To Hal and Major Jaffey, who had silently watched so much go on in this particular room that evening, this was the last straw. At first Jaffey was inclined to dismiss the whole affair as a practical joke, but by the time Rex Pebble had begun to call for drinks in so realistic a fashion, the Major began to feel that anything was possible. He took a very cautious look around the room just to be sure nobody was about to surprise him with a magic baptism. To Hal, whose mouth was fixed in a permanent sort of gape, he whispered, "Look here, old man, I don't think we'd better drink any of the water around this place. As for bathing, I wouldn't be caught near a bath-tub."

Suddenly twisting himself in Nockashima's cuddling arms, with the Jap tut-tutting over him, Rex spied his two male friends. "Major," cried the infant in arms, "well, for the love of Pete, am I glad to see you?" The baby's face beamed. "And accompanied by bottle and glasses." Rex reached a tiny chubby hand of pink crinkled flesh toward the Major. "Gimme one, old scout, will you?" pleaded the child.

Major Jaffey pretended not to notice that he had been addressed. Indeed, he wondered whether he had been addressed. It was perfectly possible still that these two madwomen and the willing Japanese had conspired to take advantage of his and Hal's somewhat credulous condition.

"All right, all right!" screamed the baby to whom Nockashima clung with difficulty. "Just wait till I get out of this diaper. Just wait till I get my strength back. I'll beat you two eggs up so you won't know each other. Is this gratitude? I take you in and give you a big evening, and then what happens? You make out as though you didn't know me, just because I happen to have shrunk and have to wear a bath towel around my middle." Res tugged at the safety pin with his small pink fists.

"Boss best to leave honorable towel around loins. Very draughty, also likely to shock ladies present."

"You too, Nocka?" cried Rex Pebble. "Going back on me, making fun of me? After all the years I've known these two women," it was a strain to distinguish just what the tiny, thin voice was saying, "that I should give either of them a shock. You make me laugh!"

"Great shock possible from disappointment," murmured Nocka, adjusting his charge's pseudo-diapers. "Nockashima somewhat surprised himself."

"Keep your surprises to yourself, you Japanese limb of Satan," remarked Sue Pebble, "and let me have my husband. I'll fix him!"

Spray took up the battle cry. "He wants milk," she said, "hot milk."

"What gave you the maternity complex?" the baby asked acidly. "I never noticed you going round trying to feed babies hot milk or catnip. You were much more likely to be feeding hot babies whisky."

"May I take a close look at the little fellow?" asked Major Jaffey unsteadily, hoping to detect a fraud.

"Help yourself," answered Sue Pebble. "It's no treat. We aren't going to put him in a side show. That's the trouble. He's a perfectly ordinary baby."

"My old friend Rex, at his age," observed Major Jaffey, "really should prove something a little unusual." "If he is, it's escaped us," snapped Sue.

"I think," said Spray sweetly, "that if you just let me have the child for a few minutes, I can work wonders with him."

"I lent him to you for twenty years," said the man's wife, "and I quite agree that you've worked wonders with him. Next time I lend anyone a husband, I'm going to have him insured."

Rex Pebble was addressing the Major fiercely between beautiful little white baby teeth, "You get me a drink, you pop-eyed, evil-minded old wreck, or I'll batter your face to a pulp when I get back my years," he muttered.

The Major, however, was literal-minded. "I should think, Rex," he chided, "that you would learn to get what you want by being a little gentleman and behaving yourself. You can't bully people, remember, because it's going to be years and years before you grow up into a big strong man again."

"Just for old times' sake," begged the baby, "hand me a small finger. It won't hurt me. I'm still myself."

"Beg honorable pardon," interrupted Nockashima in the interests of truth, "but that no strictly so. Nockashima already forced change bath towel twice. Hard on laundry. Mr. Pebble not man he used to be."

"I'll tell you what we'll do," said Spray Summers, with compassion in her lovely dark eyes. "We'll let the child have some sherry. That will be all right for him. It's in the cellar. We'll all have some. I like sherry late at night. Remember, Rexie?" the young woman asked, with a curiously knowing look.

"Yes," answered the baby, gritting its teeth.

CHAPTER XV

ALL IN A NIGHT'S WORK

THE idea of giving poor little Rex Pebble a drink of sherry was a charitable one, to begin with, but in execution the scheme took on a slight tinge of manhandling. Spray Summers had suggested the wine with the best of intentions, out of genuine sympathy for this man whom she loved, now so pathetically reduced to the shape and the figure of a babe-in-arms.

But it had been a long time since Spray Summers had been to her cellar. Rex himself was in the habit of getting up what was required in drink, or else Nockashima would go scuttling down the steep, tortuous steps into those regions. Spray didn't realize how dark the place was until she led the party of wine seekers thither. It smelled musty and sweet, as indeed it might, in view of the rows of shelves so amply stocked with choice liquids of all kinds, including a fine wine supply.

"Ooh! how dark!" squealed Spray. "I can't see a thing."

"There's nothing to see that I can make out," responded Sue Pebble suspiciously. "You aren't now conspiring to lure me down into this imitation afterlife and bump me off, are you?"

"Why should I clutter up a perfectly good cellar with extra bodies?" inquired Spray Summers. "If I were going to dispose of you, I think I'd find a pleasanter place to do so. Out of the way, something quiet and retiring, to match the corpse."

"It is dark," admitted Major Jaffey, who was experiencing some difficulty in locating each next step. "I just don't think I can find a thing around here."

"Now, Major," warned Spray, "remember, we're all going to behave down here in this nice dark place."

Spray led the parade, followed by Sue, then Hal, who was muttering incoherently to himself about the absurdity of going down into cellars in the pitch black of night. After that came Major Jaffey and Nockashima bearing Rex Pebble.

"Stop being so silly," screamed the baby, "just take me back upstairs and give me a drink of whisky. That's all I want."

"No, you must have wine," said Sue; "it will be good for you. This is the first time I ever had a chance to have a hand in regulating your diet, and I think I'll just be pretty firm about it."

"Look here, after all," remarked Major Jaffey, "I can't see why the whole bloody lot of us should be diving down into this hole. We could send one person down and get the stuff."

"That's not a bad idea," agreed Sue. "Let's just sit down here nice and cozy in the dark and have a little drink on the steps while we're waiting for Nockashima to come back. I'll hold Rex."

"Oh no, I hardly think so," said Spray. "This is my house, and I'll hold him." Both women made a snatch for the man-child, one in the dark clutching a small leg, while the other grabbed a hand; both tugged.

"Let go of me," screamed the infant. "What do you think I am—a mere thing, a mama-doll ?"

"Best leave honorable boss alone," suggested Nockashima timidly as he held on to Rex with the idea of protecting him from the overzealous wife and mistress. Sue and Spray, however, continued to grab at the man until he piped at the top of his tiny voice:

"Goddamn it, leave me alone!"

Hal, the fireman, sensed the tensity of the situation. "Hold on," he said, "let's think of some way we could all share Mr. Pebble."

The baby groaned.

"No, best I hold master," objected Nocka. "Have seen ladies loose with babies. Impossible to predict what happen to this one should fall into clutches."

Both women laughed sneeringly, but Hal pursued his idea. "Why not tie a string to his safety pin and lower him down to find the bottle himself ?"

It seemed a little hard on the child, but since it was practically impossible for any member of the party to regard Rex in any other than an adult light, the thought was considered a good one. Of course, the baby might bang his nose, or he might bump into a large healthy rodent, or Nockashima might even let go of the string, by mistake. Human bodies seemed so comparatively easy to obtain that evening that no one except Rex Pebble took these hazards as serious.

"If I ever get back to where I was," breathed Rex Pebble, "I'll fix you two women."

"Is that a threat or a promise, you shrunken shadow of a husband?" inquired the man's wife.

Nockashima took a firm stance and began to lower the body, hand over fist, into the deep well of darkness. Hal held the Japanese around the waist, while Major Jaffey clung to Hal. It was a little ridiculous, as Rex Pebble, since his magic reducing swim, could have been held by one little finger. However, the men above him panted and held to each other in desperation, as though they were letting a grand piano over a cliff. The baby screamed. "Ouch!" it cried, "you're banging me against the stairway. Keep clear to the right. Ouch! Look out for that stone wall. You hit me behind."

"Watch your grammar!" called Sue Pebble sharply. "You sound like an Irishman."

"You'll find the bottle over by the coke bin," instructed Spray Summers sweetly. "You may have to look around a little, but it's there all right. Only don't get the wrong one. There's some absinthe around there somewhere."

There was no sound from Rex.

"When you're ready to come up, just tug on the string," called Hal, originator of the idea. Hal had read about pearl diving. The weakest and least professional part of their equipment, he had pointed out, was the string. No diver would go down unless he was sure that his rope was strong enough to withstand pressure. Hal had just happened to find this string around a packing case. It wasn't awfully strong.

"I hope he comes back sometime," murmured Spray, "I think there're a lot of things I could still do for him. Things that make you sad when you think of them," she sighed.

"I should think they would make you sad," remarked Mrs. Pebble, "but considering his present state I think that you did quite a bit for him! What's the little fella doing now?"

There was silence from the depths of the cellar. Everyone's ear was cocked, but nothing happened. No tug came on the rope; no sound was heard. "Drop the string a little farther, Nocka," said the Major. "Perhaps that will bring him to."

"It ought to bring him to something," added Hal. "He must be at the bottom by now."

"Well," suggested the Major, "I think we ought to give a little toast to Mr. Pebble's expedition. To the Rex Pebble Research Foundation!" The bottle was passed.

As the party sat huddled on the basement stairs waiting for news from below, there was a great clatter above in the bar and the kitchen. Evidently Baggage had returned with her latest catch, young Kippie. Sounds indicated, however, that there was a third person accompanying the couple, and that this person was being most unwillingly dragged around.

"It's no time of night to go about telling fortunes," remonstrated an elderly female voice, "and I can't understand how you could find that many people up at this hour to have their fortunes told them, anyhow. Just give me that drink you mentioned, and I think I'll be going along."

"Oh no, you won't," cut in Baggage. "There're a lot of things these particular people ought to be told, and you're going to do it. Besides, the way we happened up with you is anything but creditable to your character. Suppose I were to tell?"

The party on the steps listened in tense silence.

"Yes," interrupted Kippie heatedly. "I never would have imagined that even a fortune teller could be so base."

"I can't see anything wrong with what I did: it's what you were doing that was so shameless," protested the strange woman's voice.

"Answer me this," demanded Baggage, "and we'll call it quits: would you have known we were in that hedge if you hadn't been psychic?"

"Well, my dear," returned the voice, "I can only say that even a medium uses her ears."

"Very good," said Baggage, "however it was, I'm expecting you to help us out. We're lucky to have you around. Come, Kippie, my pet, I think we'll just let Alma do her stuff. Where are my friends now?"

On the floor above the group there came the sounds of the tap-tapping of a cane. "Holy Christmas," murmured Hal, "she's got a witch after us!"

The tapping wavered in apparent uncertainty as to direction for a moment, then headed straight for the head of the stairs. "I should say they are somewhere in this neighborhood," wheezed Alma. "What is it?"

"I can't see what they'd be doing in there," Baggage speculated, "but you may be right. There's no telling what these people are likely to do. What are you doing to find them?"

"I'm following a mystic call for help," returned Alma. "It seems to come from the lips of a babe. This child seems to have fallen into bad company. The words it uses are anything but polite."

"Is this babe a gentleman or a lady?" inquired Baggage. "I know a couple of babes here, but both of them use that kind of language."

"Neither a gentleman nor a lady," snapped the woman, "as far as I can tell. It seems to be making a terrific effort to do something."

"That must be Uncle Rex trying to get away from Sue and Spray," guessed Kippie.

"Well, open the door. They can't be up to any good if they're all down there in the dark," returned Baggage. "Let's see what they're doing."

"Aha," sneered Alma the medium, "who's being curious now?"

The door to the stairway was opened, dropping a plane of bright electric light across the men and women on the steps. Faces flashed around guiltily. Hal and the Major grinned sheepishly, standing close around Nockashima's bent-over body, hoping to conceal the little man and his nefarious operations.

"So!" Baggage packed a wealth of meaning into the word.

"How long has this been going on?" inquired Kippie. "And where is my dear harassed uncle Rex?"

"Oh, he's hanging around," Sue Pebble informed the girl, with some degree of truth.

"Who's that," countered Major Jaffey, "that you have with you?"

Baggage was not to be thrown off the track. "It's a fortune teller and character reader," she said, "and I want you all, including Rex Pebble, to come up here right now and have your characters read."

"You flatter us," Spray Summers said sweetly. "Do you read between the lines?"

"I tell everything I see, the whole story," said Alma the medium, with professional pride.

"Tell you what," proposed Major Jaffey, "if she tells everything she sees and she can see without light, why not have her sit down right here and talk to us in the dark? That won't be any hardship on her, and it may save us a lot of blushes." There was no tug on the string from the Pebble infant. The whole party was beginning to undergo distinct misgivings as to Rex's whereabouts and condition. Supposing the poor creature had bashed in its head on the hard cement floor or strained its baby figure by the band around its middle? Any one of many horrible things might have overcome that small, bawling, protesting wine seeker in the dark of the underground place.

"All right," Baggage conceded dubiously, "I guess we can do that. How about it, Alma?"

"O.K. by me," responded the medium blithely. "All I need is a hand to look at, and a crack of light from the door here"—she seated herself—"will fix that."

Baggage and Kippie joined the band on the stairs. "Who's first?" asked Alma.

This threw the company into considerable confusion. Spray maintained that Sue, as the wife of Rex Pebble, should be first. Sue, on the other hand, declared that Spray Summers, as the mistress of the house, should be first. Alma spied Nockashima.

"Bring him here," she commanded.

Major Jaffey, of those in on the secret about little Rex Pebble, was the first to use his wits. "Oh, he's permanent," the Major said. "You can't move him. He has to stay there. Anyway, he'd be too hard to read."

"I could read that fellow myself," remarked Baggage. "Come, come, there're a lot of fortunes to be done here tonight."

"You couldn't do him," Alma objected in a hurt tone, "but I can, and I like 'em hard. Give me your hand, fella."

Nockashima extended his left hand, with the right still clinging to the rope that held Rex Pebble. "No, the other," said Alma. "Don't be dumb." With the agility of Orientals, Nocka switched hands without letting go of the rope, on which there now came a violent tug.

"What's the matter?" asked Alma. "Are you afraid? That's the way with guilty minds." The hag bent inscrutably over the hand. It was wrinkled and tiny and difficult to see, but to the fortune-telling mind it contained a secret of great import. Alma started up in alarm. "He has something to do with a baby, something to do with that baby I was telling you about." She addressed Baggage. "There's some mighty funny business going on here."

"I quite agree," said Baggage, "but that's not news. Now, get your mind off babies and tell us what you see."

Alma, however, was insistent in her messages of alarm. On the rope from Rex came heavier and heavier tugs of warning. Nocka found it hard to keep the rope in his fingers. He tried to slip it to Major Jaffey, but Alma intercepted him.

"Stop twitching," she commanded. "Do you do that all the time? You Japanese have too much ju-jutsu in your blood." She scrutinized the hand. "I see blackness and a bottle and a baby and a rope."

"It sounds like the difference between a hanging and a cocktail party," said Baggage. The girl was growing impatient; there was a great deal to be done. Somehow, in the last few hours, she had begun to have her doubts as to whether or not mortals were ever happy. Give them youth, restore their physical attractions, smooth out their wrinkles, their memories, and what happened? What use did they make of their happiness, of this good fortune? Baggage remembered all her years on the marble column, the days of boredom and the nights of yearning. She thought of Rex Pebble and the graceful, manly form she had watched change with the years into the lines of age, distinguished though it was. There was a great deal, she felt, that she could tell human beings about their lives, and she longed for the opportunity to do so. Baggage had a growing feeling that, with an apparently incompetent medium in charge, she should take over the works and reveal what was on her mind.

"Here," said the girl roughly to Alma. "Stop jabbering about babies, and I'll tell you a few things." She grabbed Nocka's hand. So excited was the little man with these rapid developments that he almost dropped the rope.

"Excuse, madam," he murmured, "but greatly disturbed in mind. Impossible to have fortune told. You miss fortune."

"I think I'm beginning to understand that you're all hiding something from me. Which hand shall I take?" Baggage grasped Nocka firmly around the waist and wrested the rope from him. "So," she said. "Maybe the old girl wasn't so wrong after all. Whose body is on the end of the string?"

"That's what we've been disagreeing about," Major Jaffey informed her as she hauled the rope up hand over fist. The whole party looked aghast, watching with horror for the sight that should meet their eyes when Baggage drew in the last few feet of rope.

The sight was deplorable but altogether different from what might have been expected. Rex Pebble held a bottle in one hand while with the other he swung his makeshift elevator from side to side. He was singing to himself. The voice was small, but it was hearty. The song was something about a French girl who had three lovers and what happened when they all went to war. Its tone was lewd, but Mr. Pebble, in his infantile way, seemed to find it highly amusing.

"Hello," said the baby, interrupting his song. "So this is Baggage. Well, well, well! Where've you been since I dropped out of the picture? Have a drink, anybody?" Rex had gotten into the whisky section. His small, sweet mouth put forth a large, offensive breath. "If you won't give me a drink, I guess I'll just have to go around cellars grubbing for myself."

Both Sue and Spray reached for the child as his body drew alongside the stairs. "Hi, there, Sue old girl," he sang out. "Been thinking about you. Business is better. I've got something big coming up."

"That," remarked Sue, "would be news to me. Give him to me," she demanded. "I'm his wife."

"Yes, and I'm his mistress, and this is our anniversary," complained Spray Summers.

The women struggled to get at the baby. To Baggage, observing the pathetic situation of Rex Pebble, this was a crowning blow. For years she had worshiped the idea of the man. Had it not been for him, she would never have dived off the pedestal. Then he had been restored to youth; but so had Spray, dashing into the water in angry jealousy, and so had Sue, because Baggage her. self, out of pity and jealousy, had helped her. Baggage looked at Kippie. He was young and handsome, and he looked amazingly like the young Rex at whom she had gazed longingly for so many hours from her classic imprisonment, but there was something of Rex that the youth lacked. Baggage grew thoughtful. What was that escaped quality? Was it that she had grown used to Rex, had watched him so long that without the gestures he had acquired with time Kippie seemed lacking somehow? And was it that no one else in the world, however attractive he might be, or how near a replica of the original, could bear for her the same charm?

Nockashima had rescued Rex Pebble from his two wrangling women, but they continued to fight for possession of him. The rest of the party looked on in awed silence. Things seemed to be drawing to a dramatic climax. Rex Pebble's face was a study in changing emotions; something magic and curious seemed to be working in it.

"Here," said Baggage suddenly to the astonished Alma, "give me your hand and I'll tell you a thing or two."

"I see two women fighting over a man," Baggage broadcast. "One woman has loved him a long time but never quite enough. The other has loved him a long time also, but too much. I see that their struggles over him have put lines into his face, because, even if they were given eternal youth, human beings would always fight over each other and make themselves old. I see that the longer they fight the older they grow before their time. I also see that something very strange is happening to a baby named Rex Pebble."

As indeed it was. For, as the women argued, Rex grew older with each sentence, and the older he grew the tighter his home-made diapers fit him.

"For heaven's sake, shut up," said Rex, "or you'll have me busting this bath towel." He was almost full-grown now, and the towel stretched around him like the skin on a very fat pig.

"I think I know what you need," suggested Baggage, pushing the full-grown man off her lap. "Come with me," she said.

"I think I can see that, for all your charity, you're still up to your old tricks," remarked Spray, who had not lost her grip.

Rex Pebble, in splitting bath towel, sped up the steps, followed by the whole pack of guests and relations. He felt somehow gayer and more elated than during the whole evening, for the world had taken on a surety of beauty that he had not known before. After all that had happened, things seemed rather beautiful in the ways in which they best belonged. That is to say, being a distinguished old man would never seem quite so much a hardship again, he considered, provided one had a certain amount of wisdom not to wish for too much, and a lusty, unvarying sense of the ridiculous. He looked behind him as he sped, completely naked now, because the towel, unable longer to stand the strain, had burst asunder. Baggage was running almost as fast as he, and she was catching up. At his heels leaped the gay bloodhound puppy, Mr. Henry. After that came Spray and Sue, two beautiful, bounding figures of blonde and brunette youth, shouting wisecracks at one another as they sped. Then came Nockashima as fast as his short legs would carry him, Hal, and the Major. Alma, the old crone, lagged by the house, smirking and cursing.

Rex wondered about his two women. The magic of the pool had given him a new light on them both, and the evening had been a curious kind of beautiful adventure, unique in the world. Sparkling satisfaction of the senses was all right, but he wouldn't care now if it came to a sudden end. For there was Spray Summers, a delightful, incurable wanton—Habeas Corpus was her middle name—and Sue Pebble, a strangely faithful and harshly helpful wife, both of whom loved him, and both of whom he loved.

Baggage was the unattainable. When it came to running, he couldn't even keep up with her. She sped past him now, shedding her clothing as she ran.

"Come on, Nurmi," she called, and her voice seemed almost to vanish in distance as she passed. "I'll race you to the pool."

Rex Pebble exerted his last ounce of effort, with Sue and Spray hot after him. He wondered what the water would mean to them this time. It was clear to see where Baggage was headed: straight for the empty pedestal. If that was what the girl was going to do, what would he and Sue and Spray Summers do? The magic of the evening had not failed. Rex was not uneasy. Whatever might happen now, he was practically sure that it would be fun.

THE END

THORNE SMITH'S WRITING AS THORNE SMITH SAW IT:

"WITHOUT so much as turning a hair I freely admit that I am one of America's greatest realists. And I'm not at all sure that this calm statement of facts does not take in all other nations, including the Scandinavian.

"Like life itself my stories have no point and get absolutely nowhere. And like life they are a little mad and purposeless. They resemble those people who watch with placid concentration a steam shovel digging a large hole in the ground. They are almost as purposeless as a dignified commuter shaking an impotent fist after a train he has just missed. They are like the man who dashes madly through traffic only to linger aimlessly on the opposite corner watching a fountain pen being demonstrated in a shop window.

"Quite casually I wander into my plot, poke around with my characters for a while, then amble off, leaving no moral proved and no reader improved.

"The more I think about it the more am I convinced that I'm a trifle cosmic. My books are as blindly unreasonable as nature. They have no more justification than a tiresomely high mountain or a garrulous and untidy volcano. Unlike the great idealists and romancers who insist on a beginning and a middle and an ending for their stories mine possess none of these definite parts. You can open them at any page. It does not matter at all. You will be equally mystified if not revolted. I am myself."